Glasgow Rogue

by

Cynthia Breeding

Cover Art by *Teddi Black*

The Wild Rose Press, Inc.
PO Box 708
Adams Basin, NY 14410-0708
Visit us at www.thewildrosepress.com

Publishing History
First Edition, 2025
Trade Paperback Print ISBN 978-1-5092-6331-8
Digital ISBN 978-1-5092-6332-5

Previously Published by Highland Press 2020
Published in the United States of America

Chapter One

Glasgow, 1817

The bane of Annie Ferguson's existence, at least for the past two weeks, walked through the breakfast room door of her mother's boardinghouse. She tried to ignore the Highlander, which wasn't easy to do.

"Has anyone ever mentioned that ye are as prickly as a thistle, lass?" Niall MacDonald asked as he pulled out a chair next to her.

Annie gave him her best no-nonsense look. "Did I ever mention that ye are a *thorn* in my side?"

Niall grinned amiably, his smoky gray eyes crinkling a bit at the corners. "Aye, ye might have a time or two."

A time or two. More likely a time or two every hour of the waking day for the past two weeks, which was precisely how long he'd been following her around. "If ye would stop hounding me—"

"*Escorting* ye, lass," Niall said. "'Tis a bit of difference."

She managed to keep from rolling her eyes. Just barely. "Whatever ye call it, I doona need someone hanging on to my apron strings."

He raised a brow. "I doona think I have ever seen ye sport such a garment."

Annie shook her head in frustration. "Ye ken very

well what I mean. Ever since the incident at the tearoom, ye have nae left me in peace."

"Incident? Ye and my sister-by-marriage were accosted by men meaning to abduct ye because they are angry about that club of yours—"

"The Women for Progress and Liberty have every right to meet!" Annie practically sputtered. "We have a *right* to protest that the merchants' and weavers' unions in Glasgow are closed to women."

"I am nae arguing the point, but when ye march about the streets, ye make yourselves an easy target."

"'Tis the only way we can draw attention to our cause," Annie said.

"Och, aye. Ye definitely got noticed outside the tearoom," Niall replied. "If my brother had not been following—"

"Aha! Ye admit Alasdair was following us! Is it a family trait, then?"

A corner of Niall's mouth quirked up. "Ye must admit, 'tis a trait that comes in handy."

Annie bit back a retort. It was true that things might have turned out quite differently if Alasdair MacDonald hadn't been looking for his bride, Bridget, that afternoon. Still. That didn't mean his brother had to dog Annie's every step since then.

"Come now. Admit it," Niall coaxed. "Ye doona mind me escorting ye as much as ye say."

"Nae. I mind it more than I say." Annie lifted her chin. "I am only exhibiting proper manners by refraining from comment."

The quirk broke into a grin. "Since when are ye concerned with proper manners, lass?"

She scowled at him. "Are ye insulting me now?"

He shook his head, managing to straighten his mouth, although a hint of humor lingered in his eyes. "Nae. Prim and proper women are nae that interesting."

Annie continued to frown. "It that a compliment?"

Niall cocked his head to one side and studied her. "Are ye wanting one?"

She felt herself blush, hating the fair skin that redheads were so often cursed with. "Of course not. I doona need compliments."

"Every woman needs compliments."

Annie bit her lip, hoping the heat she was feeling wasn't turning her cheeks the color of a ripe tomato. Hadn't she learned her lesson about glib remarks years ago? "Not me. I'm nae interested. Ye can save such drivel for proper ladies who are naïve enough to believe it."

"I told ye proper ladies doona interest me. Especially naïve ones. Ye, though, are a thistle, Annie Ferguson."

"I am nae even going to ask if that is a compliment," Annie replied. "Ye have made your point that ye think I bristle too much."

"Ye misunderstand.." Niall's gaze intensified and he leaned forward in his chair. "A thistle has a lovely bloom the same color as your eyes. Has anyone told ye that?"

Annie stared at him. She knew better than to believe such nonsense, although she had to admit it was original. Worse, Niall sounded so sincere. But then, so had the man who'd taken her virginity. Annie blinked. She hadn't thought about *that* in a long, long time.

"My eyes are dark blue, nae purple."

Niall smiled easily. "I will have to study the color, then."

She wondered if it was possible for a body to spontaneously combust. Her face felt on fire and that heat was rapidly spreading throughout the rest of her. Blast it. Annie pushed back from the table to stand. "I am going to call on the Sisters of Mercy this morning. They have several elderly patients who need someone just to talk to. There really isn't any reason for ye to come along."

Niall laid down his napkin and stood as well, a thoughtful expression replacing his smile. "Ye can be as easily assaulted on your way to the home as anywhere else. I will accompany ye."

"I'm sure ye doona want to sit around for two hours or more waiting on me."

Niall shrugged. "I will escort ye there and then go to the shipping office to check on some things Alasdair mentioned before he left. Then I'll return for ye."

Annie sighed. If Niall thought she was a thistle, he was as difficult to avoid as a briar patch on a narrow, rocky trail. "If ye wish."

He gave her a suspicious look and she almost smiled. If he could unsettle her with a silly compliment, maybe she could unsettle him as well.

It was worth a try.

****

Niall definitely did not trust the demure answer Annie had given him as he escorted her to the Sisters of Mercy Home for the Infirm and Aged. In the few weeks he'd been staying at the boardinghouse, he had not seen—or heard—one demure thing come from Annie. She had a fiery temperament and never hesitated to speak her mind, a trait most men wouldn't like, but one Niall found refreshing. His younger sister, Margaret, had the same qualities, but then, she'd had to hold her own with ten brothers, none of whom were known to be even-tempered either. Heaven forbid that Annie and Margaret should ever meet.

If ye wish, Annie had said. She'd even said it again when he left her at the door to the Sisters' communal home. Somehow, that docile tone made him wary. However, he did have other matters to attend to. He just hoped she'd stay put while he was at the marine office.

"Good morn," Gustav Fredrickson, the harbormaster, greeted him as he entered the office a short time later.

"Good morn to ye," Niall answered. The harbormaster was a large, middle-aged man with the permanently bronzed skin of one who'd spent years at sea but now coordinated the dockings along the quay of the River Clyde. Niall's half-brother, Robert Henderson, said even a skiff didn't pass by unnoticed by Gustav.

"Any ships due in for the Henderson line?"

Gustav reached for a sheaf of neatly stacked papers and thumbed through them. "*Ja*. The *Sea Lady* should be in day after tomorrow." He handed a sheet to Niall. "Looks like she'll be carrying a load of kelp."

Niall nodded as he took the paper and went to the small office that Robert rented at one end of the building. He left the door open as he rounded the desk and sat down behind it to study the paper. This end of the shipping business was new to him. At his home in Arisaig, his part in farming for kelp—the seaweed that would be burned for its soda ash and used in glassmaking—was limited to visiting the Hebrides in search of new underwater fields. But Robert's house in Arisaig had been struck by lightning, and while he was rebuilding it, he wanted someone in Glasgow to supervise the shipments. Alasdair had done it before, but he was in London pursuing a seat in Parliament.

Niall put the paper down and reached for the ledger lying on the desk. Opening it, he flipped through several pages of transactions. Earlier entries contained small, precise numbers that were easy to read. In the last few pages, the entries were larger, some of the numbers overlapped, as if made by a hand not used to accounting. That probably wasn't surprising since Alasdair had told him the original bookkeeper, Mr. Graham, was recovering from a bad bout of consumption and his nephew, Gordon Monroe, had taken over the books. Niall looked over to the smaller desk in the corner where the accountant normally sat. It was empty now because the nephew had claimed a sudden family emergency that needed attending.

Looking back at the ledger, Niall sighed and shut it. Accounting was not his strong suit either, but surely he could manage for a few weeks until Robert could return. Besides, it was a perfect excuse to stay in Glasgow…or more precisely, at Annie's mother's boardinghouse.

He grinned suddenly. Exactly why Annie intrigued him was something of a mystery, but intrigue him she did. Perhaps it was her independence. Or perhaps it was because she appeared to be immune to his ability to captivate. The idea was somewhat offsetting since he had a well-deserved reputation for wooing lasses. Even the other ladies of the Liberty and Progress Club weren't oblivious to him. They might not be as openly flirtatious as debutantes, but he'd caught their furtive looks and smug, little smiles when he paid them compliments. Annie was the only one unfazed. In fact, she actually didn't seem to like compliments at all.

His grin faded. He'd been sincere about the color of her eyes this morning. They were such a deep, dark blue that they did look violet. He hadn't been overly solicitous either, yet she had all but rebuked him. As far back as he could remember, that had never happened before. Ever. Not even when he was a green lad getting to know what girls liked. Only two of his brothers, Gavin and Braden, had as many women surround them at a feast or ball. Good thing they were both up north. They'd never let him hear the end of their taunts if they heard Annie's responses to his efforts. Niall shook his head as he stood to leave. Annie was a challenge.

But then, he did like challenges.

****

"Dearie?" Mrs. O'Connor, the elderly lady Annie had been reading to, inquired as she leaned forward in her chair. "Is there something in there that ye don't think I should be hearin'?"

Annie blinked, suddenly realizing that she had been wool-gathering and lost track of what she should be doing. She'd been reading Walter Scott's epic poem, *Marmion*, when her thoughts had drifted to the conversation with Niall MacDonald. Drat it. She glanced at the book now and smiled at Mrs. O'Connor. "Unless a man lusting after a lady who is already betrothed to another shocks ye, no."

The old lady shook her head. "I'm thinkin' no much can shock me at my age," she said and then smiled, a hint of a dimple in her right cheek. "Besides, I know how the tale ends."

"Why didn't ye say so?" Annie asked, closing the book. "I can find something else."

"No need to be doin' that," Mrs. O'Connor answered. "I'm rather likin' the idea that a nun who broke her vows gets walled up alive. 'Tis rather fittin'. One should always uphold an oath, don't ye think?"

"Aye. A person should be held to account," Annie replied. Maybe if Broderick Fletcher, the miscreant who'd promised to fulfill her heart's desire, had been more accountable... Then she frowned. If she wanted to be honest with herself, she'd allowed the seduction, even if she foolishly had believed everything Broderick had said.

"What's wrong, dearie?" Mrs. O'Connor asked. "Ye look a wee bit troubled."

Annie shook her head to clear it. That whole, sordid mess had happened three years ago. Luckily, she hadn't quickened with child, so there was no sense in dwelling on it. "It's nothing. I was just thinking how true the line 'What a tangled web we weave...' is. Deception is never good."

"A pity more people don't remember that." Mrs. O'Connor smiled again. "But the gallant knight is reunited with his betrothed, so *Marmion* has a happy ending."

Annie smiled back. "Are ye a romantic? Someone who believes in happy endings?"

"Aye. Of course." For a moment, the old lady's eyes glazed as though she had slipped into another world and then she refocused. "My Gilbert and I had near fifty years together. And fine those years were."

"Fifty years. It seems unbelievable."

Mrs. James nodded. "And they went by like a salmon's flash in the stream."

"Did ye never argue?"

"Argue? Nary a day went by that we didn't." Mrs. O'Connor's pale blue eyes twinkled. "But then, there was the putting-it-all-to-rights that followed. Mr. O'Connor had a talent for doing that, right up to the time he died."

It took Annie a moment to realize what Mrs. O'Connor meant. "I dinnae…" Annie stammered, not sure how to continue.

The older lady smiled again, the dimple reappearing. "'Tis not just young folks that feel frisky, ye know. Some feelings don't change just because we age."

Annie felt her face heat. "I'm sorry! I dinnae mean it that way. I… 'Tis just that I doona think I could ever have such strong feelings for a…for anyone."

Mrs. O'Connor tilted her head and studied Annie. "Not even for that young man who accompanied ye here this morning?"

Annie's face warmed again and she shook her head quickly. "That man has been the bane of my existence for the last two weeks. He won't leave me alone."

"Perhaps he is smitten with ye, dearie."

Annie gave an unladylike snort. "Hardly. He insists on escorting me every time I leave the house, as if I don't have enough sense to take care of myself."

"Why would he think that?" Mrs. O'Connor asked.

"I doona ken…" Annie shrugged. "Well, there was an incident where his sister-by-marriage and I were almost attacked, but—"

"Ah. And did the young man rescue ye?"

"Nae." Annie shrugged again. "His brother did."

"And ye could have been hurt," Mrs. O'Connor said. "'Tis not a bad trait for a man to want to make sure that doesn't happen."

Annie frowned. "I doona need a man to protect me."

"Not even one so braw and handsome as him?" When Annie shook her head vehemently Mrs. O'Connor continued, "Ye have to admit, dearie, that he does present a formidable presence."

Annie's frown deepened. It might be true that more than one of her club members had gazed at Niall with interest, although she'd attributed that to his wearing a kilt the first time he escorted her to a meeting. He'd had a broadsword strapped to his side and black-handled knives sticking out of each boot as well. Who wouldn't stare at someone dressed like that? She had to admit that he did present a striking appearance. His longish black hair that resembled a wild mane did make him look a little bit animalistic, too.

Mrs. O'Connor winked. "Ye might want to rethink."

Annie felt herself blush again. She sincerely hoped this blushing thing wasn't going to become a habit. It was quite annoying. Just like Niall MacDonald. "I doona need to rethink. I have nae need for a man in my life."

"Ummm."

Annie was tempted to ask what that meant, but she really didn't want Mrs. O'Connor to indulge further in some fantasy of Annie being a damsel in need of rescuing by some knight errant. She was *not*. "Truly. It seems some sort of punishment that the Fates landed Niall MacDonald at my mother's boardinghouse. There are plenty of other establishments around."

Mrs. O'Connor blinked. "Punishment? Ye are lookin' at it wrong. 'Tis nae the Fates who have a hand in this. 'Tis the Fae."

Annie blinked too. "The Fae?"

"Aye. Faeries. *Sidhe*. They do enjoy a bit of

meddling, just like our Irish leprechauns."

Annie opened her mouth, then closed it. Mrs. O'Connor had always seemed quite lucid, but perhaps at her age she was a trifle touched in the head. Right now, the elderly lady was tipping her head to one side like a bird and fixing a bright-eyed look on Annie.

"Ye don't believe, do ye, dearie?"

"Ah…" Annie swallowed, not sure how to respond. If Mrs. O'Connor was having a delusionary bout of some sort, would it be better to play along or to correct it? She didn't have experience with flights of fancy due to aging—or, for that matter, flights of fancy, period—but Annie had never been one to lead someone on. She shook her head. "I doona think such creatures exist."

Mrs. O'Connor was quiet for so long that Annie was afraid she'd insulted her. She was about to apologize when the woman smiled.

"Perhaps ye will one day."

"Perhaps." Annie wanted to say she doubted it, but she didn't want to sound argumentative with the kindly, elderly lady.

"Good." Mrs. O'Connor's eyes brightened again. "'Tis all that can be asked."

That remark left Annie feeling disconcerted, but before she could comment, one of the nuns came to escort Mrs. O'Connor to prayers. She turned in the doorway before she followed the sister out and looked back at Annie.

"Humor an old lady and don't push that young man too far away, aye?"

"Aye," Annie replied, more to appease Mrs. O'Connor than anything. She suspected she wouldn't have any more luck pushing Niall away figuratively than she would if she actually tried the physical act of moving him. However, she might be able to elude him…especially if she left the home early. The other lady she normally visited had her daughter here today, so there was no need to see her, which meant that Annie had nearly an hour free.

The club had scheduled a meeting at the tearoom near the toll booth. She hadn't *promised* Niall she would wait for him after all. She had merely acquiesced.

So why wait? Nothing bad was going to happen in broad daylight.

Chapter Two

"Annie—Miss Ferguson—*left*?" Niall started to curse, then remembered he was standing in the presence of one of the Sisters of Mercy. She was already frowning at his tone of voice. He managed to assume a more agreeable inflection. "Where did she go? When did she leave?"

The sister tucked her hands into the sleeves of her habit and studied him, as though she were deciding whether to answer. It was all Niall could do not to tell her to hurry the reply, but he doubted it would do much good. He tried giving her his most winning smile...the one that diffused even the most suspicious of mamas. The nun simply tightened her lips into a flat line. He sighed inwardly.

"Annie—Miss Ferguson—might be in danger."

The sister looked at him suspiciously. "Why?"

Again, he curbed his impatience, although he had the feeling he was wasting valuable time. Why couldn't the lass have waited like he asked her to? *If ye wish,* she'd said. He should have known better than to believe Annie was going to listen to him. Now she was God-knew-where, without the benefit of an escort. "Miss Ferguson is known to be part of a ladies' club that is not well-liked by certain groups of men."

"You mean the Liberty and Progress Club?"

Naill didn't try to hide his surprise. "Ye ken of it?"

13

The nun nodded primly. "Just because we are cloistered does not mean you should think us ignorant of what takes place outside these walls."

"I dinnae mean ye were ignorant of such things." He gave her another smile. "Ye seem to be quite intelligent."

One eyebrow went up, but she said nothing. Niall wondered if somehow his notorious ability to charm females had been banished once he entered the convent. Strictly speaking, he wasn't *in* the convent but in the home associated with it. Perhaps when nuns took their vows, they became immune to any type of commendation. In any event, the sister did not appear to be moved one bit. Rather like Annie. Although comparing Annie to a nun was rather like comparing lemonade to good Scots whisky. He tried a different approach.

"I assume ye are also aware that the ladies' march with signs protesting the unions nae allowing them to work?"

"Annie has mentioned it."

"Then ye have probably deduced the men in those unions are very angry about it."

The sister frowned slightly. "Why should they be angry?"

The nuns were obviously sheltered, after all, although Niall thought it prudent not to point that out. "The men think the women would take away their jobs and their income." When the sister's face remained impassive, he added, "There was an incident several weeks ago where Annie came close to being abducted by two such men."

The nun eyed him speculatively. "She never mentioned an incident."

Niall sighed again. It would be just like Annie not to talk about it. He'd had the devil of a time prying the information out of her and he'd been at the boardinghouse when Alasdair had brought her and Bridget back, both disheveled. Annie insisted the attack was a one-time occurrence and she was too stubborn to admit otherwise.

"Miss Ferguson is lucky to be alive."

Alarm flickered in the sister's eyes. "Someone really tried to harm Annie?"

Normally, Niall would soften his answer to such a question, but time was of the essence and he'd already tried cajoling, to no avail. "Aye. She may nae be so lucky next time." He gave that a moment to sink in. "The lass is nae safe walking the streets by herself right now, which is why I need to ken where she went."

The nun shook her head. "I don't know where she went, but she left about thirty minutes ago."

"Thank ye!" Niall turned and raced out the door before waiting for a reply, but once on the sidewalk, he slowed his pace. Glasgow was a large city. Looking for Annie would be like searching for a lost sheep in the Great Glen. He'd already spent an additional ten minutes trying to wheedle out information. Where the hell did he start? He was fairly certain there were no protests planned for today or Annie would not have come to the Sisters of Mercy, but he couldn't remember if the ladies had planned to meet. Not that Annie would tell him. Damnation. Protecting the lass would be a lot easier if she weren't so determined to thwart him at every step. And he'd been wary all morning that she would try something like this.

Something niggled at the back of his mind and then

he remembered. He'd been about to enter the kitchen yesterday when he heard Annie mention something to her mother about meeting several of the club members at that tearoom near Tolbooth this afternoon. She didn't know he'd heard her, since he'd backed away silently, thinking he'd surprise her by appearing out of nowhere to escort her. He'd halfway harbored the hope she'd think he had an uncanny ability to read her thoughts, which was a rather stupid idea, in retrospect. But at least he had an idea of where she was headed.

As Niall turned in the direction of High Street, the hair at his nape began to prickle. His unease grew as he picked up his pace.

****

As Annie walked along Argyle Street on her way toward the Tolbooth steeple, she paused at the corner of Miller Street near a sand-colored Georgian mansion that had been owned by one of the Tobacco Lords who became prosperous before trade with America had been cut off because of the war. She always had mixed feelings about the "Virginia dons" who owned these homes. The wealth they accumulated allowed them to live like aristocrats—much to the dismay of blue-blooded, titled Englishmen—not that any self-respecting Scot gave a thistle about what the English thought. The trade in tobacco just proved what ordinary, common men could accomplish. The problem was that only *men* could achieve monetary goals. Their wives were still relegated to pouring tea in parlors.

Annie grimaced as she began to walk. It wasn't like women weren't educated. Her friends in the club were not only literate but most were quick with sums as well, yet they weren't considered employable as accounting clerks or secretaries, let alone working directly in the trades. When would males ever acknowledge that females were just as intelligent and capable as they were?

An absolutely perfect example of such addled thinking was in the form of Niall MacDonald. Honestly! The man thought Annie could no more fend for herself than a bairn still in leading strings. She had managed quite well to get along for twenty-two years. Her mother had come to rely on Annie the past few years, since her father's death, but even her father had encouraged her independence. Perhaps because he had no sons, but still.

Then Niall MacDonald had arrived on her doorstep, exuding pure masculine bravado, coupled with the ability to sound so sincere she almost believed his sweet-talk. Almost. When Niall wasn't trying to bully her into obeying him, he tried to soften her up with compliments. Neither strategy was going to work. The sooner he learned that, the better off both of them would be.

At least, she'd managed to elude him this time. It was a start.

A block later, Annie paused again at Virginia Street. New office buildings had gone up in the past three years, once Napoleon had been defeated and the shipping lanes reopened to the Americas. How she would love to work in one of those offices! She hesitated a moment and then turned up the street. It wouldn't hurt to have a closer look. Her club meeting didn't start for another half hour anyway.

As she neared the third building, the door opened and three burly, unkempt men stormed out. It was evident from the raised pitches of their voices and their agitated expressions that all three of them were angry.

"'Tis nae a fair price they're offering," the first man said, his fists clenched.

"What do ye expect of an oaf of an Englishman?" the second one asked and spit on the ground.

"Aye. The damn fools think they can move into Scottish cities and act like they own us," the third one replied. "They learned nothin' from the wars. The French got tired of money being squandered on gold-gilded palaces and the Americans didn't fancy taking orders from an English king. Neither do we Scots."

"Right," the first man affirmed. "'Tis as bad as takin' orders from a woman."

All three men smirked at that and then, as they noticed Annie on the sidewalk, their attention shifted. She didn't like the looks in their eyes, but she resisted the urge to turn and run.

"Well, well," one of them said. "Perhaps our luck is changin'."

Another man grinned. "Ye may be right. A woman out alone is usually looking for one thing."

"And she's in luck too," the third man said and guffawed. "There's three of us to be had."

Annie found her voice. "I am simply on my way to tea."

The first man made a show of looking around. "Ain't no tearoom on this street."

"I know that." Annie lifted her chin. "I was simply admiring the buildings."

"Admirin' the buildings?" the second one asked and laughed again. "Are ye sure ye ain't lost? There's boardinghouses a couple of blocks over, down by the river—"

"With rooms to let by the hour," the third one

finished. "'Tis a bit early for doxys to be wandering about, but we doona mind." He looked to the other two men. "Do we?"

"Nae," they said in unison and started walking toward her.

Annie willed her feet to move. Her shoes felt like they were filled with lead. "Ye doona understand—"

"Nothin' to understand," one man said. "We'll just flip a coin to see who is first."

"The first to die."

Annie jumped at the sound of Niall's voice. Before she could turn, he was beside her, one of his knives in each hand. The blades flashed as he flicked the handles, ready to throw.

"Any takers?" he asked.

All three men shook their heads as they backed up. "We dinnae mean nae harm," one said.

Another added, "We thought she was a doxy."

"She is nae a doxy." Niall barked, his voice as sharp as his knives. "I am itching for a wee bit of practice with my blades, so unless ye want to be targets—"

"We're leavin'," the third man said and nearly knocked over the other two as they all turned at once and proceeded to run in the other direction.

Niall watched them go and then flicked the knives again with a deft motion that had each in its boot sheath before Annie could do more than blink. Slowly, she looked up at him. His face could have been chiseled out of stone. No doubt she was in for a lecture.

"That was impressive," she said to avoid the scolding. "I had nae idea ye could handle knives like that."

Niall shrugged.

"Ye must teach me."

He raised a brow.

"Really. I...I could defend myself."

The other brow went up.

Annie shifted her weight from one foot to the other. Niall wasn't standing that close, but she could feel heat steaming off him. Anger? "For someone who is so glib with words, ye certainly are nae saying much," she said, a shade too brightly. "I was on my way to tea—"

"Ye dinnae *wait*." The words came out, hard as stones tumbling down a crag. "Ye dinnae wait for me."

He *was* angry. "One of the ladies I normally read to had a visitor, so I thought—"

"Ye dinnae *wait*."

Her own temper began to flare. "Ye doona have to sound like a parrot. I heard ye the first time."

His mouth tightened. "Ye promised to wait for me."

Annie frowned. "I dinnae *promise*."

"Ye agreed with me. Ye said 'if ye wish.' 'Tis the same." His gray eyes penetrated hers. "Or does your word mean nothing?"

Oooh. That was too much. "Ye doona have the right to say such a thing. When I make a vow I keep it!"

One black brow rose again, and Annie willed herself not to fidget beneath Niall's steady stare. "I just dinnae see any reason to wait for ye. 'Twas nae that long a walk to Tolbooth."

"It was a long enough walk to place ye in danger, lass."

She glanced away. "That was a fluke. Bad timing. I've walked Argyle Street a hundred times by myself. The chances of something like that happening again—"

"Once is enough."

"I could have outrun them. I was just about to…"

Niall crossed his arms, making her aware of the powerful muscles in them and how broad his shoulders were. How strong his hands were, too, and how quickly he'd handled his knives. As much as she hated to admit it, his presence had stopped what could have been a bad situation. Probably *would* have been a bad situation…well, all right. It would have been bad. She cringed inwardly as Niall just stood there, waiting.

"I suppose ye might be right."

"*Might* be?"

Annie scowled. She hated admitting she was wrong. "I might not have been able to outrun those men, even though they were overweight."

"'Tis nae what we are talking about."

She grimaced. "All right. I owe ye a big 'thank ye' for following me. This time."

"Ye owe me nothing, lass." Niall shifted his stance and tucked her hand inside his arm to begin walking. "The next time ye promise to wait for me, do it."

Annie looked up at him. "Only if I *promise*. I'll nae have ye ordering me about like a wee bairn."

Niall shook his head and grunted something unintelligible in Gaelic. Annie decided not to ask. Besides, she needed her strength to keep walking for, suddenly, her knees were shaky.

****

Annie Ferguson was going to drive him completely barmy. Niall was sure of it. He'd probably be sprouting gray hair soon if he stayed in Glasgow much longer. In the four days that had passed since the incident on Virginia Street, the lass had managed to lead him all over the city, attending a meeting of the Progress Club at the tearoom and a visit to the museum that housed, of all things, legal documents related to the Magna Carta, as well as taking him on not one but three outings to look for a proper bonnet, which she hadn't found. Not that she wore bonnets to begin with. Niall suspected Annie was deliberately trying his patience with escorting her everywhere.

Well, he hadn't survived growing up with nine rowdy, devious brothers not to know a thing or two about biding his time.

But tonight was different. This wasn't just another wild goose chase. Somehow, Aileen Douglas, the club's president, had managed to secure ten minutes of speaking time during the Tuesday night meeting at the Trades Hall. Niall had been wary when Annie told him about it, but she'd insisted that a representative of the chairman had personally approved the request that all of them—Annie, Aileen, Cora, Fenella, Nairna, Kiara, Deirdre, and Inis—were allowed to attend.

Just to be sure there was no question that he was escorting the women and was prepared to defend them, Niall had chosen to wear his full tartan, complete with broadsword and several knife sheaths on his sporran belt. Not to mention leaving the handles of the sgian dubhs in his boots visible.

His apprehension only increased as he followed the ladies up the staircase to the Grand Hall. The first thing he didn't like was that the stairs appeared to be the only exit. As they stepped inside the crowded room, the din of voices fell to a hush as the men realized they'd just been invaded by eight women. Women who held their heads high and marched, nearly in unison, toward the front of the room without looking right or left. The ensuing rumble of voices grew increasingly louder, and Niall didn't like the tone of them, either. He fingered his blades as he sat down at the end of the front row of chairs that the ladies had claimed. Skilled as he was, he was no match for the large gathering. For once, he would have liked to have all his brothers with him.

A man—Niall supposed it was the chairman—appeared at the front of the room and gestured for the others to take their seats. An uneasy silence fell, but Niall could still hear harsh whispers. He really wished the women had decided to sit near the back, both because they would be closer to the exit and because they wouldn't draw so much attention. But then, attention was what they wanted, wasn't it? Niall resigned himself to shifting his chair slightly so he could have a partial view of the men behind him.

"What are those women doing here, Mr. James?" one man asked before the meeting could start.

"This is not a social gathering," another one added, to which a number of men concurred with loud murmuring.

Mr. James frowned. "It seems we have some unexpected visitors."

Unexpected? Niall felt his ear perk up like a buck scenting danger to his doe. He glanced at Annie beside him and kept his voice low. "I thought ye said this had been approved."

"I thought it was."

"Ye *thought*? Ye were nae *sure*?"

"Well…" Annie shrugged. "The man Aileen talked to said he'd mention it to Mr. James."

"He'd *mention* it…" Niall let his voice trail off and raked a hand through his hair. By the devil's horns! Did the lass not realize the danger she was in by infiltrating this meeting uninvited? The weavers had just finished a strike and the tailors and hat-makers were two trades the women had recently targeted. If their chairman didn't welcome the women, things could take an ugly downturn quickly. Didn't Annie realize that? Or was she just too stubborn to care? Niall didn't need anyone to answer that question. "We should excuse ourselves and leave."

Annie looked at him as though he were a foreigner not speaking English. Then her expression changed and when she spoke, it was in the tone one might use for a rather dimwitted bairn.

"We came here specifically to speak. We cannae—willnae—leave before we accomplish that."

Niall suppressed a Gaelic curse. Barely. "Well, have Aileen get on with it, so we can go."

"Oh, Aileen is nae going to speak. I am," Annie said and rose to move forward before Niall could reach out to stop her.

Hell's fires. The lass truly was going to drive him barmy. Silence swept the room as Annie approached the chairman. He did not look welcoming. Niall swore under his breath and fingered one of his knives.

"Mr. James," Annie said, sounding as though she were greeting a guest at her mother's boardinghouse. She gestured toward the other ladies. "Our—"

"Who are you?" one man shouted.

"I think they're part of that damn women's club that marches around town," another answered.

"The ones who think they can take our jobs?" a third voice asked, followed by loud grumbles.

Niall started to rise as the chairman held up a hand to quiet the crowd. Slowly, Niall sat back down.

"I have no idea of why you are here," Mr. James said to Annie. "Obviously, there has been a misunderstanding."

"We were led to believe," Annie continued as though she hadn't been interrupted, "that we would be allowed ten minutes to speak."

The chairman raised both eyebrows. "I can assure you I did not issue an invitation."

"They need to leave!" another man shouted.

"Get out! We don't want them here," a second one yelled. "They want our jobs!"

Annie turned on them, eyes shooting sparks. Niall wasn't sure her hair wouldn't catch on fire, it was blazing so red. For a fleeting moment, he pictured her as the ancient warrior queen, Boudicca. Then he was on his feet, hand on the hilt of his sword.

Before he reached her, though, a middle-aged man stood and held up a hand for silence. Mr. James nodded quickly, looking relieved for the distraction. "Mr. Haines. You wished to speak?"

"Aye. I do." He turned to the rest of the crowd and grinned at them. "It's been my experience that if a woman is determined to speak her mind, that is what she is going to do." He waited until a few twitters of laughter died down. "Now, the way I'm looking at it, let the lady have her ten minutes and then they'll leave and we can get on with our meeting."

There was some grumbling, but when Mr. James nodded, the noise died away. Mr. Haines smiled at Annie. "Miss…?"

"Annie Ferguson," she answered, "and thank ye."

The older man nodded affably and sat down. Niall took his seat too, although he'd rather have stayed standing. Then he groaned as Annie began to speak about why women were marching. She couldn't take a more diplomatic approach, considering the odds weren't exactly in their favor? He heard low rumbling behind him. Niall raked his hand through his hair again. The lass was definitely going to drive him to an early old age…if they made it out of here alive.

Chapter Three

"I think that went quite well," Annie said to Niall once the group was out on the street fifteen minutes later. From the way Niall stared at her as though she'd just grown another head, she knew he did not agree. In fact, he looked as though a lecture was going to be forthcoming. She smiled brightly. "I did get to speak my piece, so the evening was a success."

"The only thing successful is that all of you are out here, safe and sound," Niall muttered.

"Oh, pish," Aileen retorted. "What were they going to do to us?"

"We are nae witches," Nairna, one of the twins, said.

"No one has been burned at the stake in three hundred years," Kiara, the other twin, added.

"And no one had a bucket of hot tar either," Fenella said.

"Probably because they dinnae ken ye were coming." Niall grimaced. "None of ye can possibly think those men took ye seriously?"

Annie lifted her chin. "No one laughed."

"Ye miss the point," Niall replied. "Boos and jeers are not usually considered sympathetic."

"The tradesmen are civilized, for all that," Aileen said. "They were nae going to harm us."

Niall shook his head. "I am nae so sure, ladies. I doona think it safe for ye to continue with your marches

27

and demands."

"Even with ye to protect us?" Inis asked and deliberately batted her eyelashes at him. "Who would dare to accost us when we have a braw man like ye around?"

Niall smiled and gave her a lavish bow. "I am glad one of ye lasses sees the wisdom in that."

Annie gaped at him. Had he not recognized the sarcasm in Inis' voice? True, she was petite, with delicate features and hair so blonde it gave her an ethereal look, but Inis had a sensible, no-nonsense approach to life. Right now, she was looking a little bewildered.

"Pay him nae mind," Annie said. "What he means is that I have nae such wisdom."

Niall turned to her. "Those are your words, lass. Nae mine." His eyes darkened slightly. "But ye might consider the benefits of having an escort."

Annie opened her mouth, then closed it. She had hardly forgotten the incident on Virginia Street, even though neither of them had spoken of it. In truth, it had left her shaken more than she cared to admit, even to herself. Niall must have sensed as much or he wouldn't have agreed to follow her around—shopping for bonnets, no less—the past few days. Drat it. She really did not need a bodyguard. Worse, now the rest of her group was glancing from Niall to her, waiting to hear how she would respond. She gave an indifferent shrug.

"Well, ye cannae escort each of us," she said to Niall, an idea coming to her. She batted her eyelashes at him too, although it felt ridiculous. "But if ye insist on being our Lord Protector, we could each schedule a day for your company perhaps."

"That title belongs to Cromwell, I think," Niall answered, "and what he protected was his own interests, nae lasses."

"King Arthur, then," Inis said. "I doona ken a woman who would nae appreciate such support."

Annie glanced at her. Inis hadn't sounded sarcastic at all. She wasn't batting her eyelashes, either. In fact, she was smiling. A real smile. And Niall was smiling back.

"I am nae King Arthur and I have nae knights to summon," Niall replied and then widened the smile. "but I do have eight available brothers in Arisaig."

"Are they all as braw as ye?" This came from Cora. It didn't sound sarcastic either.

Niall shrugged. "Nae man has ever bested any of us in a fight."

Annie gave him an amused look. "Are ye bragging a wee bit?"

Niall shrugged again. "We've each honed skills that come in handy."

She sobered, remembering how deftly he'd brought out his knives on Virginia Street. She also remembered how Alasdair had thrown his dagger to save Bridget from the mad woman, as well. The idea of eight more of Niall's brothers riding down to Glasgow was a bit daunting.

"I am sure that will nae be necessary," Aileen said, sounding authoritative. "As I said before, Glasgow is civilized."

"But 'tis kind of ye to offer," Inis said, and the rest of the group nodded.

Annie gave them all a startled look. This wasn't the usual reaction any of them had to manly offers of help.

Were they that impressed with a man brandishing a broadsword and looking a bit like a medieval warrior in that kilt? It definitely did show off a pair of very well-muscled calves... Not that she had studied men's legs. But the members of the Progress Club weren't helpless damsels, after all. Yet Annie could see no dissent on their faces, only something that looked suspiciously like admiration.

What in the world was going on?

****

Niall shuffled through the stack of papers that Gustav had given him when he got to the marine office the next morning. How could so much paperwork pile up in just four days? Of course, if he'd been able to spend time in the office, instead of traipsing through half the millinery shops in Glasgow, he'd have been able to keep up.

But that would have meant letting Annie roam the streets by herself. Having a sister equally as strong-willed as Annie had taught Niall and his brothers to tread lightly when trying to be protective, but Margaret was in Arisaig, hardly more than a village. Annie was in a city. She might not think she was in any danger, but contrary to what Aileen had said, Niall didn't agree that all of Glasgow was civilized. What kind of men booed a woman who was speaking? They may not have thrown rotten fruit—probably because they didn't have any—but the atmosphere had been far from friendly.

At least, Annie had promised—he made sure she said the word *promise*—to stay at the boardinghouse this morning so he could attend to ship's business.

Niall put aside the Bill of Lading for the kelp. That had already been taken care of. The next shipments were bolts of woolens and barrels of barley being shipped to America. Luckily, they were already warehoused and all he would have to do was make sure the inventory count was accurate.

He glanced at the empty accountant's desk. Gordon Monroe had not returned from whatever family emergency he'd gone to take care of. Gustav hadn't had any word either, which meant that Niall would be responsible for entering the payments into the ledgers. He hoped he didn't make a mess of it.

It was several hours later when Niall finally had— he hoped—put everything in order. He cursed when he realized it was already past one o'clock. Annie had promised to stay in during the morning. It would be just like her to be gone when he got home and then defend herself by saying she didn't leave the house until after the noon hour.

To his relief, he heard her voice when he entered the foyer a quarter of an hour later. Then he heard a man's voice as well. The sounds were coming from the small parlor across from the main public room. Niall headed straight for the room. What man would be paying a call unannounced?

Niall stopped inside the door when he recognized the middle-aged man who'd spoken at last night's meeting. Haines, he thought the name was. The man had just taken some papers from the tea table in front of the sofa and was putting them in his satchel. Annie put down the pen she'd been holding.

"What did ye just sign?" Niall asked and then wished he hadn't sounded quite so blunt. No doubt she'd be irritated with his demand and tell him it wasn't any of his business. To his surprise, she smiled instead.

"Mr. Haines has just offered me a job," she said.

"A job? Doing what?"

A flicker of annoyance showed in her eyes and then she suppressed it. "I will be managing his warehouse."

"His warehouse?" Niall repeated, feeling confounded.

The man rose. "Allow me to introduce myself. Archibald Haines, owner of Haines Consolidated Warehousing. I house stores for several shipping lines."

"Niall MacDonald," Niall replied.

"Yes. I remember you from last night. You seem quite protective of Miss Ferguson." He gave Niall a speculative look. "Are you her fiancé?"

"Nae!" The word came from both of them at once.

Mr. Haines glanced from one to the other. "I see."

He probably didn't see at all. Good God. Just because Naill found Annie interesting—even intriguing—didn't mean he wanted to marry her. He hadn't even considered marriage. To anyone. From Annie's forceful answer, neither had she. Niall frowned. Actually, her response was more forceful than his was. And louder. In his experience, women always wanted to get married. Didn't they? He shook his head to clear it. "I am escorting Miss Ferguson while I am a guest at the boardinghouse, just as any gentleman would."

Annie made a strange sound he couldn't quite identify, so he ignored it and continued. "Why would ye want Miss Ferguson working for ye?"

This time, full-fledged indignation showed on her face and also in her tone. "Why would he nae?"

Niall gave her his most contrite smile, which did absolutely nothing to diminish her scowl. Why was this one woman so damn unimpressionable? He turned back to Mr. Haines. "I would think ye would already have a manager in place."

"Oh, I did," Mr. Haines replied, seeming not to notice the exchange between Annie and Niall. "But he was involved in a bad carriage accident several weeks ago. Killed, actually. I've had to manage the job myself since then."

"So why did you choose Miss Ferguson?" Niall asked, risking infuriating Annie further. Out of the corner of his eye, he could practically see her hair bristle. Interesting how the color seemed to glow brighter when she was angry. And he had no doubt she was.

"To tell you the truth, I had not considered a woman managing the place before last night," Mr. Haines answered. "But when I heard Miss Ferguson speak…" He smiled and nodded at Annie. "…I realized there was no reason a woman could not handle the position."

"There. Ye see?" Annie said to Niall before she turned to Mr. Haines. "Thank ye. It certainly is assuring that *some* men see value in women."

"I dinnae say ye had nae value," Niall said. "Ye do."

"Just nae when it comes to holding an actual job," Annie shot back.

Niall started to protest, but then decided against it. He wasn't going to win this particular argument. At least not now. If he wanted to tell Annie how much value she had, he wasn't going to do it in front of Haines. The conversation could—would—get personal. Annie probably wouldn't appreciate that either. In fact, he was probably going to get another glare, if not worse, from her when he asked his next question.

"So what will this job include, exactly? I doona want Miss Ferguson injuring herself."

He hardly had the words out before he could hear her start to sputter. Luckily, Haines interjected before she could unleash a tirade.

"Nothing like manual labor," the man said. "I have a number of young men who can do the heavy lifting and moving things around."

Niall didn't like the sound of that either. He didn't want Annie surrounded by a lot of young, strong men. It wouldn't be safe. "I doona think a lady should be—"

"By the saints! Will ye stop?" Annie gave him a look that might have withered another man, but Niall just set his jaw.

"I doona think being the only woman working in a warehouse is a suitable job for ye," he said stubbornly.

"'Tis my decision," Annie replied, equally defiant.

"Perhaps I could interpose," Mr. Haines said mildly.

They both stopped glaring at each other to look at him. He smiled benignly.

"I can understand Mr. MacDonald's concern," Mr. Haines said smoothly, "but Miss Ferguson will mostly be in the office handling the paperwork. The only time she need be on the floor is to make sure the inventory is correct before it leaves. She will have to vouch for that."

"Which is something I can do," Annie said, blue fire flashing from her eyes in Niall's direction. "Unless ye think me utterly a nitwit."

"Nae," he replied and then realized Annie had outmaneuvered him with that last comment. Damnation! Then another thought came to him as he recalled something he'd seen on one of the invoices in the marine office earlier. He smiled and turned to Mr. Haines. "Does your warehouse hold woolens and barley for Henderson Shipping?"

The man looked surprised, but it was quickly masked as he nodded. "It does. Why do you ask?"

"I am temporarily managing Robert Henderson's office here in Glasgow," Niall replied, "so I will be stopping by the warehouse myself."

Annie made that strange sound again that he couldn't identify. He looked at her, allowing his smile to widen into a grin. "It looks like we might be working together, after all."

****

Archibald Haines locked the door of his walk-up flat on the East End and walked over to the serving cart that held a decanter of bourbon and poured a half-snifter. The liquor wasn't premier stock from either France or the States. The decanter wasn't Waterford crystal, either. But soon, *soon*, he would be able to afford the best.

He tossed the liquor back and poured another, taking this one with him to the brocaded sofa beginning to show wear in spots, much like the scratched mahogany table in front of it. Those items would be replaced soon as well.

Archibald looked around the room. The wallpaper was still intact and showed no signs of yellowing. The carpet—not Aubusson—still looked relatively plush. There really was nothing wrong with the place, other than that he longed for one of the mansions on Buchanan. He *deserved* one of those. His father had owned one, only to lose it—along with the family fortunes—when the Revolutionary War brought the tobacco trade to a halt. Damn the Americans. Damn the British. And, for that matter, damn the French too. With all the sea blockades in place, nothing had been easy to trade. Now, at long last, goods were coming across the Channel and

35

going across the Atlantic too.

He took another swallow of bourbon, more slowly this time. The interference and regulations would be rectified once the Committee for Organizing a Provisional Government put their full plan into action and declared Scotland's independence. And when they did, he would be ready. He would become one of the most powerful rulers of the new country.

Last night's meeting at the Trades Hall had been a godsend. Initially, he had reacted like the rest of the men when the group of women from that idiotic Club for Liberty and Progress showed up. Then the red-haired chit began to talk and Archibald thought perhaps the Fates were beginning to smile on him at last.

Not that he agreed with anything she said. Every man knew women weren't capable of managing anything other than household staff. They certainly didn't know a thing about how businesses were run.

Which was why Annie Ferguson was perfect for the job. She'd concern herself only with the inventory count—even a female could compare the number on an invoice to the actual product—and not question the *contents* of the shipments.

Archibald took another swallow. Every barrel of barley had a false bottom. Beneath that bottom, powdered opium—for which he used smugglers in order to avoid the huge excise taxes the English government demanded—was carefully packed for shipment to the state of Virginia. Once there, the barley and opium would be unloaded and replaced with tobacco for the return trip. The false bottom would contain gold, which he would meticulously count and then turn over to Gordon Monroe, the unscrupulous accountant at

Henderson Shipping, to invest for him.

Unfortunately, the man had disappeared a few weeks ago. Archibald thought it had to do with Monroe's connection to an insane woman who tried to attack the wife of Alasdair MacDonald. At least, Archibald hoped that was the case and not that MacDonald had discovered that Monroe was also altering the books at the shipping company.

Archibald finished his drink and stood to get another. Damn the MacDonalds too. When Alasdair left for London, Archibald thought the coast was clear. Then the brother showed up. Not only that, but Niall MacDonald had made it obvious he was the Ferguson hoyden's watchdog.

Archibald poured more liquor and stood staring out his third-story window, although he paid no attention to the scene below. He needed Annie Ferguson as a foil. He wasn't a man of violence. He much preferred aristocratic pursuits, but if Niall MacDonald interfered with the plans too much, there were dockhands on the quay that could make a man disappear into the murky waters of the Clyde.

Chapter Four

"How exciting! An actual job in a man's world!" Cora exclaimed as Annie shared her news with the Progress Club in the tearoom the next afternoon.

"We're so happy for ye!" Kiara added, while her twin nodded.

"What we really are," Aileen said drily, "is jealous."

Fenella practically bounced in her chair. "Tell us all about it!"

"Wait." Deirdre opened her reticule and withdrew a small flask. "I think this calls for a celebration first."

Everyone laughed and hurriedly drained the tea in their cups so Deirdre could pour the whisky she'd confiscated from her unsuspecting brother. Annie grinned too. They usually finished their meeting with a bit of *uisge-beatha,* but as Deirdre said, this was cause for celebration.

"Ye remember the man at Tuesday's meeting who stood and said we should be allowed to speak?" When everyone nodded, Annie continued, "Such a kind, wonderful gentleman he turned out to be," she said and told the group what had transpired, finishing with another grin. "Obviously, Mr. Haines is intelligent as well since he thought I would be perfect for the position."

"Most men wouldn't even consider hiring a woman," Cora said wistfully.

"What did Niall—Mr. MacDonald—have to say about this?" Inis asked.

Annie shook her head. "He tried to dissuade me, of course. Said a warehouse was not the proper place for a woman."

Aileen snorted. "Men think only one place is proper for a woman."

Nairna frowned. "Men shouldn't think all we can do is run a household—"

"I doona think Aileen meant that," Deirdre said and poured a bit more whisky. "Most men think a woman's proper place is in bed, lying beneath them naked."

Nairna colored and her twin's eyes went wide. Annie felt a twinge of empathy for them since they were the youngest of the group, barely eight-and-ten, yet there was a shred of truth in Deirdre's comment. Annie had thought Broderick agreed with her when she'd told him of her ambitions, only to realize too late he only encouraged her to gain her trust. She felt her own face heat with shame and quickly took a swallow of whisky.

Deirdre glanced at her and raised both brows. "Did I say something wrong?"

"Nae," Annie said. No one, not even her mother, knew what had transpired. Her mortification wasn't so much that the man had ruined her, as far as marital prospects went, but that he had laughed when she'd asked if he was going to propose after the deed was done. He had *laughed* and asked why he should. She hadn't been much older than the twins. Just a foolish girl. "Nae," she said again.

"Perhaps we should go back to the original topic," Inis said. "Did Mr.MacDonald escort ye here today?"

Annie gave her a cursory glance. Inis certainly

seemed to be interested in Niall since Tuesday. Not that Annie cared. "Aye," she said, "but he went to the marine office to do some work."

"Is he going to let ye walk home by yourself this time?" Aileen asked.

Annie tried not to squirm in her chair. Niall had made her promise not to leave without him. He'd even made her say the word twice, as though she didn't understand what the word meant. "I told him I'd wait."

When Aileen arched a brow, Inis intervened. "I think it very chivalrous of him."

"Since when do we need chivalrous men?" Deirdre asked. "That's just another way of ordering us around."

"Is it? I must admit, I was a bit uncomfortable at the Tuesday meeting." Inis shrugged. "Mr. MacDonald did make for an imposing figure draped in all that weaponry."

"He wanted to make a statement," Annie replied.

The twins giggled. "He did."

Fenella laughed too. "I can just see him escorting Annie to the warehouse dressed like some medieval warrior. That ought to ensure Annie's safety and impress even the dockworkers."

"Is he planning to escort ye to work every day?" Aileen asked.

Unless she planned to shimmy down the rose trellis by her window before dawn every morning, yes. Even then, Annie wouldn't be surprised if Niall were waiting on the ground. The man had an uncanny sense of timing. "He did mention something about it."

Aileen snorted again. "If we want to be respected as independent women, we don't need a man dogging our footsteps."

Annie had lost that argument after the Virginia Street incident. "He calls it escorting me," she said, hoping she sounded nonchalant. She didn't even want to think what the group would say if they found out Niall planned to work with her as well.

"I think it is a courteous thing to do," Inis said. Annie gave her a guarded look. How much of Inis's interest was personal?

Not that Annie cared. She didn't.

****

"Ye can leave me here," Annie said to Niall the next morning as they approached the door to the office warehouse. "I doona think I'll be accosted in the next fifteen feet or so."

Niall's jaw set. "I will see ye inside."

Annie stopped, her hands on her hips. Good lord. The last thing she needed was for Niall to walk in with her, wearing his tartan and all the same equipment as he'd worn to the Tuesday night meeting. She doubted the king's guard was that well armed. "If ye escort me inside, it will look like I cannae handle this by myself. I am supposed to be the *manager*."

"And I am going to make sure every man understands that," Niall said and started walking toward the door.

"*What*? Wait!" Annie hurried after him and grabbed his arm. The muscle flexed beneath her fingers, as hard as granite. She dropped her hand quickly. "Ye cannae just go in there demanding such a thing!"

"I willnae demand. I will just tell them they will have to deal with me if—"

"Nae!" Annie managed to get herself in front of him, blocking his path. He halted, so close that if one of them moved the slightest bit, she would be against his chest. A broad, chiseled chest that was probably equally hard as his arm. His gray eyes turned dark. For one dizzying moment, she felt almost pulled toward him, to close the space between them. Then she stepped back and licked her suddenly dry lips. "I must earn the respect myself. Ye cannae force it."

His gaze followed the movement of her tongue and then he looked back into her eyes. "Aye. Ye will have to earn their respect." He stepped around her. "But having them see ye have a protector will make it easier."

Annie started to refute that, but the stubborn man had already reached the door and was now holding it open for her. She sighed and picked up her skirts to climb the three steps. "Nae one word," she hissed as she passed him.

Niall gave her an enigmatic smile which she chose to ignore and stepped inside.

The office was larger than she'd thought. Her attention was immediately caught by the open area on her left. It contained an ensemble of Sheraton furniture. The dark blue velvet cushions of the cherrywood sofa contrasted nicely with the maple veneer along its back. A low table of the same wood fronted the sofa and two padded chairs sat on either side, lyre-backs carved with bow-knotted wheat ears and sprays of other foliage. A large watercolor of what Annie assumed was a southern plantation house on a cream-colored wall. Light blue satin brocade drapes hung across the one window that fronted the street.

To her right was the expected work counter with a large, rolltop desk behind it and shelves full of ledgers along the wall. Mr. Haines rose from the desk.

"You are right on time, Miss Ferguson." As he glanced at Niall, a slight flicker of annoyance crossed his face, which he quickly masked.

Annie couldn't blame him for that. Niall's insistence on coming inside was unneeded. "I always try to be prompt."

"Excellent," Mr. Haines replied and then gestured. "How do you like the office?"

"It looks like a parlor," Niall said before Annie could respond. "I thought this was a place of business."

Annie shot him a warning look and then smiled at Mr. Haines. "I like it. It feels homey."

"My point. I see no reason not to surround myself with a few creature comforts even if…" Mr. Haines paused and gave Niall a pointed look. "…it is a place of business."

Niall seemed oblivious. Instead, he pointed to a door on the far side of the room. "Does that lead to the warehouse?"

"Yes, but it's restricted," Mr. Haines said as Niall crossed the room and opened the door.

Niall glanced back. "I am representing Henderson Shipping and Henderson Shipping stores some of its stock here, nae? That gives me the right to inspect the place." He turned and disappeared without waiting for an answer.

Annie bit back a groan. She knew what kind of an "inspection" Niall was about to make. And he was going to get an earful of what she thought about blundering through the warehouse with all his weaponry. "I am so sorry…" she started to say and then was surprised when Mr. Haines just smiled.

"Perhaps it is good that your…*escort*…sees where

43

his products are. That way he will know everything is on the up-and-up and can only hold himself responsible for any mistakes in his shipments."

"That is verra accommodating of ye, Mr. Haines," Annie said. She couldn't imagine any mistakes being made regarding shipments, especially since she would be the one in charge of making sure counts were accurate, but she did appreciate Mr. Haines not taking offense. What a kind, understanding man he was.

****

Niall finished making entries in the shipping ledgers and laid down his pen, suppressing a yawn. Accounting was definitely the most boring thing he'd ever done. He glanced at the brass clock on the wall, startled that it was already late afternoon. He'd spent hours with the damn books. No wonder he was bored.

Getting up to put the ledgers back on the shelf, Niall wondered how Annie's first day on the job had gone. When he left her this morning, Haines had been explaining something about a running inventory control. Annie had hardly looked up, but Niall suspected that was because she was still upset with him.

He was pretty sure he had made the proper impression on the men working in the warehouse this morning when he'd done his "inspection." He'd counted fifteen of them as he'd walked the narrow paths between boxes and barrels piled nearly to the ceiling. Niall also made sure he had met every man's eye before he left as well as told several that he considered Annie—Miss Ferguson—to be under his protection. Those men had promptly looked at the array of weapons he carried and nodded their assent.

Annie would more than likely want to throttle him

for that if she found out. He doubted she would, though, since the men were not likely to admit such a thing to her. But they weren't likely to forget it either, even if Niall showed up the next time wearing breeches and waistcoat. He'd simply exchange his sword for a musket and make sure at least two knife handles showed from the tops of his boots.

"I heard Archibald Haines hired Miss Ferguson," Gustav said as Niall closed the door to Robert's office and came into the larger front one.

"How did ye find that out?" Niall asked, not bothering to hide his surprise.

"Haines Consolidated is one of the largest warehouses for shipping, and some of the dockhands have relatives working there." Gustav shrugged. "Word travels fast along the quay. The news probably got here before you did."

"Um," Niall replied noncommittally. It seemed men gossiped as much as women did. "I did a walk-through of the warehouse this morning, just to make sure it was a safe place for Annie—Miss Ferguson—to work. Everything seemed to be in order."

The harbormaster nodded. "Haines runs a tight operation. He makes sure his deliveries arrive to the ships on time and, ever since one of the dock hands dropped a barrel of barley and cracked the lid, Mr. Haines always makes sure everything is loaded by the same workers each time so no damage occurs."

"That sounds a little drastic over a barrel of spilled barley," Niall said and hoped Haines wouldn't be too harsh on Annie, especially since she wasn't trained. But then, if Niall heard anything like that happening, he'd just have a talk with the man. A *strong* talk, if needed.

"*Ja*," Gustav agreed, "but the man's father was a tobacco lord and Haines is determined to get back the wealth that was lost."

"I cannae blame him for that," Niall said.

"I guess not," Gustav answered. "A lot of the heirs to those lost fortunes meet regularly at Walker's Hotel on Buchanan to discuss how to get their fortunes back."

"Now that the shipping lanes have reopened, they will have the opportunity," Niall said.

"What they want is government reform," Gustav replied. "Lower tariffs on both imports and exports. The merchants complain all the time that the price of goods is too high."

"And the trades people, like the weavers, complain their wages are too low."

Gustav nodded. "That sums it up. There is a storm brewing as sure as the winter ones sweeping in from Iceland."

Niall didn't particularly like the sound of that and mulled it over as he walked over to the warehouse to collect Annie. For centuries, the Scottish clans had skirmished amongst themselves. There had even been major clan wars. The English had never been welcomed north of the Borders, even with the Act of Union that made them all one country. It seemed to Niall that that unrest remained, only to take a somewhat different form, now that the world was becoming industrialized. He only hoped the warehouse, being in somewhat of a neutral position of simply moving goods, would not be caught in any of the unrest.

Niall heard Annie's laughter even before he entered the office. Opening the door and stepping inside, he saw the reason why.

A tall man hovered near Annie's shoulder, leaning much too close as they both studied what looked like a map on the counter. The fellow's long blond hair was tied back in a queue and he wore only a waistcoat over a linen shirt that had its sleeves rolled up and remained open at the neck. Why was the man dressed so informally? And, a better question…who the hell was he? Niall had taken inventory of the workers that morning and this man hadn't been present.

Niall frowned and placed a hand on his belt, causing the knives and sword to rattle.

Annie looked up at the sound. Niall's frown deepened as the man looked up too. He was probably Niall's age and looked like a bloody Viking with eyes the color of glacier ice. And just as coldly penetrating. Niall widened his stance, a thumb on his sword hilt. "Who are ye?"

Annie sighed and shook her head. "Good afternoon to ye, too." Then she turned to the big brute. "Allow me to introduce Niall MacDonald. He is staying at my mother's boardinghouse."

"I am also Annie's personal escort," Niall said, deciding to use the familiar name rather than the formal. He saw something flicker in the other man's eyes briefly and stared him down. "I still doona ken who ye are."

"John Kingsley," he answered brusquely. "I am the foreman for the warehouse."

That at least explained the informal attire. "Ye were nae here this morning."

This time, a brow rose and the man looked at Annie.

She sighed again. "Niall decided to make sure there were no villains or brigands lurking about in the warehouse to accost me whilst I counted boxes."

The Viking laughed. "I assure you, Miss Ferguson, that I will take care of any who attempt such a thing."

Niall barely managed to refrain from scowling. Protecting Annie was his job, dammit. Once a Highlander vowed to do something, he did it. And he wasn't checking for criminals in the warehouse. He was making sure—very sure—that the workers understood what—*who*—awaited them if they insulted Annie in any way. "Ye were nae here this morning," he repeated.

"No, I was not," Kingsley answered as Mr. Haines came through the back door of the office. He gave the briefest of nods to Niall and then looked back to Kingsley and Annie as he pointed to the paper on the counter. "Were you able to figure out a way to make more room?"

"I think so," Kingsley answered. "I was just asking Miss Ferguson what she thought about my moves."

What damn moves was the man talking about? Niall clenched a muscle in his jaw. Kingsley was still standing too close to Annie, although she didn't seem to notice. Instead, she put a finger on the paper, which Niall could now see was a layout of the warehouse. "I think Mr. Kingsley's idea to move the first row of stock directly against the wall was a good one."

Haines nodded as he followed her gesture and then he looked up and smiled. "I think the two of you are going to work well together."

Niall stifled a growl. Those were words he didn't want to hear.

****

John Kingsley watched Annie leave with MacDonald and wondered how much trouble the man was going to be. After all, one didn't often see

Highlanders in tartans on the streets of Glasgow, let alone one armed to the teeth as though he had just been dropped onto a nineteenth-century sidewalk from some ancient Scottish battlefield.

And, if Kingsley read the man correctly—he most likely had, considering he'd spent years honing that skill in order to keep alive—MacDonald was a man loyal to his cause. In this case, the cause being Annie Ferguson.

He would have to tread carefully. Loyalty, like honor, were rare traits, but Kingsley never underestimated the power of either of them. Both could turn seemingly mild-mannered men who normally abhorred violence into mindless, brutish avengers when tested. There was nothing mild-mannered about MacDonald, and John suspected the man had no qualms about using the weapons he wore either.

The Crown didn't expect him to make mistakes, which meant he would have to rethink his plan, but being flexible had helped him survive other situations, so this was merely an annoyance at the moment. The prime minister had received messages of a possible secret committee that was forming in Glasgow to overthrow the government. John had already spent months casually visiting Walker's Hotel and ingratiating himself with the disgruntled heirs of the Virginia Dons to gather information. Although they all grumbled about the downturn of the British economy along with high prices, he'd not been able to gather anything actually incriminating.

Part of the unrest was an outflow of the French and Americans both revolting against monarchy rule. Part of it also had to do with the trade unions which had formed and that were demanding better working conditions and higher wages. Neither of which was terribly surprising. The third part, though, was more elusive. Some merchants, particularly those dealing in overseas trade, were accumulating wealth that did not correlate with the amount of tariffs that were collected at the Custom House. The fear was that those men could and would finance a Scottish revolution and then take control of the country themselves. One of the prime suspects was Archibald Haines.

Getting to Archibald Haines meant his manager had to die. It was simply a price to pay so John could snatch the opportunity to apply as his replacement, concocting a story on being down on his luck. Archibald had said he needed to think on it and had offered a position in the warehouse instead. John had accepted the job and worked to gain the trust of the foreman. When the foreman unfortunately met his demise a few weeks ago by drinking tainted ale—a drop or two of wolfsbane went a long way—Haines promoted John.

He'd hoped to soon advance to the manager position where he could get a look at the books. *That* plan had to be revised when Annie Ferguson showed up with that medieval-looking Highlander. But Kingsley was nothing if not innovative. He would persuade the woman to show him the books. His first thought had been to charm her— another trait in which he had skill—but soon sensed that she was not taken with flattery. However, there was more than one way to flatter a female. This one thought she was intelligent, so he would ask for opinions and advice, eventually having her "teach" him to do accounting. If all went well, she wouldn't even know she'd been a contributor to his plot.

John Kingsley's mission was to find the men who

might be plotting a revolution against England and, as Liverpool put it, "take care of the problem."

Which he planned to do. If MacDonald were lucky, he wouldn't be a casualty.

Chapter Five

Annie glanced sideways at Niall for at least the fifth time in their walk back to the boardinghouse. She had fully expected him to be tossing critical remarks about her working, but instead he had remained stonily silent. Even his face looked like it was carved from granite. His mouth was set, his jaw jutted forward, and his eyes looked like flint. She sighed.

"Ye might as well come out with it."

"Come out with what?"

It was amazing that his lips hardly moved with the question. Annie was tempted to look around to see if someone else had uttered the words. "Ye ken what."

"I ken nothing."

Annie stopped, her hands on her hips. "Now ye are being stubborn, to boot."

Niall halted as well. "'Tis a trait we share."

"'Tis nae the point," Annie replied. "Come out with what ye have to say."

"Nae." He started walking again.

Annie caught up with him. "Aye."

He stared stoically ahead. "What would ye have me say, lass? Ye ken I doona think it good that ye are working in a man's environment with nae protection."

"I have a right to have a job!" To her frustration, Niall didn't answer, only picked up his pace. Annie glared at his back. Did he have to walk so fast? "Ye might be proud of me for landing the position."

That stopped him. He turned, a quizzical expression on his face. "This has nae to do with being proud of ye. 'Tis your safety I am concerned with."

Annie shook her head. "We have been over this protection idea before. Ye already insist on escorting me to and from the place. What harm can come to me in a warehouse full of working men?"

One black brow went up. "Ye are nae that naïve, are ye?"

Annie felt her face flush, partly from the insinuation and partly from anger. If only Niall knew how very much aware she was of allowing herself to be in a position where a man could take advantage. That was not going to happen again. "I am nae a nitwit nor am I planning to loiter in the dark corners of the warehouse like some doxy."

Niall blinked. "Now ye have given me another concern for my list."

"Your *list*?" Annie narrowed her eyes. "I should have kenned. 'Tis nae like ye to be so compliant. Ye've been thinking up reasons for me nae to take this job."

He frowned. "I doona need to think up reasons. They all stand out, clear as words on paper."

She scowled. "Then read this imaginary paper to me since I fail to see it."

Niall folded his arms across his chest, which made him seem bigger and more imposing. Annie was sure he did such a thing on purpose and drew herself up to her full height, crossing her arms too. "Well?"

He glanced down at her stance and a corner of his mouth quirked. He relaxed his arms and then began ticking reasons off on his fingers.

"One. Ye and Bridget were accosted just weeks ago coming out of a club meeting—"

"That was because—"

"Two," Niall continued, "there have been trade strikes all over Glasgow the last year. The weavers, in particular, are still angry with their lot."

"That doesnae have to do with me."

"Nae? Your club has marched past their shops with signs—"

"Only to make a point."

"Three," Niall said, quitting the argument. "Warehouse workers are like dock hands. They are nae used to dealing politely with ladies—"

"I will earn their respect."

"They will probably nae think ye a lady at all. Have ye thought of that?"

Annie lifted her chin. "If I treat them fairly, they will. I can be polite and civil."

Niall shook his head and went on. "I observed the men this morning when I went into the warehouse. Ye will nae be able to control them with polite, civil speech."

"John Kingsley promised me I will nae have trouble with the men."

Niall's eyes turned steely-gray. "Is he going to be in charge, then?"

"Nae!" Annie shot back. "I am the manager. Mr. Haines made that quite clear today. He wants me to personally count the inventory and sign off on each shipment and log it into the ledgers as well. Mr. Kingsley will only be in charge of directing the men to load the boxes and barrels."

"I doona like ye being out in the warehouse at all,"

Niall replied. "Can ye nae just stay in the office and keep up with the numbers?"

Annie shook her head. "If I am to sign off on something, I need to be responsible for it. That's one of Mr. Haines' policies."

"I doona like it."

"Ye have made that clear." Annie huffed a breath and then put a hand on Niall's arm. "'Tis nae that I doona appreciate your concern. I just doona need that kind of protection. Truly."

Niall looked down to where her hand rested and she quickly removed it before he thought she was trying to use some kind of feminine wile on him. She felt her cheeks warm again, knowing that was a lie. She'd removed her hand because she'd felt his hard muscle flex beneath it. For just a fleeting moment, he had seemed like a knight of auld. She certainly didn't need to indulge in that kind of idiotic thought.

Niall muttered something in Gaelic under his breath and started walking again. She wished she understood the language.

****

The first person—and the last one Niall wanted to see—the next morning when he entered the warehouse office with Annie was John Kingsley. The man was standing across the room, studying the plantation picture on the wall. He reminded Niall more of a bloody Viking this morning than he had the day before. Niall's own Nordic blood began to stir. *Enemy.* Niall shook his head. Where had that thought come from?

Kingsley turned as they closed the door behind them. His glance raked over Niall. "I see you've decided to dress in civilized fashion today."

Niall managed to keep from clenching both fists. The only reason he'd worn breeches and boots was because he was going to be at the dock, taking care of the kelp shipment coming in on the *Sea Lady*. "I am nae without my weapons though."

The other man's gaze traveled to the musket at Niall's hip and then down to the knife handles protruding from his boots. "One never knows when a battle may erupt on the streets of Glasgow."

It was meant as a taunt, but Niall chose to ignore the tone. "Ye speak more truth than ye ken."

"Oh, for heaven's sake!" Annie said. "I hope ye are nae thinking of starting something."

Niall cocked an eyebrow at her. "Where?"

She grimaced. "Anywhere. Doona start trouble."

He heard the warning tone in her voice and shrugged. "Only if trouble finds me, lass."

Annie looked heavenward. "Why do I think that would be easy to do?"

Niall grinned. "I like to keep my skills sharpened just like my blades."

Annie opened her mouth, then snapped it shut, her cheeks turning slightly pink. The unexpected blush made something else stir in Niall. He hadn't meant the remark as an innuendo, but had she perceived it like that? If she had, then her reaction could mean the little vixen might be a wee bit more interested in him than her prickly behavior let on.

It was an interesting idea.

Niall became aware that Kingsley was watching them. While it was tempting to push the conversation a bit further just to warn the man off, Niall didn't want to embarrass Annie.

"I need to get to the marine office. I will come to collect ye this afternoon," he said and then smiled. "I will look forward to the moment." Taking her hand, he brushed a kiss across her knuckles and heard her sharp intake of breath. When he looked up, she was staring at him with widened eyes.

He managed to keep from grinning as he turned and left.

****

Although it had been the merest touch of his lips, Annie's hand tingled from the effect. What in the world had made Niall do that? She couldn't remember him ever acting courtly before. He sometimes gave her high-sounding compliments that she knew better than to take seriously, but most of the time he raised her ire by chiding her about one thing to another. He certainly never said he'd look forward to seeing her again. He'd never kissed her. Her *hand*. He'd never kissed her hand before. Why…

John Kingsley coughed and suddenly Annie knew why Niall had acted as he did. Like a stag protecting his doe, Niall was staking his territory, warning John to keep his distance. Not that it was warranted. She was simply going to be working with the man during the day with plenty of people around. It was typical of Niall to assume he knew what was best for her. It probably had something to do with Highland men expecting their women to follow their orders. Bridget had even mentioned it once. Annie shook her head in disgust. She wasn't going to put up with anyone ordering her about.

Annie walked toward the picture and smiled at John. "Do ye suppose Mr. Haines kens the owner of such a place?"

Kingsley gave her a thoughtful look before turning his attention back to the painting. "The plantation is Dogwood Lane near Jamestown. I believe Mr. Haines' father had a stake in it."

"Really?" Annie studied the painting with renewed interest. Medium-sized trees, covered with so many white flowers that they looked snow-laden, lined either side of a long, straight gravel drive. At the far end the lane circled around a flower garden awash in brilliant red, yellow, and blue blooms. Behind that stood a large, three-story rectangular white house with green shutters. Porticoes graced the top floor along with a belvedere crowning the roof. Stone pillars supported an open-air porch that ran the length of the house. Annie could imagine sitting in a rocking chair on that porch enjoying soft, warm breezes.

"It's verra pretty," she said. "Does Mr. Haines still own part of it?"

"Doubtful. When America declared her independence, most of the British not living there forfeited ownership to the lands."

"It seems like such a loss," Annie said.

Kingsley contemplated the picture again and then he nodded. "I am sure that it was."

Mr. Haines came through the front door just then and they both turned to greet him. He glanced at the painting.

"I see you have been admiring Dogwood Lane."

"'Tis beautiful," Annie said. "Have ye been there?"

"Once, as a child," Mr. Haines answered. "My father was a tobacco lord."

Kingsley nodded. "With the trade lanes open again, the tobacco trade will resume. Do you plan to purchase land over there?"

"Perhaps," Mr. Haines said evasively. "I would have to do research on how economically feasible it is."

"Ye could talk to Robert Henderson," Annie said.

"Of Henderson shipping?" Kingsley asked.

"Aye."

"And how do you know him?"

"Only in a roundabout way," Annie answered. "Robert is a brother of sorts to Niall MacDonald."

"MacDonald?" Kingsley riveted his gaze on her. "What do you mean, 'of sorts'?"

"My friend Bridget told me the story when she married Alasdair MacDonald." Annie shrugged. "Robert's father sailed from America and married Alasdair and Niall's mother, who was a widow with seven bairns. Then they had three more."

"That is all very well," Mr. Haines interjected, "but what does it have to do with the economy in the States? And tobacco?"

"Och, I dinnae mean to run on," Annie replied, feeling her face warm. "I meant to say Robert lived in America until last year. He would be able to tell ye the state of things there."

"Hmmm," Archibald said contemplatively. "That *is* interesting."

Kingsley gave him a speculative look. "Yes, it is."

"Of course, ye will have to wait until Robert returns to Glasgow," Annie said.

"When will that be?" Mr. Haines asked.

"As soon as he gets his house in Arisaig rebuilt," Annie answered. "Maybe a few weeks."

"And MacDonald is supervising Henderson Shipping until then?" Kingsley asked.

"Aye." She grew quiet. Once Robert returned, Niall would be leaving. She would be rid of the thorn in her side. Only…it hadn't felt quite so much like a thorn lately.

"Perhaps I should pay a visit to the office," Mr. Haines said. "Just to check on the status of the barley and woolens I ship through the line and make sure everything goes smoothly."

"I could accompany you to answer any questions MacDonald might have," Kingsley added.

Mr. Haines frowned. "I doubt that will be necessary. All you have to do is make sure the correct numbers are sent to the docks."

"As you wish." A muscle ticked ever so slightly in Kingsley's jaw.

Annie saw the small movement and a wave of appreciation swept over her. How kind both Mr. Haines and Mr. Kingsley were to be concerned for Niall. She was more convinced than ever that she had done the right thing in accepting this job.

****

The *Sea Lady* was just docking when Niall made it down to the pier. He was surprised to see his older brother Aidan standing on the deck.

"What brings ye down to Glasgow?" he asked as soon as Aidan had descended the gang plank.

"We've found a number of good, rich kelp beds on Skye," Aidan replied. "Robert thinks it would be wise to open a small office there to make sure the shipments get loaded properly. He sent me to learn how to set up the books so they correspond to the ones in Glasgow." Aidan hoisted his duffel bag. "Are ye staying at the Widow Ferguson's boardinghouse?"

"I am, but she has a full house," Niall answered.

"Well, I will bunk with ye tonight. I can find another place tomorrow."

"One night," Niall replied, "and ye will have to sleep on the floor."

His brother grinned. "I suspected that."

Niall nodded. "Tomorrow I can show ye the books."

Aidan lifted a brow. "Numbers were never your strong suit, brother. I had best take instruction from the bookkeeper."

"And I would be more than glad to let ye do that," Niall replied, taking no offense. "But Mr. Graham is recovering from consumption and his nephew who was in charge has taken off."

"Robert dinnae mention that."

"'Tis because he doesnae ken it." Niall shrugged. "I saw nae reason to make him fash." Aidan looked doubtful, but then he'd always been the most levelheaded of any of them. "Besides, the harbormaster is there as well."

Aidan nodded. "We will make do."

"Aye," Niall replied. "So where is the office going to be? The small port at Armadale?"

Aidan shook his head. "Off Loch Bracadale."

Niall felt his eyes widen. "That far north? 'Tis MacLeod country."

"That may be, but the sea belongs to no one," Aidan answered.

"True, but the MacLeod own the shore." Niall frowned. "Robert is American. He doesnae understand how far back the clan wars go."

"The one on Skye was finished over two hundred years ago," Aidan said.

Niall lifted a brow. "Are they ever really over, brother? Land is important to Scots—"

"Doona forget that Robert married a MacLeod and so did Alasdair."

"But nae the branch of Tormod."

"But MacLeods, just the same," Aidan answered. "Besides, when we were on expedition there a few months ago, I met with the laird at Dunvegan. He is nae opposed to the operations."

Niall's eyebrow went up again. "Nae?"

"Nae." Aidan shrugged. "I offered him a percentage of the profits for using his land."

Niall scowled at him. "Ye could have said so in the first place."

"I was planning to," Aidan replied, looking definitely pleased that he had managed to irk Niall. "Another reason the laird agreed was because Owen MacLean was prowling the waters around Indrigill Point—"

"Owen MacLean?" Just saying the name made Niall want to ball his fists. The MacLeans had lands bordering the MacDonalds and were always hungry for more. Reiving cattle and stealing brides might be things of the past, but the MacDonalds had been ambushed passing through MacLean land a year ago. Owen's father swore that it had been brigands, not MacLeans, but suspicions remained. And Owen was cunning. He'd clerked for Nathan Rothschild's bank in London before he'd returned to Scotland. Worse, having learned city ways, he acted like a dandy. Women flocked to him like bees to a hive. Even Niall's own sister, Margaret, had not been immune to his smooth talk.

Niall grimaced. "No wonder the laird agreed.

MacLeans are nae to be trusted."

"Och, well…" Aidan shrugged.

Niall stared at him. "Are ye forgetting all the times—"

"I am nae forgetting the on-going spats between us," Aidan said, "but the decision on MacLeod's part was strictly business. Uniting with us MacDonalds will keep MacLean—and anyone else intent on harvesting kelp on Skye—a safe distance away."

"I suppose ye are right," Niall said grudgingly.

"I always am," Aidan replied.

"And ye are nae conceited about it either," Niall returned, "but doona forget who is the stronger of us."

Aidan grinned. "Are ye so sure of that? Do ye care to find out?"

"Any time."

Aidan's grin widened. "I will check my calendar, then."

"I will look forward to besting ye, brother."

"We will see," Aidan said. "Meanwhile, shall we see to getting the kelp unloaded?"

"Aye," Niall grumbled, knowing they probably would not even spar. With any of his other brothers, a conversation wouldn't even have taken place. They'd just swing a fist. Not that Aidan was less strong than the rest of them. He just didn't believe in unnecessary violence.

Several hours later, after they'd hauled close to a hundred bales of dried kelp into carts, Niall was beginning to rethink the sparring challenge. Aidan had not even broken a sweat with the heavy lifting, but Niall had. Actually, it was just a bit of dampness on his face. But still. The idea didn't sit well that Aidan might best him in a match after all.

Adding to his frustration, he found Annie had left the warehouse before he arrived. Aidan had looked amused at that and Niall had spent the entire walk home explaining how the lass took foolish chances and was making his hair grow gray.

At least, she was home. He heard her voice as they climbed the steps to the boardinghouse. The door had been left slightly ajar and he caught a glimpse of her standing by the counter. Pushing the door open, he stopped and groaned.

Owen MacLean was standing by the counter too. He and Annie were laughing.

Aidan cleared his throat. "I was going to tell you that Owen plans to open an office in Glasgow also."

Chapter Six

Niall didn't think he'd ever heard Annie laugh as much as she did at dinner that night. He didn't see anything particularly humorous in MacLean's stories about London, but Annie apparently did.

"You look quite enchanting this evening," Owen was telling Annie now.

"'Tis kind of ye to say so," she replied.

Niall nearly choked on the sip of ale he'd just taken. 'Tis kind of him? *Kind* of him? Anytime Niall gave Annie a compliment she either rolled her eyes or made some comment to the contrary. Now…*kind* of him? Niall stabbed a piece of meat.

Aidan arched a brow at the gesture. Damn it. His brother had always been overly observant. Niall refused to look at him, not wanting to see a smirk appear on Aidan's face. His brother had better not make a comment either or they *would* be sparring after dinner.

"Tell me about this office ye plan to open," Niall said to Owen before he could wax forth on another compliment.

Owen turned his dark gaze to him. "I am finishing the negotiations I started the last time I was here. The kelp harvest on Eigg and Rhum has been plentiful. Enough so that I do not want to entrust an independent agent to handle things on this end. Having a MacLean office in Glasgow will also help me procure more financial backing when I go to London in the spring."

"If ye need someone to manage the office, I have several friends who might be interested," Annie said.

The ladies of the Progress and Liberty Club, no doubt. Niall wasn't surprised that Annie would try to promote one of them. MacLean didn't strike him as someone who would want a female managing his business though.

"Who would that be?" Owen asked.

"Well, there are several. Aileen Douglas. Fenella Grant. Deirdre Gordon. Cora MacBain."

A shuttered expression crossed Owen's face. "They are all women?"

Aha! Niall had been right. Owen didn't want a female working in his office. Although Niall had to admit the man had hidden his surprise well and kept his tone neutral. Something for Niall to keep in mind.

"Aye," Annie replied. "I—"

"Doona forget Inis Russell," Niall said. "She has both beauty and intelligence."

Annie gave him an annoyed look. Niall bit back a grin. "Not as lovely as ye, of course."

The annoyed look changed to a scowl before she turned away, then smoothed her features to speak to Owen. "What I was trying to say is that I have recently been offered a job managing a warehouse which shows at least one businessman is a progressive thinker. I thought ye might be of the same caliber, having lived in London."

"Thank you for thinking so highly of me." Owen gave her a wry smile. "Most of London's ladies are kept quite busy pursuing social events. Unfortunately, those not involved in society have not achieved equal status in the business world either."

Annie looked disappointed. "'Tis the same there as here, then."

"I am afraid so," Owen replied and then tilted his head to study her. "What kind of a warehouse do you manage?"

"Haines Consolidated," Annie said. "'Tis close to the wharf."

Owen nodded. "I have heard of it."

"Henderson Shipping uses it," Annie said and gestured toward Niall. "I have a shipment of barley ready to be loaded onto one of their ships tomorrow."

Owen turned to Niall. "Has Henderson used it long?"

"I am nae sure—"

"For several months at least," Annie interrupted. "According to the ledger, the accountant at Henderson Shipping approved the site."

"The accountant?" Owen asked. "Why not Henderson?"

"Probably because Robert's house in Arisaig was struck by lightning and he hasn't been here," Niall replied. "I am keeping an eye on things for now."

"Ummm," Owen said and then turned back to Annie. "We have several orders for shipment to France this fall. I'll need a place to store the kelp bales until I can contract with one of the shipping lines. Would you have room?"

"Aye. I am sure we do," Annie said, looking delighted.

"Good." Owen gave her an engaging smile. "I will look forward to working with you, then."

Niall barely refrained from growling. First he had to

worry about the male crew at the warehouse, to say nothing of Kingsley's unwanted attention toward Annie. Now MacLean was adding himself to the list. Damnation. If Annie had to pursue a job, why couldn't it be one that didn't involve a score of men?

Aidan coughed discreetly as Niall stabbed another piece of meat. He ignored the smirk he knew would be on his brother's face.

****

"Have a care with my dishes," Annie's mother said mildly as they were cleaning up the kitchen after the meal.

"Sorry," Annie said and put down the plate she'd been drying less forcefully. Her mother liked using the bone china once a week for gentility's sake. She said it reminded them to maintain good manners.

Her mother had just chosen the wrong night.

Annie had known Niall would be upset to find her gone from the warehouse this afternoon and he'd shown his displeasure as soon as he came in the door of the boardinghouse. He had barely been civil to Owen, instead asking why she hadn't waited for him.

She might have told him that Mr. Haines had wanted her to meet Oliver Nolan, a business partner of his, and that he'd dropped her off in his carriage later, but before she could say anything, Niall had practically ordered her to wait for him next time. His brother—who had never met her—had tried to hide a grin. No doubt he thought she deserved the scolding for not obeying Niall. Annie glowered at the glass she'd just picked up.

"Careful," her mother said again. "'Tis nae Waterford crystal, but still expensive to replace."

"Sorry," Annie repeated. "I will take more care."

Her mother glanced at her before plunging her hands into the soapy water in the basin once more. "What ails ye? Is the job nae what ye thought it to be?"

Annie shook her head. "'Tis nae the job. I have a lot to learn, but I think I will like it."

"Then what is it?"

When her mother used that no-nonsense tone, Annie knew she couldn't sidle her way out of the conversation. She sighed. "'Tis Niall. He is bossy."

Her mother raised both brows. "Like ye?"

"Nae. I doona order people around." Silence met that remark and Annie frowned. "At least, I doona expect anyone to sit and wait like some loyal hound for its master."

Her mother smiled at that, which only made Annie's frown deepen. "Well, I doona."

"And neither does Niall." Her mother took the towel from her and dried the next glass herself. "But it might help if ye doona bark at him so much."

Annie gaped at her. "Bark at him? How can ye say such a thing?"

"Ye could be kinder to the man," her mother answered. "He is only trying to protect ye after what happened to Bridget and ye."

"But that was a one-time thing," Annie replied, trying hard not to raise her voice. "I doona need protection!"

Her mother set down the glass and gave her a direct look. "As much as I admire your independence and as much as I agree that women *should* be allowed to work, there are many who doona agree."

"Men, ye mean," Annie said.

"Aye. And whether we like it or not, having

someone to protect ye is nae such a bad thing."

Annie opened her mouth to protest and then closed it. She knew her mother worried about some of the things the club did, especially in light of recent workers' strikes and general unrest, but she didn't understand how much Annie didn't want to depend on a man for anything ever again.

"Niall means well," her mother said.

Annie nodded, more to end the conversation than to agree with it. She started putting the dishes away, careful not to crack anything.

Niall MacDonald had a talent for vexing her. Except for the fact that it would probably have given him great satisfaction, Annie would have gotten up and left the table after his remark about Inis having both beauty and brains. He didn't have to point that out, as it was obvious to anyone who did not need an eyeglass to see. And then, he'd added insult to the remark.

Nae as lovely as ye, of course.

Did the man think she was such a fool as to actually believe something like that? Oh, there might have been a time when she had. When she'd *wanted* to believe such a thing. But she'd come to terms with herself after Broderick left her. She was tall and angular, not dainty and curvy. Her hair was straight as a nail, not softly curling. She even had a splattering of freckles, thanks to a fair skin that burned in the sun. She didn't smile demurely or bat her eyelashes.

Not that she was *enchanting* either, but Owen MacLean had lived in London and that was just one of the things that gentlemen said to flatter ladies. She knew he didn't mean it any more than Niall truly thought she was *lovely*. The idea that she was some sort of a seductive siren nearly made her giggle. She ought to be able to laugh off Niall's remark as well. So why hadn't she?

Annie closed the cupboard door, wishing she could close off her thoughts as well.

****

"I really doona need two of ye to accompany me to work," Annie said the next morning as both Niall and Owen awaited her by the door.

"I would like to meet Mr. Haines in person if I am going to be using his warehouse," Owen said and then smiled. "But I agree, MacDonald doesn't have to come along."

A muscle twitched in Niall's jaw. "'Tis nae out of my way."

Annie closed her eyes briefly, then shook her head and started down the steps of the boardinghouse, leaving the men to follow. They did, one on each side of her, their assortment of knives, swords and muskets rattling with every step. Apparently, clan rivalry was still alive and well, for they both also wore tartans. Even a bairn still in leading strings could probably figure out the two of them had no liking for each other, but they seemed to have decided to play some kind of competition-like game to which only they understood the rules. She just hoped they weren't regarding her as some kind of trophy.

She was tempted to point that rather important fact out, but since neither of them had actually alluded to her in the game in which they were engaged, she could hardly say she didn't want to be the prize. And maybe she wasn't. Judging from the way both Niall and Owen tried to stay a step ahead of each other, they probably wouldn't even notice if she stepped back and let them continue on jostling one another for position.

She tried it. Three steps later they both stopped, turning about as precisely as soldiers in a drill.

Niall frowned. "Why did ye stop?"

"Are you all right?" Owen asked.

"I… 'Tis a bit crowded walking three across," Annie replied.

Owen nodded. "MacDonald can go ahead to his own office since I need to meet Mr. Haines."

Niall gave him a steely look. "I told Annie's mother I would escort her."

He was bringing her *mother* into this? Annie was about to tell him that was nonsense, but then remembered her mother's words to be more kind and bit back the retort. "There really is nae need, gentlemen. No one has accosted me or even come near."

Niall and Owen each put a hand on their swords' hilts.

"'Tis because they ken to respect the MacDonalds," Niall said.

"And to *fear* the MacLeans," Owen added.

Annie sighed. She hadn't intended to encourage the rivalry. "'Tis a safe walk. Nae a person has even looked at me this morn."

That much was true. Everyone that had been on the sidewalk had given startled looks to two highly-armed Highlanders and given all three of them a wide berth.

"Ye doona need strange men looking at ye," Niall stated.

"Indeed, although it is difficult for a man to ignore a beautiful woman," Owen said smoothly, "but that is why I am here to keep you safe."

Niall glowered at him. "'Tis why I am here."

Annie looked heavenward. She couldn't stop herself. If she didn't put a stop to whatever silly game they were playing, they'd probably end up in fisticuffs or worse, given the assortment of weapons they each carried. "*Gentlemen*. May we continue? I doona want to be late for work."

Owen adjusted his sword belt and stepped to her side. "Of course. I should have thought of that."

Niall adjusted his belt too as he stepped to Annie's other side. "Aye, I should have thought of that too, lass."

"Very well," Annie answered and picked up her pace. It was only two more blocks to the warehouse. Surely they could make it.

****

"Excellent!" Mr. Haines said when, after they managed to arrive intact with no one wounded a short time later, Annie explained that Owen was interested in renting space. "I am sure we can find a spot. I will leave it to Kingsley, since I have a meeting this morning."

Kingsley unfolded a layout of the warehouse and spread it on the counter after Mr. Haines left. "We will need to keep the kelp bales in a dry spot. Which location is best, Miss Ferguson?"

Finally. A man was treating her as an adult and not a dimwitted bairn. John was asking for her actual opinion on something and not just assuming he knew the answer. She smiled at him and moved toward the counter. Then she realized that both Niall and Owen had moved with her. She was tempted to look at her waist to see if they had woven a rope around it to stay attached.

"I think I am capable of handling this," she said, her jaw so tight she hoped she didn't crack a tooth.

"I want to make sure the spot is dry," Owen said,

"since I could lose substantial money if the kelp rots."

He was right, drat it. "Of course." Annie sidled to the left to give him more room to look and bumped into Niall. He didn't budge when she glowered at him.

"I need to make sure I didn't overlook any areas when I checked out the warehouse the other day," he said.

"I'm sure ye missed nothing," she replied and then realized that her skirts were still brushing his thigh. He glanced down at their closeness and she stepped quickly back, feeling her face warm. It heated even more when he grinned at her. "'Tis true I doona miss much, lass."

"Miss Ferguson?" Kingsley sounded slightly annoyed at her delay.

He wasn't more annoyed than Annie was. "Here," she said and pointed to an area along the inside wall adjacent to the office. "It is the farthest from the outside doors and should keep the wind out as well as the rain."

"Good choice," Kingsley said.

"Thank ye." At least someone thought her capable of making right decisions.

Kingsley folded the layout of the warehouse and tucked it under the counter, watching as Niall and Owen finally left. Then he gave Annie a curious look. "Do you really feel the need for bodyguards?"

"Nae!" The word came out a bit louder than she intended and Annie lowered her voice. "I have tried to tell them so, but they doona listen."

"They should. You seem to be quite an intelligent woman."

Aha! At least one man had sense. "Thank ye."

"No need to thank me for what is obvious," Kingsley replied. "But why do you think they hound you so? Especially MacDonald?"

Annie gave a frustrated sigh. "He just wants to make sure nothing goes wrong with my job."

Kingsley gave her a sharp glance. "Like what?"

"My safety here, for one thing."

"Well, he can put that fear to rest. As foreman, I will make sure the workers all know their place. You will not be accosted."

Annie nodded. "I told him as much." She remembered that Niall had muttered something in Gaelic.

"I know MacDonald is handling the books for Henderson Shipping temporarily." Kingsley paused and then frowned. "Does he think you are not capable of keeping the ledgers here?"

"I doona ken about that."

"Another fear to put to rest. I am here to help you, Miss Ferguson."

"'Tis kind of ye," Annie said.

"Just a part of my responsibilities. In fact…" Kingsley looked thoughtful. "…it might be a good idea if we went over the accounts together until you become more familiar with the accounting system."

"I will have to check with Mr. Haines about that."

"Absolutely, if you think you must," Kingsley answered, "but he did hire you to be the manager." He shrugged and lifted his palms upward. "He might consider it a weakness if you feel you have to ask his permission to do something that is simply a part of your job."

Annie drew her brows together. "I hadn't thought about it like that."

"Do give it some thought. Two people checking the

accounts cannot hurt." Kingsley smiled at her. "After all, you do not want Mr. Haines to rethink his decision on hiring you because of simple arithmetic errors that could easily be avoided with a second set of eyes."

She definitely did not want that to happen. "I realize Mr. Haines has taken a risk in hiring a woman, but I will nae let him down."

"Forgive me. I did not mean to imply you would. Mr. Haines doesn't even need to know that I did any checking." Kingsley smiled again. "I am only here to assist you, Miss Ferguson, not to undermine your authority. Trust me, please."

How she wished Niall—and even Owen—had been present to hear that statement. Maybe then they'd stop treating her like someone incapable of making decisions. Annie nodded slowly. "In that case, I will accept your help, Mr. Kingsley."

Chapter Seven

Annie was so elated over the way the day had gone that she didn't even get annoyed when both Niall and Owen showed up to escort her home. She noticed they'd both changed into regular street clothes and the swords were gone. Owen was even carrying one of those fancy walking sticks the English favored. Perhaps they had put their rivalry behind them. At least, they wouldn't scare the other people off the sidewalks on the way back home.

"Why are ye here?" Niall asked Owen as Annie went to get her shawl. "'Tis nae your responsibility to escort the lass."

"I had to return the storage contract," Owen answered and then held the door open as Annie joined them. "Besides, maybe I enjoy Miss Ferguson's company."

"Ye would see Annie at supper," Niall muttered as they walked outside and down the steps.

One of Owen's brows rose. "If you are on such familiar terms that you address Miss Ferguson by her first name, perhaps she needs a chaperone from you."

Niall scowled. "Are ye challenging MacDonald honor?"

Owen smiled easily. "Only if you think it justified. Rumor in Arisaig has it you left a trail of brokenhearted lasses."

The scowl deepened. "Ye may think on your own

reputation, MacLean. Ye had more than one father ready to lock up his daughter while ye were in town."

Annie sighed. So much for thinking their silly game was over. "I would really nae want to hear of your conquests with ladies."

Niall blinked at her. "I doona discuss such things."

"Neither do I," Owen said.

"Good. Then it's settled," Annie replied, although she had a feeling nothing was settled between the two men. Neither did she have any doubt that both of them left an assemblage of disappointed ladies behind. She had to admit that Niall and Owen were good-looking and braw to boot. Even if they weren't scoundrels like Broderick and didn't make promises they didn't intend to keep, they were smooth-talking enough that naïve, innocent girls of marriageable age would read intent into their words. Annie grimaced. At least, she wouldn't fall into *that* trap. She decided to change the subject and turned to Owen.

"Ye will be glad to ken I cleared the space ye wanted for your storage."

"All of it?" Owen looked surprised. "There were a good number of barrels taking that space."

"Aye. Barley barrels bound for the States," Annie answered, "but I moved them."

"I dinna think ye were going to be working in the warehouse," Niall said.

"Doona fash. I did nae handle them," Annie said. "Mr. Kingsley instructed the workers. I only assisted in taking count."

Niall gave her a stubborn look. "But I thought ye said ye would be managing the paperwork."

Annie tried to hide her exasperation. "How do ye

think I can count the barrels if I doona actually see them?"

"Is that nae what the foreman is for?"

Although she was grateful that John had gone over the books with her this afternoon—they had caught two minor subtraction errors—she didn't want to relinquish what authority she had. Men were quick to take total control if given the opportunity. "I am responsible for the entries I make in the ledger."

Niall set his jaw. "But ye were nae moving the stock to a ship, so there were nae entries to be made."

Annie wanted to stomp her foot, but that would be equivalent to a childish tantrum. The man was incredibly stubborn and had the single-mindedness of a hawk soaring over its prey. "I just want to make sure everything is accounted for."

"Which I think is a very good thing," Owen said before Niall could reply. "I will rest easy knowing my kelp bales will be watched over."

Annie gave him a grateful smile although she wasn't sure how serious he really was being. "Thank ye for trusting me to do my job."

Owen returned her smile. "I have no doubts you will."

Beside them, Niall made a noise that sounded like a growl.

Annie smothered a grin.

****

Her good humor quickly faded the next morning when she entered the office. Mr. Haines was pacing by the counter. Kingsley stood on the other side. Neither of them looked pleased. In fact, Mr.Haines actually looked angry.

"Is something amiss?" she asked, glad that Niall for once hadn't come inside with her. She didn't need him coming to her defense over her job.

Mr. Haines turned as she came in. "The barley barrels were moved."

Annie frowned. "Aye. Mr. MacLean is expecting a shipment of kelp to arrive soon. That location is the driest in the warehouse."

Mr. Haines looked as though he were debating what he wanted to say. Kingsley stood quietly watching him. "Did I do something wrong?" she asked.

"No." Mr. Haines paused. "You are quite right that it is the driest location, but that is why I put the barley barrels there. If the wood gets damp, the barley will rot by the time it reaches the States."

"I dinnae realize that," Annie replied, "but the side wall should be dry as well."

"That may be, but I prefer the barrels to stay where they were. Delivering the barley—dry—produces more profit than simply storing kelp bales for a short period." He opened the door leading into the warehouse. "I will have them put back. In the future, please see to it they remain where they are."

He left before Annie could respond. She gave Kingsley a puzzled look. "Both places should be dry. I just thought the one closest to the office would be better for the kelp with less wind to blow through."

"You are correct about that," Kingsley answered, "and the barrels are set up on blocks so even if the floor did get wet, the bottoms would remain dry."

"Then why do ye think Mr. Haines was so upset?"

Kingsley looked thoughtful. "I am not sure."

****

Annie was still pondering over it late that afternoon when Niall arrived to walk her home. Mr. Haines had not come back into the office. When she'd checked the warehouse, all forty barrels—she'd counted them twice—were back in their original place. She hoped Mr. MacLean wouldn't mind the switch in location.

"Where is Owen?" she asked Niall as they started back toward the boardinghouse.

Niall frowned. "Why do ye ask?"

Goodness, but he sounded irritated. And Niall thought *she* was prickly? She'd merely asked a question. "'Twas a change in location for storing his kelp at the warehouse. I wanted him to ken."

"Oh." His expression smoothed. "I have nae seen MacLean since this morning. Why was a change made?"

"I am nae sure. Mr. Haines seemed quite upset that the barley had been moved."

Niall stopped walking. "Did he insult ye?"

Annie stopped too. "Nae. He just…just was adamant that the barrels should stay where they had been. He even had them put back."

"But he did nae offend ye?"

She shook her head quickly and started walking again before Niall decided to go back and have words with Mr. Haines. "I cannae take offense because my boss requests something so simple. 'Tis my responsibility to follow his wishes."

Niall caught up to her in two strides. "Aye, but ye are a lady. I'll nae allow the man to mistreat ye."

A part of her should feel indignant because Niall thought a woman couldn't handle criticism, but he sounded so concerned that Annie wondered if he might actually care about whether she was treated like a lady.

Unbidden, an image of Sir Walter Raleigh spreading his cloak over a puddle floated through her mind. Another emotion stirred inside her—one that she'd not allowed to surface in a long time—one that made her suddenly feel feminine and maybe even fetching. She pushed the thought back. That path was one she'd walked down before, only to be thoroughly disillusioned.

"I am nae so stubborn that I cannot accept an order."

One of Niall's black brows rose. "Ye willnae accept an order from me."

"Ye are nae my…" Annie stopped talking, mortified that the word "husband" had almost slipped out. Where in the world had *that* come from? First, Sir Raleigh and now…*husband*? What was wrong with her that a simple statement from Niall could make her thoughts spin in directions for which they had no reason to go? Niall was looking at her oddly. She needed to say something.

"…employer. I am earning wages at the warehouse."

"Aye, but that does nae give Haines the right to disrespect ye."

That strange feeling shot through Annie again. "At least Mr. Haines did nae shout at me like some men have." She managed to shrug and hoped she sounded nonchalant. "Our Progress Club is nae exactly popular with men."

"That is nae excuse," Niall replied as they reached the boardinghouse. "Nae one will shout at ye again if I am around, lass, unless they wish to see what a Highlander can do with a sword."

Having seen the assortment of weapons—including a claymore which Niall thankfully didn't wear—Annie had no doubt he meant the words. Highlanders seemed to have their own code of honor to follow. Still, her heart fluttered a little as Niall opened the door for her and she silently walked inside.

****

"As long as the kelp stays dry, I do not mind it being put in a different location," Owen said after Annie told him of the change in plans later that evening at the supper table.

Niall watched her covertly, thinking she looked far more relieved than a mere move of goods warranted. Had Haines been more critical of her than she mentioned?

"'Tis a good spot," Annie said. "Thank ye for understanding."

Owen grinned. "I try to be accommodating…at least, with charming ladies."

Annie's face turned pink. "I am nae sure I ever charmed anyone."

"You do not give yourself enough credit, then," Owen said. "You are quite captivating."

Hell. MacLean was flirting with her. Annie's blush had deepened. She didn't blush when Niall gave her a compliment. Her face might turn red, but it was more oft from a fit of temper at one of his remarks.

"Ye are verra kind," Annie passed a bowl of mashed turnips to him.

"I am sincere," Owen replied, taking the bowl.

Niall put a forkful of meat into his mouth to keep from telling MacLean to stop it. Not that he had the right to say anything. He didn't. He'd offered—well, Annie would say *insisted*—to escort her simply because he didn't want her being attacked again. Any red-blooded Highlander—and certainly a MacDonald—would do the same.

Not that Annie didn't intrigue him. She did. Stubborn. Proud. Independent…and immune to his own flirtatious comments. That was probably why he resented Annie's seeming acceptance of MacLean's remarks. They were like a gauntlet thrown down in Niall's path. A challenge. Nothing more. He certainly was not jealous.

"Allow me to serve you," Owen said as he spooned turnips onto Annie's plate.

Annie smiled at him. "Thank ye."

"It is my privilege," Owen replied. "Would you like some oat pudding as well?"

"Aye, that would be good."

Niall tore off a piece of bread and stuffed that into his mouth too. Had Annie suddenly lost the use of her own hands to put food on her plate? And what was MacLean trying to do, acting like some damn English courtier?

Owen glanced at him, a side of his mouth turned up in what looked like a smirk. "You are being awfully quiet this evening, MacDonald."

It was a good thing his mouth was full or he would have said something he'd likely regret. Not that words mattered right now. MacLean had issued an unspoken challenge to gain Annie's approval. Niall wasn't one to turn down a fight. The gauntlet had been thrown. He was determined to win.

And he was *not* jealous.

****

"Really, the way ye run on about Mr. MacDonald and Mr. MacLean, I am wondering if ye doona kind of like the attention," Nairna said Saturday afternoon as the Progress Club met at the tearoom.

Her twin, Kiara, giggled. "I ken I would."

Annie glowered at them. "I am nae running on."

Fenella smiled. "Aye, ye are a bit."

"I am nae…" Annie paused and then sighed. "Och, ye are right. But I am doing so because the two of them are acting like bairns."

"With all those weapons he wears, 'tis hard to imagine Mr. MacDonald as a wee bairn." Cora laughed.

"Aye. He is verra braw," Inis murmured.

Annie drew her brows together. This wasn't the first time Inis had made that observation. "I dinnae say he was *wee*. I said he was acting childish. They both are, always trying to best each other, like lads in a schoolyard."

Last night at supper had merely proved the point. For some unknown reason, Owen's remark about Niall being quiet had seemed to pique his ire. Not only had he started talking, complimenting everything from the gravy she'd made to the gown she was wearing, but he'd sliced the cake and heaped extra frosting on her plate and then insisted on pouring her more wine—a gesture that nearly spilled the whole bottle on her mother's linen tablecloth since Owen reached for the bottle at the same time. A tug of war had nearly ensued.

Even now, they had stationed themselves outside the door, assuming wide stances with arms folded across their chests, looking like two feudal warriors in their tartans. Annie sighed again. "I hope they are nae scaring customers away or we will be asked to leave."

Cora looked around. "I doona think we need to worry about that. I think they may actually be drawing in customers."

Inis nodded. "'Tis nae every tearoom that has two good-looking men standing at the door."

"Aye. I think more women have come in since we've been here," Fenella said.

"Of course the place if full of women. Ye doona expect men to come to a tearoom, do ye?" Annie asked.

Both twins giggled. "I doona think Annie's beaus will allow men in," one of them said.

"They are nae my beaus!" Good Lord in heaven. She certainly didn't need that kind of a rumor to get started. Niall and Owen might be giving her compliments, but she knew better than to believe smooth words. Besides, it was obvious there was some unspoken rivalry between the two, probably relating to some feud that could be decades, if not centuries, old. All Scots had long memories, but Highlanders had acquired special acumen in that area. "They are guards, if anything. Not that they are needed as such."

"'Tis true," Aileen had not spoken until now. "Is it possible to slip away from them on Monday evening? We are scheduled to give a speech at the Trades Hall and I'd rather we try to persuade the tradesmen that we are sincere about wanting—and having the ability—to work alongside them. If we're shadowed by your two armed guards, we will appear weak and nae able to fend for ourselves."

Annie grimaced. She didn't need to be told that Aileen was right. They needed to appear strong, not in need of benefactors. "I will find a way."

Chapter Eight

Aileen looked past Annie's shoulder as she entered the Trades Hall Monday evening. "Did ye actually convince Mr. MacDonald nae to escort ye?"

"I said I would find a way," Annie answered, although she didn't elaborate. She hadn't *convinced* Niall of anything since he didn't know she was coming here, but she didn't want to add a lie to her somewhat dubious scheme. Not that it was totally deceitful. She had told both Owen and Niall that Mr. Haines had planned a meeting for this evening, which was partially true since he would be in attendance tonight. And she'd asked Kingsley to send a rented hack, so she could at least claim the carriage was arranged by the office.

"Good," Aileen said. "The men here, especially the weavers, need to understand we women are capable of the same work they are."

"Ye doona have to convince me," Annie replied and switched the subject before Aileen could question how she'd managed to elude Niall. "Where are the others?"

"They are waiting down the street," Aileen said. "We thought it best to have the men arrive first and allow the meeting to get started, unlike last time."

Last time. Niall had been here. Annie glanced over her shoulder, half-expecting to see him on the steps. That somehow he'd found out where she was headed. But he wasn't there.

She remembered his scolding them that they were lucky to have gotten out of that meeting with just boos and jeers. But tonight was different. Mr. James knew they were coming. They were even on the agenda of the meeting, so the tradesmen would not be surprised as they had been the last time.

"Ah, here they are now," Aileen said as the rest of the women came through the door. "We are last to speak, so we have a bit of time to gather our thoughts."

Even though they were well-prepared, with Aileen doing most of the talking and the rest providing support, Annie still felt a bit of queasiness as they entered the Grand Hall upstairs twenty minutes later. A sudden hush fell over the audience as the women appeared, but that was to be expected. In a way, they were breaking ground simply by being here. Annie looked for Mr. Haines and spotted him at the far end of the hall. She didn't see Kingsley anywhere, but then the warehouse foreman probably didn't need to attend a tradesmen's meeting.

This time, Mr. James gave a proper introduction, requesting the men to refrain from booing and jeering. But Aileen had only begun to speak before the shouting began.

"We doona want women in our workplaces!"

"Why nae?" Aileen shot back. "We can do the work."

One man stood up. "Weaving is a skill that takes years to learn. Ye cannae just step in."

"Many women ken how to use a loom," Aileen answered.

"Stick to making dresses," another man called out.

"Seamstresses doona make good wages," Cora said. "The weavers' union has forced the government to bring

88

back decent pay."

"Aye," the man standing said. "Because we *are* a union. We pay dues and we stick together. We had to go on strike to make the government believe us. Those wages support our families."

"Women have families to feed too," Cora replied. "We should be paid as well as men."

"Nae in the weavers' trade," the man answered. "We fought for those wages. We'll nae let someone—man or woman—come in and steal from us."

"We are nae stealing…" Aileen began, but half the hall was already on their feet, starting to move out. "Wait! Where are ye going?"

"The weavers' union is walking out," the original standing man said. "We have nothing more to say."

Fenella and Deidre began to protest, but Aileen held up her hand. "Let them leave. Perhaps we can convince the remainder."

It took Mr. James several minutes to quiet the rest of the audience down. He turned to the women. "I suggest you conclude your remarks quickly."

Annie frowned. First the union workers walked out—she'd also seen Mr. Haines follow them, more than likely to insure their goods would stay at the warehouse—and now their group wasn't supposed to finish speaking?

Aileen took a deep breath. "We just want to let the rest of ye ken that we just want the right to work—"

"Then be a seamstress," someone yelled.

"Seamstresses doona make good wages," Aileen answered. "We—"

"Doona expect tailors, cordwainers, or milliners to let ye take away their jobs," another man interrupted.

"We doona want to take your jobs," Cora said. "But some women have families to feed too."

"Then get married and let your man support ye!"

Annie felt her temper rising. "Maybe we doona want to be chattel!"

"'Tis your place. A man provides a roof over your head and ye should be grateful."

"What if we want to be independent, just like ye?"

A rumble of voices followed that remark. Mr. James hurried over. "I think you had best leave."

Annie turned to glare at him, her hands on her hips. "Why?"

The answer she waited for did not come from Mr. James. Instead, several dozen rotten pieces of fruit and vegetables came raining down on them. Annie had started to duck, but a large cabbage hit her head. For a moment everything sparkled around her and then all went black.

****

Niall stomped up the stairs to the warehouse, found it locked, and started pounding on the door.

"You are making enough racket to wake the dead over at the Necropolis," Owen said mildly. "Everything is dark. I do not think Annie is here."

Niall didn't think so either, but he kept pounding. "There was a light in the back of the warehouse when we passed by."

"I thought she had a meeting with Haines. What would Annie be doing in the warehouse?"

"Hell, I doona ken," Niall answered, "but she should have been home by now. If she's nae in the office, where else can she be?"

"Did Haines say they were to meet here?" Owen

asked.

Niall paused, rubbing his sore knuckles. Had Annie mentioned the location? She'd just said she had to attend a meeting with Haines and she'd insisted that Niall not accompany her or Haines would start to think she was not competent. He'd argued the point, but when she accused him of considering her a dimwit, he'd acquiesced. He didn't want her feeling he thought she was stupid. "I doona think she said."

"I think she may have given us the slip," Owen said.

Niall gave him a sharp look. "Us?"

Owen shrugged. "I did not try to stop her either."

"Well…" Niall started to go down the steps when he heard a bump and then a muffled voice on the other side of the door and turned back. "Someone is in there."

"Aye. It sounds like someone bumped into something," Owen said and started rapping on the door with metal head of his walking stick.

Niall glanced at it. "I guess that comes in handy for something."

"Actually, this thing comes in quite handy as a quarterstaff when used correctly," Owen replied. "London does not favor men walking around with long swords strapped to their sides."

"Good point." Niall resumed hammering on the door. "I ken someone is in there. Open up or we'll break down the door."

There was another muffled sound, closer this time, and then the door opened. Kingsley held up a lantern. "Good God. Do the two of you want to have the night watchman come running?"

"I doona care if he does," Niall answered. "Where is Annie?"

"With Haines, I imagine."

Niall held onto his temper. Barely. "And where were they meeting?"

Kingsley frowned at him. "The Trades Hall."

"The Trades Hall?" The hair at Niall's nape began to prickle. "Why would she be going there?"

"The union workers are holding their monthly meeting." Kingsley shrugged. "She said that women's club of hers was going to speak—"

"Hellfire and damnation!" Niall didn't wait for him to finish, but started running down the street, Owen beside him. He should have suspected something when a carriage had called for her, since they usually walked to the warehouse. The last time the women had gone to the Trades Hall, they'd been lucky nothing had happened besides being shouted at. The mood of the crowd hadn't been good then, and with wages still not up to what they had been two years ago, those workers would not be inclined to welcome anything the Progress Club had to say.

Niall increased his pace as they turned onto Glassford Street. "I was a damn fool to let Annie talk me into letting her go alone."

Owen didn't break his stride. "That makes two of us."

Niall gave him a sharp look. For once, they agreed on something, but now was not the time to discuss it. He bounded up the stairs of the Trades Hall, pushed open its double doors, and ran up the steps to the meeting room, Owen right behind him.

It took only a moment to assess the melee. An assortment of rotten food littered the floor near the speaker's stand. Several men were approaching it while the women huddled around another form on the floor.

Annie.

He sprang toward her, cursing himself that he hadn't chosen to wear his sword this evening. One man had almost reached Annie and Niall landed a fist on the man's jaw, hearing a satisfying crunch and flattened the nose of another who'd picked up a cabbage to throw. And then Owen was in front of him, wielding the cane like a claymore, swinging the walking stick low to crack the knees of a third man and lifting it as he reeled around to strike the shoulder of a fourth.

"Get the lass out of here," Owen said, crouching into a fighting stance, holding the staff ready. "I've got ye covered." Then he turned back to the men who stood gaping. "Which one of ye cowards is next? 'Tis a while since I've had a good fight."

Niall hardly noticed that Owen had lapsed into a Scottish burr. Instead, Niall gathered Annie in his arms—God, was she breathing? She was so still. Let her be breathing… He breathed a sigh of relief as he felt Annie stir and moan. He jerked his head toward Aileen. "Get your friends out of here. I'll follow."

She didn't need to be told twice. They all scurried toward the stairs. Niall glanced back before he started down. Owen was still holding his position, but Mr. James was shouting at the men to stand down. There probably was no need to tell them, since they hadn't moved after four of their friends were passed out cold on the floor. Niall managed a quick grin in spite of the situation.

It seemed MacLean was still a Highlander, after all.

****

Kingsley watched MacDonald and MacLean race off and then muttered a soft curse as he closed the office door. That had been a bit too close for comfort, but at least neither of them had asked what he was doing here.

He set the lantern down on the counter. Maybe he was getting soft. He couldn't afford to be careless in the spy business, yet light from the lamp must have leaked from the one window in the warehouse, even though he'd pulled the oiled cloth over it before he began investigating. He'd had a jolt when the banging began, thinking for a moment that Haines had returned from the meeting early, but then quickly realized the man had his own key. He'd remained still when he recognized the voices, figuring they'd soon leave, but when he went to check if they had, he bumped into a damn chair. Another mistake. He had no doubt they would have broken the door if he hadn't opened it.

The prime minister had spent too much time slowly tracking down the suspected culprits in the plan to overthrow the English government for Kingsley to botch things up. Liverpool would have little tolerance, if any, if his own scheme was discovered. As it was, Kingsley had not succeeded in identifying who the actual head of the Committee for Organizing a Provisional Government was or if it truly existed or was just rumor. All Kingsley could do at the moment was begin to ferret out the men who met at Walker's.

The ledgers at Haines Consolidated Warehousing had been of little value. He might have saved himself the time it took to persuade the Ferguson woman to trust him enough to double-check the books. The accounts seemed to be in order, with stock entries matching the numbers in inventory, which nixed his first theory that more stock was being sent out than was reported. Yet the prime minister had documentation of investments Haines had made that required more money than his profit margin showed he was earning.

Kingsley hadn't had a chance yet to check on whether shipments received agreed with ledger entries, since none had come in while he'd been here. A tobacco shipment was due from the States next week and he would take careful count, but Kingsley's instincts told him he was looking down the wrong rabbit hole.

And his instincts were rarely wrong.

Which had brought him to the warehouse tonight. If the inventory numbers were accurate, than maybe something was out of order with the inventory itself. He'd examined bolts of linens and woolens stored on shelves, opened—and closed—boxes of glassware, and even inspected empty barrel drums that a cooper had brought in just that morning. He'd been about to look at the barley barrels when MacDonald and MacLean had started pounding on the door.

Kingsley picked up his lantern and headed back into the warehouse. He circled the space where the barley had been placed on wooden pallets to keep the barrels dry. It has seemed peculiar to him that Haines had insisted they occupy this space only since the other wall was equally dry. The Ferguson chit had been right that this spot would be better for kelp bales since it was also out of the wind. So why had Haines been angry and insisted the barley be moved back? And, Kingsley remembered suddenly, Haines had also said that, in the future, barrels were not to be moved. Why?

Was it possible there wasn't barley in those barrels? Kingsley pulled out a pocket watch. The meeting at the Trades Hall would end soon. He had no way of knowing whether Haines would come by the warehouse or not, but he certainly couldn't be caught opening one of the barrels.

He glanced over at the empty barrels the cooper had brought. Miss Ferguson had counted them, but Haines hadn't been in today, so he would have no way of knowing if one was missing. Kingsley doubted that Miss Ferguson would check either since the barrels weren't due to ship out for several days. He could fill one with dirt and use it as a placeholder while he took one of the barley barrels to his flat. If all the barrel contained was barley, he would return it and no one would be the wiser.

Fifteen minutes later, the barrel was in the back of his phaeton and Kingsley was on his way home.

Chapter Nine

An annoying buzz hovered over Annie's head and she tried to swat the interference away. She wanted to stay nestled where she was, in cocoon warmth against a broad chest, held by strong, muscular arms, enveloped in a delightful scent of fresh soap and leather and floating in a foggy haze.

A face came into focus. Niall. He lowered his head, his lips brushing across her cheek gently. Not her cheek. Her mouth. She wanted his firm lips on her mouth…

The buzz became a faint murmur of voices. Annie burrowed further into her dream. She was content to remain here forever. *Niall was about to kiss her…*

Someone gave her shoulder a gentle shake. "Open your eyes, Annie."

A male voice, but not Niall's. Her shoulder was shaken again, a bit harder this time. "Annie. Wake up."

She didn't want to. She liked where she was, if only they would let her alone. A putrid odor suddenly invaded her nostrils and she sputtered, then blinked her eyes open. The physician was waving smelling salts under her nose. She sputtered again. "Take those away."

He moved back. "She sounds normal."

"Thank God. We have been so worried."

Annie turned at the sound of her mother's voice and then looked around. She was in her bedroom, lying on her bed. Behind her mother, she could see the members of the Progress Club crowding the doorway.

"What happened?"

The doctor looked at her gravely. "How much do you remember?"

Annie frowned, trying to recall. "We…were at a meeting. The Trades Hall. I…I was speaking…" It hurt to think. Her head ached. Annie lifted a hand to her forehead and felt a lump, wincing as the pain increased. "How did I hit my head?"

"I believe something was thrown at you," the doctor replied.

"A cabbage," Aileen called from the doorway. "Some lily-livered idiot threw a cabbage." The doctor gave her a mild look which she ignored. "Niall and Owen are trying to find out which one of the louts did it."

So Niall wasn't here then. Annie didn't know whether to be relieved or sorry. Had he really kissed her cheek or did she just dream it? But why would she dream something like that? It didn't make sense. But then, neither did it make sense if he really did kiss her. Her thinking must be muddled. She began to shake her head to clear it, then stopped from the pain.

"Easy now," the doctor said. "I think you have a mild concussion, so the less you move your head the better.

"A concussion?"

He nodded. "It is fairly normal when someone is struck and loses consciousness. The fact that you remember most of what happened is good." He picked up the small oil lamp by the table and held it close to her face. "Your pupils are not dilated. Another good sign." He put the lamp down. "But I want you to stay in bed and rest for two or three days."

"Can we nae talk to her?" Fenella asked.

"Talking is fine. It's better if she stays awake." He gathered his things and put them in a satchel and turned to go. "Just do not excite her."

"That is easier said than done," Cora said as the women flowed in after the doctor left. "Too bad ye were not awake to see what happened!"

Annie touched her head again. "I am nae sure I want to ken."

"Aye, ye do," Deidre said. "Well, maybe not the part about the rotten fruit—"

"Someone actually threw rotten fruit at us?" Annie asked.

Aileen nodded grimly. "Lots of it too."

"But why? We had permission to speak. Mr. James put us on the agenda."

"Which just gave the jackanapes time to gather their ammunition," Deidre replied. 'They had nae intention of even listening to us."

"So what happened after I was knocked out?"

"Oh! Well, that's the best part!" Kiara said.

"Aye! I have nae seen anything like it before!" Nairna added.

"Like *what*?" Annie asked.

"Niall—Mr. MacDonald—was magnificent," Inis said. "He—"

"When he saw ye on the floor, he practically flew across the room!" Kiara interrupted.

Nairna nodded. "I've nae seen a man move so fast."

Fenella grinned. "His fists were quick too. He smashed the nose of one of the swine and I think he broke the jaw of another. I heard a nice crack."

Annie winced. "Were the men still throwing rotten

fruit, then?"

"Nae. I think they'd run out," Aileen answered, "but some of them were coming at us."

Annie felt her eyes widen. "Why? What were they going to do? Beat us?"

"Who kens? They had become a mob."

"But doona fash." Fenella gave Annie another grin. "They didnae get a chance to do anything."

"Niall stopped all of them?" Annie asked.

"Owen—Mr. MacLean—helped," Kiara replied.

"I dinna ken a walking stick was a real weapon," her twin said.

"Ye are nae making sense." Annie hoped the bang to her head wasn't worse than the doctor thought. "What did Owen do?"

"He called the entire crowd cowards," Fenella said, "and then asked who wanted to fight him."

Annie lifted both brows. "With only his walking stick?"

"Aye, but the way he handled it, it could have been a sword. He felled two men practically in the same move," Fenella answered. "I think maybe he broke the knee of one of them. Maybe we can get a count of the number of bones broken?"

Aileen frowned. "That hardly matters."

"It was amazing the way Niall and Owen fought with bare fists and a walking stick. They acted like knights of old." Inis smiled. "If they'd been dressed in their tartans and carrying their regular weapons, those men would have turned tail and run."

Fenella nodded. "Some with wet trousers, too."

"That does nae matter either." Aileen shook her head. "Having four of them passed out on the floor stopped the rest of the mob."

"Thank God," Cora said.

"But what do we do now?" Deidre asked. "How can we make our voices heard if we are nae safe speaking in front of what was supposed to be a civilized group?"

"We cannae back down," Fenella replied.

"Nae. We cannae let them think they frightened us," Cora said.

"We could organize a protest march," Aileen answered. "We can use what happened to shame those men. We'll make signs and gather in front of Glasgow Cathedral on Sunday. Pelting innocent females who had permission to speak at their meeting is both dishonorable and base. If we take the righteous stance of being wronged, their wives will no doubt make them pay for it, even if the ladies don't believe in our cause."

"And as a follow-up, we can march down George Street in front of the city chambers on Monday," Fenella added.

A chorus of "ayes" went up from the club. Annie didn't even want to think of what Niall was going to say about that. She'd no doubt be in for the lecture of her life as well. In fact, she'd be lucky if he let her out of his sight to use the necessary room.

****

Annie didn't see Niall until the next evening since her mother insisted she follow the doctor's orders and stay in bed. She didn't really mind having a breakfast tray brought up—dining in bed was a rare luxury, especially with a boardinghouse full of guests, but by the time the noon meal came, Annie was already restless. There was no way she could stay cooped up in one room for another two days.

Niall was seated at the dining table in the small room off the kitchen her mother used for their private meals when she entered. He stood. "Are ye well enough to be out of bed?"

"I will go stark raving mad if I have to stay inside four walls." Annie motioned him to sit as she helped herself to mutton stew from the cauldron on the table. "Why are ye eating alone?"

"I wanted the peace and quiet," he replied, breaking off a piece of bread. "I had two ships arrive today and every worker on the dock wanted to ken what happened last night. I could barely get them to unload the wares. When I got home, every boarder hounded me as well."

"I suppose they are curious, especially since I've been tucked away out of sight."

"Curious is putting it mildly. Owen said they were worse than London's *ton* scenting scandal."

Annie looked around. "Where is Owen?"

"He and Aidan are making the rounds of clubs this evening."

"Carousing? I've only met your brother once, but he dinnae seem the type."

"He is nae. And they are nae. Carousing, I mean."

"Then why are they visiting the men's clubs?"

Niall chewed a bit of bread and swallowed before answering. "MacLean thought it might be wise to get the feel of things. See what pockets of unrest are still there."

"That could lead to brawling."

Niall shook his head. "That is why Aidan went with him. My brother prefers to negotiate and smooth things over when possible."

Annie smiled. "Are ye sure he's your brother?"

"I dinnae say he could nae fight," Niall replied.

"When we were lads, he could beat all of us. Well, except for Alasdair."

Annie remembered Alasdair's rescuing Bridget and herself. He'd arrived just in the nick of time, much like Niall had last night. She shifted uneasily in her chair. So far, Niall had been pleasant. That didn't mean a storm wasn't brewing and about to be unleashed.

"So let us talk about last night." Niall laid down his spoon.

Annie nearly toppled off her chair. Had she spoken her thoughts out loud? He couldn't have read her mind. "Ummm. It seems I owe ye a big thank ye."

Niall watched her. "I doona want thanks."

"Ah…the girls told me that ye were quite magnificent to watch."

He shrugged.

Annie swallowed hard. "It was verra good of ye—and Mr. MacLean—to come to our defense."

"We are Highlanders."

As if that explained everything. Well, it probably did to him. But he wasn't giving any quarter in this conversation. His eyes were turning even darker, like a squall line forming. She tried not to wiggle. "I doona ken why the men got so angry."

Silence. Niall's face could have been chiseled in stone.

She tried again. "We did have permission to speak at the meeting."

One black brow went up. "That dinnae matter much now, did it?"

Did he have to look so formidable? He must not have shaved since yesterday, because stubble shadowed his face, which just made him look darker and more contentious. And she had dreamed that he had gently kissed her? Annie felt her face warm. "The men dinnae want to hear us."

"Well, at least we agree on that." He lowered his brow. "'Tis good ye are embarrassed about going there."

Annie blinked. He thought she was embarrassed about attending the meeting? What she was embarrassed about was the dream…especially the end of it when he was about to kiss her. Dear God! Worse, she had *wanted* him to. In the dream, that is. Dear God. How could she have even dreamed of such a thing? Niall's mouth—she gave it a fleeting glance—was so set it could have been sculpted of marble. Definitely not kissable. She needed to forget that blasted dream, yet it had seemed so real… Her face heated even more.

Niall frowned. "Ye are verra flushed, lass. Are ye sure ye are nae running a fever?"

Drat her fair skin. She certainly couldn't tell him the real reason her face was on fire. He'd probably be horrified that she had even thought about what his lips would feel like on hers. Or worse, he'd laugh. Like Broderick. She felt her face flame and put her hands to her cheeks, hoping to hide the color.

She had to leave. Annie pushed back her chair and stood. "I think perhaps I do need to return to my room."

Niall stood too. "Do ye want me to walk with ye? Ye doona look well."

"I…I will be fine." Annie forced herself to walk, and not run, to the door. "I just need a bit more rest. I'll be better in the morning."

Niall looked unsettled. "Until morning, then."

She nodded and turned into the hall. At least, she could be grateful that she had escaped the lecture she was sure Niall had planned. But her relief was short-lived, since Niall called after her.

"In the morning, we will discuss why ye slipped away from me."

****

Niall sat back down after Annie left. He didn't think he'd ever met such a stubborn female, and that was saying something, considering his own sister was willful and tenacious, not to mention his sister-by-marriage being equally headstrong and obstinate. Niall had actually laughed at Alasdair when Bridget flaunted his orders. *Requests* really, not orders. It wasn't so funny now. Annie was worse…she was intractable.

What had possessed those women to think they could march into the Trades Hall and talk to union workers about taking their jobs? Did they think the men would just sit there and listen to them politely as though they were asking for donations for the almshouse? Niall sighed. That was more than likely exactly what they thought. And that was where women were different from men. Women *trusted*. Women were *civil*. Niall couldn't remember a single meeting of opposing Highland clans—even to discuss truces and alliances—where everyone wasn't well-armed and only a step or two away from brawling.

Didn't those ladies of the Progress Club recall their last encounter at the Trades Hall? Niall grimaced. He remembered Annie had thought that evening had gone quite well. They'd been lucky to leave without violence breaking out. The undercurrent had been angry, but the ladies didn't think the boos and jeers were anything to worry over. Another difference between men and women.

Besides that, women were vulnerable. They might deny it—Annie most certainly would—but that didn't change the fact. Men were bigger and stronger and, when threatened, reacted physically. Those union workers had come prepared to hurl rotten fruit and vegetables. Annie had gotten hurt. She could have been killed.

Annie could have been killed. Niall shuddered. The sight of her lying on the ground with blood flowing from the head wound had been an image he'd tried to push away all day. Now it returned in stark reality. He remembered how fragile she had seemed when he carried her down the steps. How warm and soft she had felt in his arms and how her face had nestled perfectly against his shoulder, the light lavender scent of her hair making her seem all the more delicate—a description she would no doubt denounce with some colorful words. The kiss he'd brushed across her cheek had made him want to taste the fullness of her lips…

"There ye are!" Aidan came through the doorway, followed by Owen. "We were looking for ye out in the public room."

"I didnae feel up to handling a load of questions," Niall replied. "Did ye find any answers?"

"Aye." Both men sat down and Aidan looked to Owen. "Do ye want to go first?"

"We could not find the man who actually threw the cabbage," Owen said, "but that is not surprising since there were a number of cabbages on the floor."

"Nae to mention the union workers are a tight-knit group who will nae speak against their own," Niall said.

"Aye," Aidan replied, "but Mr. James is willing to admonish the men who were involved."

"Hindsight is always sharp, nae?" Niall asked.

"Hindsight and perhaps what occurred being mentioned in the papers," Owen said. "I am sure there was probably a reporter or two there."

"'Twould be good if the rest of Glasgow kens what happened."

"Perhaps. Perhaps nae," Aidan said.

Niall frowned at him. "Nae? The union workers acted like brutes."

"I am nae arguing that point," Aidan replied, "but tempers are already running high due to low wages and the English government trying to control the unions. If the rest of Glasgow starts condemning them for what transpired, they might blame—and hate—the women in the Progress Club even more."

"Then Annie needs to cease working at the warehouse," Niall said.

Aidan raised a brow. "Somehow, I doona see her agreeing to do that."

"Of course she will nae agree to it." Niall set his jaw. "I will persuade her."

The other brow went up. "Have ye learned nothing from Alasdair? He was nae successful in curbing Bridget."

"That was different," Niall answered.

"Be that as it may," Owen said, "but the warehouse is probably fairly safe."

Niall folded his arms across his chest. "How so?"

"First of all, the barley farmers who use the warehouse are not involved with the unions," Owen replied. "Neither are our kelp shipments."

"But what of the weavers? Half the warehouse is full of woolens."

Owen nodded. "But the weavers were not there last

night. Haines assured me they had walked out before the melee started."

"Why did they leave?"

"They were nae happy with the women speaking," Aidan said.

"Which just proves my point, nae?" Niall asked. "If the weavers are angry, they might vent that on Annie while she is at work."

"Haines assured us that he will deal directly with the weavers, and Kingsley vowed to keep order at the warehouse."

Niall didn't particularly like Kingsley, but the man had the size to impose order among the workers. Perhaps Annie would be safe for a few days until Niall could figure a way to convince her to seek other employment. Meanwhile, he would double his efforts of escorting her everywhere, armed to the teeth. She wasn't going to slip away from him so easily again.

"There is just one more thing," Owen said.

Niall turned to him. "What?"

"I also spoke to Inis today." Owen had an odd expression on his face, one that Niall couldn't read. The hair at Niall's nape began to rise. "And?"

"The women are organizing a protest march."

"They are doing *what*?"

"A protest march," Owen repeated. "They intend to use what happened to Annie as a way to shame the men for their actions."

Niall was suddenly very glad he was sitting down. Hellfire and damnation. Annie Ferguson was going to be the death of him yet.

Chapter Ten

"Ye are *nae* going to march!"

They had scarcely left the steps of the boardinghouse on the walk to work the next morning before Niall made his announcement. Annie stopped in her tracks. "How did ye find out about that?"

"Inis told us." Niall narrowed his eyes. "Ye were thinking about sneaking out on me again, like ye did Monday night, nae?"

"I dinnae *sneak* anywhere. I left in a carriage."

"Ye ken verra well what I mean, lass. Ye were near killed."

Annie shook her head. "I doona think anyone meant to kill me."

"Those men were nae throwing flower petals in the air."

"I *ken* that. The stench alone made that obvious. And aye, it was rude—"

"Rude? *Rude*? Ye cannae be so…" Niall paused.

Annie lifted a brow. "Stupid? Was that what ye meant to say?"

"Nae…I…" Niall ran his fingers through his hair. "If ye cannae truly see what those workers' intentions were, then ye surely qualify for sainthood."

Annie put her hands on her hips. "Then ye *are* calling me stupid. For certain, no one has ever likened me to a saint."

Niall gave an exasperated huff. Annie had a way of turning his words around. "I meant only a saint would show mercy for what those men did."

"Ah! So we are in agreement, then." She gave him a satisfied-looking smirk and started walking again.

Niall frowned and followed her. "What did we just agree on?"

"The protest march, of course."

Niall stopped abruptly, not sure he'd heard correctly, but Annie continued to walk. In three strides he caught up to her. "I think the bump on your head may have muddled your thinking."

She glanced at him. "Now ye are calling me a half-wit?"

"Nae!" Niall felt like growling. "Ye just are nae making sense."

"Um." She turned her attention to the sidewalk. "That is what half-wits do, ye ken. Make nae sense. 'Tis why they are called such."

He was going to be half-witted soon himself if Annie didn't stop using his words against him. "I will never agree to the protest march."

"Ye doona have to."

Niall drew his brows together. "What do ye mean by *that*?"

She stopped again. "Just what I said. Ye doona have to agree. 'Tis my decision."

"I will nae allow it." As soon as the words came out, both of her brows shot up and Niall realized too late he'd probably used the wrong words. Again. It seemed Annie had a way of muddling his thinking as well. "'Tis nae safe for ye."

She inhaled deeply and Niall could practically hear

her counting numbers in her head. Finally she spoke.

"I appreciate that ye want me to be safe. I also appreciate that ye came to my rescue Monday night. I admit we were nae prepared for such an onslaught." She took another deep breath. "But this is different."

He crossed his arms across his chest. "How?"

"We are going to meet Sunday in front of the cathedral—"

"A church? Ye are planning to meet at a church?" Had the lass truly hit her head too hard? "The minister is nae likely to allow ye to speak."

"We doona intend to go in," Annie answered. "We are going to hold signs that the wives will read when they come out, so they'll ken how their husbands behaved."

Niall groaned. Men who would be turned out of their beds would be as surly and irritable as a bear awakened in midwinter. "Ye will just make the men more angry."

Annie shrugged. "Initially, perhaps."

"'Tis nae wise."

"There ye go again, telling me I doona ken how to think."

"I dinnae mean…" Niall muttered a curse in Gaelic under his breath. Annie was going to drive him barmy. "Never mind. Ye are going to be late for work if we stand here arguing over this."

"Ye are right about that, at least." Annie stomped off.

Niall sighed and went after her. She might not like his presence, but he had vowed to escort her whether she liked it or not. He wasn't going to take the chance on her being accosted on the street, but he wisely kept quiet for the rest of the walk. It wasn't until they were at the front door of the warehouse that he spoke again.

"I doona want ye to be part of that protest."

Annie hesitated on the steps and then shook her head. "Ye are nae my husband. Doona tell me what to do."

"Ye are still prickly as a thistle." Niall clenched his jaw and opened the door for her. "We are nae married. Ye are right about that. Somehow, I doona think ye would do as I asked even if I were your husband."

She gave him a startled look and then her face turned a deep shade of pink as she turned and rushed inside.

Niall closed the door and stared at it. Why in the hell had he said that? He didn't know, but the woman had the unique ability to make him say the wrong things.

****

Annie was relieved to see no one at the counter when she entered the office. She needed a moment to gather her thoughts, if not her wits. *Ye are still prickly as a thistle.* She deserved that, she supposed, given their argument. Somehow the words hurt, though, and they hadn't the last time Niall had told her the same thing. *We are nae married. Ye are right about that.* His tone had been clipped and she'd seen the muscle in his jaw twitch. He no doubt wanted her to know he was grateful they were not. Her eyes started to sting and she blinked rapidly. She should never have made the remark that he was not her husband. The words had come out before she could stop them. She should have known better than to even mention the word, given her experience with Broderick. She'd set herself up for rejection once again.

Rejection. Annie gave herself a shake. How silly to think that. She couldn't be rejected from a relationship that didn't even exist. Niall's kiss from her dream—her *dream*—had set her mind wandering in the wrong direction. How silly, too, to let a stupid comment about not being her husband bother her. After Broderick, she had vowed she would never marry. She would never succumb to *belonging* to a man like the property English law said she would be. She wanted to be independent. This job, regardless of what men thought, was proof that she could do it.

The door from the warehouse opened, breaking into her thoughts. She looked up to see Kingsley watching her.

"Are you quite recovered, Miss Ferguson?"

Annie nodded. "Aye. I just wish I had nae lost two days of work. I doona want Mr. Haines to think me a slacken."

"On the contrary. He was quite concerned over what happened."

Annie breathed a sigh of relief, only then admitting to herself that she had been afraid Mr. Haines would let her go. "I will work verra hard to make it up to him. Tell me what has transpired here while I have been away."

Kingsley went around the counter and opened the ledger. "On Tuesday, a hundred bolts of woolens were brought in—"

"A hundred bolts? That many?" Annie broke into a smile. "I was afraid the weavers might boycott the warehouse after Monday night."

"From what I understand, the weavers walked out before the…unpleasantness began," Kingsley replied.

"Aye, they did, but they were nae happy with what we had to say."

"Most men do not like to think women are as smart as they are, which makes them fools, does it not?"

Annie smiled again. "Thank ye for understanding."

"I underestimate no one's intelligence," Kingsley answered. "The weavers may not be happy with you working here, but Haines offers good prices for storage and tarps to keep the moths out of the wool. Profit takes precedence over most everything."

"Aye. 'Tis a business matter."

"The shipment of barley to the States also went out on Tuesday. Mr. MacDonald brought seventy bales of kelp yesterday and a shipment of tobacco from Virginia came in as well." Kingsley turned the ledger around for Annie. "I recorded everything so you will not have to bother."

"Thank ye," Annie replied. "Ye are a very competent foreman."

Kingsley smiled. "I always try my best."

"Aye. So do I," Annie said and walked around toward the desk. "I will just work on getting the paperwork filed, then."

"Let me know if you need me," Kingsley said. "I will be in the warehouse."

Annie immersed herself in getting things straightened out. Once she finished the filing, she decided to arrange things in a more orderly fashion. She really wanted to show Mr. Haines that she was competent, especially since he'd put such trust in her.

It was lunchtime by the time she finished. Annie walked over to the ledger on the counter. Mr. Kingsley had entered the inventory delivered in a neat, precise hand. But, since she had a bit of time, she wanted to check the counts herself. After all, Mr. Kingsley had said two sets of eyes were better than one when it came to accounts.

She tucked the ledger under her arm and went into

the warehouse. The workers had gone on lunch break, so all was quiet and still. She called for Kingsley, but received no answer, nor did she find him in any of the aisles. He'd probably gone to get something to eat too. Well, she didn't need him standing beside her just to check the inventory.

Moving to the shelves stacked with woolens, she began her count. One hundred bolts. Annie moved on to the kelp next. The slight scent of dried seaweed made her think of Niall and his ships. He hadn't ever mentioned whether he'd worked on one or if he even enjoyed sailing. Maybe she would ask this evening. The topic should be a neutral one, leaving little room for argument to occur. And, hopefully, it would keep Niall from bringing up Sunday's protest. She *was* going to attend.

Seventy bales. Annie mentally checked off the number and went over to the barrels that held the tobacco. Nineteen. She double-checked the ledger. Kingsley had entered twenty. She counted again. Nineteen. Annie did a quick walk through the warehouse, looking for the missing barrel, but found nothing. She closed the ledger and carried it back to the office. She would ask Kingsley about the count this afternoon when he returned.

Annie was just finishing the lunch she'd brought from home when Mr. Haines came in. Pushing aside the remnants of her food, she stood quickly. "I am so glad to see ye. Mr. Kingsley brought me up to date this morning, so everything is on schedule."

"Good, good. Glad to hear it. Is Kingsley here?"

Annie shook her head. "I think he left for lunch."

Mr. Haines frowned. "That is unlike him. He rarely leaves the warehouse during the day."

"Maybe he forgot to bring something to eat," Annie replied. "Or he may have had something to take care of. He will probably be back soon."

"Well, I really do not have time to wait. I have an appointment with a new merchant, Carl Cabot, who's manufacturing linen winding sheets but doesn't have enough space to store them."

Annie widened her eyes. "I hope he is nae anticipating another breakout of typhus that will require an abundance of burial sheets to have on hand?"

"Let us hope not, but people die every day, and English law requires burial in linen,' Mr. Haines replied. "I was hoping to take Kingsley to the meeting to provide reassurance that our storage facility is one of the cleanest in the city."

"Why nae take me? I can attest to that." Annie really wanted to be of assistance to make up for her missing work. "Truly."

"I am not sure…" Mr. Haines paused, considering. "I suppose I could take you. Mr. Cabot was not one of the men present at that disastrous meeting Monday night, so he should not have any animosity towards you."

Annie tried to keep herself from wincing. There was no cause for men to dislike her simply because she felt women should be able to earn fair wages.

"Just let me do the talking."

She swallowed hard. Unfair as it was, men didn't like women who spoke their minds either. If she wanted to keep her job—and she did—she needed to refrain from offering opinions at work. She'd have her chance to vent on Sunday.

"Of course, Mr. Haines. Ye are the owner." She turned away so he wouldn't detect her anger. "I will get my coat."

"I have the carriage outside," he said and walked to the door. "I will wait there."

Annie managed to compose herself in the few minutes it took to retrieve her coat, scribble a note to Kingsley, and lock the office, then proceed down the steps. She even managed to converse neutrally about the weather on the short ride to Mr. Cabot's shop, but by the time the meeting was over an hour later and she'd only been allowed two short sentences, she was ready to screech like a banshee. It was a good thing Mr. Haines had sent her back in the carriage alone or she might have unleashed a tirade of words.

Unfortunately—for Niall, at least—he was the first person she saw when she entered the office a short time later. He was leaning against the counter, one leg crossed over the other at the ankle. He looked over her shoulder through the open door just as the carriage pulled away.

Annie slammed the door shut. "Do nae even begin to lecture me on where I have been!"

One brow lifted. "I ken where ye have been."

"Oh? Did ye follow me?" Annie stormed past him, pulled off her coat and hung it on the rack. Then she turned back. "Did ye follow me?"

"Nae."

Annie frowned. "Then how did ye ken where I was?"

Niall pointed to the note she'd left.

Her frown deepened. "Ye went through the things on my desk?"

Niall straightened. "I didnae snoop."

"Then how—"

"Kingsley showed me the note," Niall replied

levelly.

"Oh."

"I doona ken why ye are so angry, lass, but I had naught to do with it."

Annie stared at him, then dropped her gaze. He was right. Suddenly she felt like a fool. She was venting her anger on the wrong person. She worried her bottom lip for a second. Apologies did not come easy for her. She looked up. "I am sorry. I dinna mean to scream at ye like a fishwife."

"Since I have nae been screamed at by a fishwife, I cannae compare." A corner of Niall's mouth quirked. "Ye remind me more of an irritated hedgehog than a fishwife."

"A...hedgehog?"

"Aye." The quirk turned into a smile. "Your hair is nigh to standing straight out from ye."

Instinctively Annie put her hands to her head to brush her hair down. "It is nae."

Niall shrugged. "Mayhap I was mistaken."

"Of course ye were." The image of an angry hedgehog caused Annie to smile. She probably did look like one. "Well, mayhap nae that much."

Niall gave her a look of mock surprise. "We agree, then?"

"Agree to what?" Kingsley asked as he came in from the warehouse.

"Um, nothing important," Annie said quickly. "I am glad to see ye back, though. I had a question about the tobacco barrels."

"What about the barrels?" Kingsley asked.

"There were only nineteen when I counted earlier. The ledger says twenty."

"Twenty is correct. I entered the number myself," Kingsley replied.

"I ken that. But I wanted to double-check the inventory that came in while I was gone," Annie said. "Ye did say two sets of eyes were better than one."

Kingsley nodded. "So I did. Why do we not go and recount?"

She didn't know what good that would do since she'd counted twice, but she didn't want to offend the foreman. "Perhaps that would be best."

"Do ye mind if I come along?" Niall asked. "Just in case of a dispute."

"Please do," Kingsley replied smoothly. "I am sure we will all find that there are twenty barrels of tobacco stored exactly where they should be."

Annie led the men into the warehouse. The barrels had been rearranged. "Someone moved them."

"I did," Kingsley said. "When I got back from lunch I realized we did not have much room in the aisle so I shifted them slightly." He gestured. "Please go ahead and do your count."

Annie used her index finger to point at each barrel so she wouldn't lose count. "Eighteen. Nineteen…. Twenty." She looked at Niall. "What did ye get?"

"Twenty."

"Good. Then that is settled," Kingsley said. "Twenty barrels."

"But there were only nineteen earlier."

Kingsley smiled. "One was probably hidden a bit behind another one. At any rate, no harm is done. We are all agreed there are twenty barrels in stock. Yes?"

"Aye," Annie said and followed Kingsley and Niall back to the office. She knew she had counted nineteen earlier. There hadn't been one misplaced, either, since she'd searched the warehouse.

Where did that twentieth barrel come from?

****

Kingsley watched Annie and Niall leave and then muttered a curse. What a bloody close call that had been. After what had taken place Monday night, he hadn't expected the chit to return to work so soon or he would have made sure he'd gotten that twentieth barrel back in place.

But then, he'd also made the mistake of assuming she wouldn't go into the warehouse and do a physical count after he'd entered the number in the ledger. Damn it. Master spies didn't *assume* anything. Not if they wanted to stay alive.

On the other hand, he now had almost all the evidence he needed.

Chapter Eleven

Annie glanced sideways at Niall as they walked home. They were almost half-way to the boardinghouse and he hadn't spoken. "Ye are angry with me still?"

Niall shook his head. "Nae."

"Ye have nae spoken a word since we left."

"Sometimes silence is better, lass."

"I cannae blame ye for nae wanting to talk." Annie felt embarrassment wash over her. "Ye doona want me to screech at ye again."

Niall smiled. "I cannae deny that, but 'tis nae the reason I am silent."

Annie furrowed her brows. "Why, then?"

"I have a sister. My brothers and I learned early to give Margaret a wide berth when her temper is riled. She has blackened more than one eye and bloodied a number of our noses."

"Your sister strikes ye?"

"On occasion. There are ten of us brothers and sometimes we tease her a bit too much."

"I have nae brothers or sisters. I cannae imagine having ten."

"Margaret would think ye lucky." Niall shrugged. "We nae doubt deserved the punches we've gotten. Besides, we were the ones who taught her to fight."

Annie felt her eyes widen. "She fights? Like a man?"

"Nae lass would win in actual fisticuffs. We did teach her to defend herself though." Niall glanced at Annie. "Something ye should learn too."

"I can take care of myself." When Niall arched a brow, she grimaced. "Well, most of the time. What happened Monday was a surprise."

"Most attacks are. 'Tis why ye need to be prepared. Have ye ever handled a dagger?"

"Nae. And doona tell me your sister handles knives like ye do."

Niall grinned. "There are few who handle knives like I do." Then he sobered. "But Margaret kens how to throw one. She can fire a musket and release an arrow straight and true as well."

"Are those skills women need in the Highlands?"

"They are skills women should have anywhere."

Annie shook her head. "I can hardly wander the streets of Glasgow with a sword or pistol at my side. And a bow would be useless in the city, if nae illegal."

"Aye, but ye can hide a dagger."

Annie glanced down to where a black handle protruded from each of Niall's boots and another knife was sheathed at his waist. "I can see those."

"But ye doona ken about the others."

"Others?" Annie frowned. "Exactly how many knives do ye carry?"

"Half a dozen or so."

"For God's sake, where?"

"About me person." Niall grinned again. "Do ye want to ken exactly where?"

Annie felt her face heat as she realized the impact of her question. "Nae! That was nae what I meant."

His grin widened. "Well, if ye change your mind,

just ask."

She didn't think her face could get any hotter, but it did. "I will nae be asking."

"Pity. I was about to divulge my secrets to ye." Niall managed to straighten his mouth. "The point is, though, that ye can hide a knife easily enough."

"I will think on it." She needed to change the subject before her face actually burst into flames. "Can we talk about something else?"

"Aye. Ye can tell me what made ye so angry earlier."

Annie sighed. That subject wasn't much better as a topic. They'd probably be arguing in a minute, but it was better than wondering where Niall kept the rest of his knives. *Not* that she was wondering. She wasn't.

"Mr. Haines needed someone to go with him to see a new client who wanted assurance our warehouse was top-notch. Mr. Kingsley wasn't in, so I offered to go. I really wanted to make up for missing two days of work—"

"Which was nae your fault. Did Haines say it was?"

"Nae. But I wanted to let him see that I could handle the job as well as Mr. Kingsley…" Annie paused and looked at Niall. "I ken ye doona think I should be working at the warehouse, but hear me out. 'Tis important that members of the Progress Club can show that women can be more than maids or nannies. They should nae be regulated to being shop clerks or seamstresses either." All the frustration of the afternoon that had built up was about to explode. Annie felt it, but could no longer stop it. "We have brains. We can think. We have intelligence. We can be bankers and accountants and solicitors and, if the blasted laws were changed, owners of property as well. We could also—"

"I think ye made your point." Niall held up his hand to keep her from protesting. "Ye doona have to prove anything to me. Margaret—to say naught of my mother—would soon put that notion to rights."

Annie frowned. "But ye doona think I should be working at the warehouse."

'Nae because ye cannae do the job. 'Tis your safety I am concerned with."

"But I have nae been accosted at the warehouse," Annie replied stubbornly.

Niall didn't seem to notice—or else he simply ignored—her tone. "But ye were knocked senseless at the Trades Hall, lass. Those are the same men who do business with Haines."

"But Mr. Haines has nae fired me. At least, nae yet," Annie answered, "which is why I need to prove to him I can do the work."

"I still doona like it."

"I ken that, but Mr. Kingsley is there too. He keeps the workers in order. I ken he would intervene if a tradesman became belligerent."

"There is something about Kingsley I doona like," Niall said.

Annie looked heavenward. "Ye doona like Owen MacLean either."

"'Tis different. Our clans tend to spar with each other," Niall replied, "although I will admit MacLean handled himself well Monday night."

Annie glanced at Niall. "So ye have a truce then? Nae more squabbling?"

Niall looked affronted. "We doona *squabble*."

Annie was tempted to roll her eyes again. "Argue,

then. Ye cannae deny that."

"We disagree on things." Niall shrugged. "But aye, for the moment MacLean and I have a truce."

"Well, at least ye have refrained from squab—*arguing*—with Mr. Kingsley. That is good."

"I doona trust the man though."

"Why nae?"

"I doona ken exactly. He talks too smooth."

Annie raised an eyebrow. "So do ye and Owen. Ye both flatter me like 'tis some game between ye."

"I cannae speak for MacLean," Niall said, "but I mean what I say. Ye do have eyes the color of a thistle bloom—"

"Must ye constantly be reminding me that I am a thistle? Besides, my eyes are *blue*."

"Ye do make it easy." Niall grinned. "Right now, I see sparks shooting from your *violet* eyes and your hair is glowing bright as a Beltane fire. 'Tis a verra pretty sight."

"There ye go again using flattery."

Niall tilted his head, his smile gone. "Why do ye nae like compliments?"

Oh, Lord! How to answer? Her face was probably glowing like a Beltane fire too. 'I…just doona put much faith in sweet words." Then, before he could press further, she said quickly, "So what other reason do ye have for nae trusting Mr. Kingsley?"

"Something just does nae seem right." Niall shook his head. "I wish my brother, Lachlan, were here. His instincts regarding a man are rarely wrong."

"I think ye are putting too much thought into this."

"Thought? Nae. Thought is logic. This is more a feeling that I have." Niall paused. "But Aidan is logical.

The most practical one among us. Mayhap I should bring him to the warehouse—"

"I doona think that necessary," Annie replied. Dear God! All she needed was another MacDonald hovering around. Along with Owen, that would make three men being protective. Mr. Haines would think her incapable for sure.

"Aidan has been busy learning the books at Henderson Shipping," Niall continued as though she hadn't interrupted. "'Tis time he see the warehousing end of it as well."

"I doona think it a good idea for Aidan to stop by the warehouse," Annie said.

"And I doona think it a good idea for ye to work there," Niall replied as they approached the boardinghouse.

Annie preceded him up the steps. "We will just have to agree to disagree on that."

"Aye, we will," Niall said, opening the door. "Then 'tis settled."

Annie gave him a side glance as she walked inside. "What is settled?"

"Ye did just say we need to agree to disagree, aye?" Niall grinned at her. "Aidan will be stopping by."

****

"Ye want me to do what?" Aidan asked the next day when Niall met him at Henderson Shipping and they were both behind the closed door of the small office.

"I need your reaction to John Kingsley. I sense something is off about him."

"I have nae the skill to read a man like Lachlan does," Aidan answered.

"True, but Lachlan is nae here. Besides, I want your

opinion on Haines' business."

"I am only in Glasgow to learn how Robert's books are set up so I can duplicate them on Skye." Aidan put down the quill he'd been using. "What reason would I use for wanting to inspect Haines' warehouse?"

"Ye would nae have to go into the warehouse."

"If Kingsley is foreman of the warehouse, would that nae be where I would find him?"

"He seems to spend just as much time in the office with Annie when he does nae need to. 'Tis another thing I find strange."

Aidan smiled. "Could that be the source of your suspicion? Are ye sure ye are nae jealous?"

"*Nae*!" Given Aidan's inquiring look, Niall realized he may have said that a little louder than he needed to. "Nae. Why should I be?"

"Ye do seem to spend a lot of time with her."

"Only for protection," Niall answered. "Annie is a headstrong lass not given to following good, common sense."

"Her own common sense or yours?"

"Mine, since I sometimes think she does nae have any."

Aidan smiled again. "I suspect she might nae agree."

"Which proves my point." Niall shook his head. "Just weeks after Annie and Bridget were attacked, the lass wanders down Virginia Street by herself and is near accosted again. How many lasses do ye ken would enter a trade union meeting and expect to be heard? Twice, mind ye. Her club was booed the first time, but did Annie learn her lesson? Nae. Back she went for a pelting of rotten fruit." A shudder escaped him at her narrow escape. "The daft woman could have been killed."

Aidan gave him a thoughtful look. "Ye care about her."

"Nae...I..." Niall paused. "Well...I mean...I like her, but she is too willful and stubborn by far."

Aidan laughed. "Which means she has nae succumbed to your charms."

Niall snorted. "Charms? The lass will nae even accept a compliment."

"That's a first for ye."

"Aye, well. 'Tis nae the topic." Niall was pretty sure Annie didn't take compliments seriously from anyone, but he didn't understand *why*. Most women craved them, even when they knew the comments were insincere. They enjoyed flirtation. Not Annie though. She acted like such a thing was an insult. That confounded him too. Annie was certainly pretty enough and, when her mouth wasn't sparking fire at him, quite a good conversationalist, quick-witted and well-informed. He *did* like her, he realized. She *did* have intelligence. She *could* think. She just wouldn't listen to him. He sighed.

"Annie talks of wanting to be more than is often a woman's lot. That they want to be bankers and solicitors and such. I ken that is the Progress Club's purpose."

"Unfortunately, Britain is nae ready to entertain those ideas," Aidan replied.

"Ye doona have to tell me," Niall said. "I think Annie kens that will nae happen, but her group sees getting the skilled jobs that weavers and wrights and cordwainers have as a start."

Aidan grimaced. "None of those are easy jobs."

"True, but the wages are far more than women's jobs pay," Niall answered. " Nae depending on a man for support is important to them."

"Do they nae realize how angry men become with just the *thought* of a woman replacing one of them?" Aidan asked. "Those workers came *prepared* to throw rotten fruit Monday night."

"Exactly what I have been trying to tell Annie." Niall lifted his hands in the air and slumped back in his chair. "Now ye understand the problem. She does nae listen to what I have to say. The lass is too headstrong, obstinate, unbending—"

"I think ye have already covered those traits," Aidan said, "but ye are nae her husband and cannae order her to stop."

There was that phrase again. *Nae her husband.* Annie had used those words herself. "I doona think she would listen to a husband if she had one."

Aidan nodded. "Ye are probably right. Alasdair doesn't fare well anytime he attempts to order Bridget about or Robert either when it comes to his wife, Shauna. But ye are doing all ye can to protect Annie."

"Well, 'tis one more thing I can do."

"Which is?"

Niall pulled a small dagger from inside a hidden sheath in his belt. "I can teach her to use this."

Aidan eyed the sharp knife. "Ye may want to rethink that. Given the lass's temper, she might be inclined to turn it on ye."

"Nae man has ever bested me with a knife."

"But a lass might, if ye let down your guard," Aidan said. "Annie is a most unusual woman."

Niall grinned. That she was.

****

An unusual woman. Aidan had no idea of how right he was, Niall thought on Saturday morning as he and

Annie stood in the small yard behind the boardinghouse. Not only had she learned the art of throwing a knife quickly, she was also hitting the target on the tree almost dead center.

"I think ye did nae tell me the whole truth when we began this lesson," Niall said as he pulled the dagger out of the tree bark. "Ye have done this before, aye?"

"Nae with a real knife."

"All knives are real. Ye mean with a dull blade?"

Annie shook her head. "I used to practice throwing sticks at that tree."

Niall would have smiled, but Annie looked so serious. "Were ye pretending to be a warrior, then?"

She hesitated. "Something like that."

He had no trouble imagining Annie playacting the part. He doubted she'd ever been a docile lass staying indoors to keep her dresses clean. "So, did ye win?"

The pause was a little longer this time. "Nae. He...that is, the *tree* is still standing."

It would have been a humorous remark, except that her tone was flat. Niall furrowed his brows. Annie had said *he* before she changed it. Had some man in the past tried to attack her? Niall didn't think she meant the recent attempts, since she said she'd *used* to practice. He started to ask, but she was holding her hand out for the blade, a determined look on her face. Niall handed her the knife. His question would have to wait.

"Try hurling it a little harder this time."

His words were barely out of his mouth when she let fly. The aim went wide, the weapon skittering off the side of the tree. Annie muttered something undistinguishable under her breath. Niall gave her a covert glance as he went to retrieve the knife.

"A word of advice, lass. Never let emotion control your throw."

She frowned. "What do ye mean?"

This time, he was the one to pause. "Either anger or fear will break your concentration."

Her chin lifted and she held her hand out for the knife. This time, she took careful aim, moved her left foot slightly forward for balance and took a deep breath as he'd instructed her to. The blade hit center.

"Verra good!"

"Thank ye." Her lips lifted in a slight smile. "Now I will ken what to do if I meet a tree I doona like."

Niall smiled too, glad to see whatever had been bothering her seemed to have disappeared. "Now I want to show ye how to use the blade in close quarters." He stepped forward and grasped her wrist before she realized what he was doing and then pressed his thumb in a strategic place between her knuckles that caused her hand to open. The knife clattered to the ground.

"'Tis nae fair! I dinna ken ye were going to do that."

"Ye will nae get fair warning if a man intends to accost ye."

"Then tell me what I'm supposed to do."

As she bent down to pick up the blade, Niall stepped to one side and reached around her waist, pinning her arms to her sides as he picked her up. She let out a surprised squeal.

"Let me go!" She squirmed furiously against him. "What do ye think ye are doing?"

Niall set her down, all too aware of how the undersides of her breasts had grazed the tops of his arms as she wiggled. How lush and surprisingly heavy they were. And how delicious her backside had felt against his groin as she struggled to get free. This might not have been the best idea he'd ever had. He stepped away, glad for once that he was wearing breeches that at least kept his obvious reaction in check. Annie's reaction was obvious too, only it wasn't amorous. Her face was red and she scowled.

"Why did ye do that?"

"I wanted to impress on ye how quickly ye could be overcome."

Her eyes shot blue flames at him. "'Tis a good thing I doona have that knife."

"Aye, 'tis," Niall said and retrieved it in one fluid motion and then carefully sheathed it inside his belt. "I think we'll be using a blunt stick as I teach ye to defend yourself, since I prefer to keep all my parts attached."

Her face went crimson and Niall hoped he hadn't pushed her too far. He wanted her a little angry so he would be able to point out to her where her weakness lay in defense. He walked to the tree and picked up a stout twig that had fallen and then went back to hand it to her.

"Pretend this is a knife. Come at me. Give it your best thrust." He felt his cock stir as soon as the word was out. *Thrust* may not have been the best word to bring to mind.

For a moment Annie glared at him and then she slashed out. He blocked the move, caught her wrist again, spinning her around, careful not to apply real pressure as he brought her arm behind her. Once again, she was pressed against him. He felt her chest heave. It took every ounce of his willpower not to let the arm encircling her waist creep upward. Damnation. Every time he touched her—

"Ouch!" Niall dropped his hands as he hopped on

one foot. Annie had brought her heel down—hard—on his other one.

Annie stepped away, looking a bit triumphant. "I did say I could defend myself."

"Aye." Niall put his foot down gingerly, grateful she hadn't gone for another part of his anatomy. "Well done."

She worried her lip. "I dinnae hurt ye, did I?"

"Doona fash about hurting your opponent, lass. 'Tis what ye are supposed to do."

"But I…we…are nae really opponents. I doona want to harm—"

"That kind of thinking can get ye hurt or killed," Niall said. "If ye are attacked, ye doona have time to think of what the cur's intentions are. Assume the worst."

Annie's eyes widened. "I…hadn't thought…"

"Exactly," Niall replied. "Ye need to react quickly, as if 'tis second nature."

"I am nae a fighter," Annie said.

"Ye are more fighter than ye think," Niall answered, "but men will nae be expecting ye to have the skills." He picked up the stick from where it had dropped. "Now let me show ye the way to thr-, to *hold* the knife so ye can do the most damage in the least amount of time." When she looked doubtful, he added, "The idea is to get away, nae stay and engage."

Annie looked at the proffered stick, but she didn't take it. "I am nae sure—"

"Ye have to decide, lass." Niall grinned. "If ye would rather I increase my presence at your side, I can do that."

Annie frowned and grabbed the stick.

****

"How many more of them are there?" Kiara asked the next morning as the club gathered outside the cathedral. They'd waited for the church service to begin, since they had no intention of entering, but Annie knew Kiara wasn't referring to any of the parishioners.

She was referring to the three Highlanders who stood a few yards behind them. Aidan had joined Niall and Owen, all three of them in tartans and armed to the teeth. Annie wouldn't have been surprised to see Niall wearing the huge claymore that Alasdair had left behind, not that he needed a weapon that would mow down men like a scythe to wheat. This was a Sunday morning in a civilized city, after all.

"Niall says he has seven more brothers at home," Annie said.

"Mercy," Kiara answered. "Are they all good-looking?"

"I doona ken. I've nae seen them."

"'Tis a good possibility though," Nairna said and giggled. "I mean, they all have black hair. Alasdair had green eyes, Niall has gray, and Aidan's are somewhere in between."

Kiara giggled too. "And Owen's are dark as the devil's."

Annie glanced at both twins. "Ye seem to have spent a lot of time looking at them."

"Och, aye. Who would nae?" Kiara asked. "They are all well formed."

"A fact, for sure, given we can see their muscular legs," Nairna added, unabashed.

"She does have a point," Inis said, coming up to them. "I rather feel like Gwinevere, surrounded by knights of the Round Table."

Fenella, standing with the rest of the group slightly to their left, gave an unladylike snort. "What silly romantic notions ye have. We are nae damsels in distress."

"She is right," Aileen said. "We should nae be dependent on men to take care of us."

"Still." Inis shrugged. "It does nae hurt to have a bit of protection after what happened Monday night."

Annie supposed she was right, although it seemed Inis had taken to acting a wee bit helpless when Niall was around. And Niall always had a flowery compliment of some sort ready. Annie could understand the twins being somewhat smitten, since they were young, but Inis? For all her dainty, fragile looks, she was solid as rock regarding their cause. Or at least she had been. Was she attracted to Niall?

Not that Annie cared, of course.

"We are nae going to have a recurrence of Monday night today," Cora answered. "I hardly think the pastor would take kindly to the smell of rotten fruit and vegetables inside his church."

"Anyway, no one even kens we are waiting out here," Deidre added, "so 'tis nae an issue."

"Aye. Our purpose today is to shame those men in front of their wives," Fenella said. "And the signs we all carry will do that without us having to say a word."

Aileen turned to Annie. "We really are nae in need of bodyguards. Can ye persuade them to go home?"

Annie glanced over her shoulder at the three men positioned with hands on sword hilts, feet spread in battle pose, and sighed. "We would have a better chance at becoming members of Parliament."

It wasn't that she hadn't tried. Niall had been adamant that she wasn't going anywhere unless he accompanied her. Owen and Aidan had stood stone-faced beside him, looking as formidable then as they did now. She'd tried to explain there would not be any violence with the men escorting their wives from church. Niall's reply had been that the Highlanders' presence would insure it. She'd even succumbed to baiting him, asking him if the training he'd given her wasn't good enough. That had backfired though. Niall had simply grinned and said he wasn't through with her training yet.

Annie felt her body grow warm as she recalled the kind of training he'd already put her through. How many times she'd been pressed against him yesterday. How many times his arms had held her pinned to him. How many times his face had been inches from hers, so close she could feel his warm breath on her nape or in her ear. And—worse—how many times her body had reacted with want. Even now, muscles deep in her belly clenched at the thought of the many ways he'd touched her, his hold firm but never harsh. Even while trying to defend herself, trying to break away from him as he instructed, her traitorous body had wanted more intimacy, more…

"Are ye all right?" Cora was peering at her oddly.

Annie blinked, pushing away what was rapidly turning into a fantasy. That path only led to ruin. She was already ruined, but at least Niall didn't know. Just like he didn't know when she practiced throwing sticks at a tree, in her mind she was really striking Broderick. But that was her secret.

"I am fine. I was just…thinking."

"Doona fash. Ye are nae going to get hurt today," Fenella said.

"None of us are, with the Highlanders here." Kiara started to giggle again and Nairna joined her.

Fenella glared at both of them. "'Tis nae what I meant. Are your brains addled?"

The twins sobered and Annie felt sorry for them, but at least they had an excuse for addled brains. They were young. She had no excuse for her own brain being in a similar state.

"Church is out," Aileen said as the front doors opened. "Signs up!"

They had rehearsed how they would stand and they now took their positions on either side of the walkway. Annie's sign read *Did your husband knock me unconscious Monday night?* while others read *Ask your man about Monday night* or *Where was your husband Monday night?* and even *Rotten fruit, rotten men.*

There were gasps from the ladies, some paling and others trying to ask questions. The club had agreed not to answer them, but merely to point to the signs they held. Red-faced men took hold of their wives' arms to lead them away while the women looked back. Annie couldn't help but smile as the last of the congregation disappeared into waiting carriages. The rumble of voices left no doubt the women were already asking questions.

"I think we succeeded," she said to the rest of the group and was met with a chorus of agreement.

"Those men will have hell to pay," Fenella said with a satisfied smirk.

"And it serves them right," Aileen said.

Cora smiled. "Hopefully their wives will refuse to cook today and those men will go hungry."

"And withhold other favors as well," Deidre added.

Annie was about to make another comment when

she felt a masculine grip on her own arm and turned.

"Let us be gone from here," Niall said. "Owen and Aidan will see the other ladies home."

She felt too good to argue. "Everything went just as we planned," she said as they walked away. "Total success."

Niall shook his head. "The only thing ye succeeded in doing was making those men mad. Time will see what happens."

Chapter Twelve

Annie wasn't quite sure if she felt like a prisoner being escorted to trial or a lady being guarded from the cruel world the next morning as Niall walked on one side of her and Aidan on the other on her way to work. Perhaps Inis had the right of it yesterday when she said she felt like Guinevere surrounded by knights…except, if the grim expressions on her escorts' faces were any clue, Guinevere was probably being escorted to the stake.

"Why are ye so glum? Everything worked out as planned yesterday."

Niall slanted a glance at her. "This is nae over, lass."

Aidan nodded. "I think 'tis the beginning."

Annie shifted her gaze to him. "The beginning of what? All was quiet yesterday. The two of ye and Owen were out on the streets and heard nothing."

Aidan lifted a brow. "Have ye ever been in a storm at sea?"

"Nae." Annie frowned. "What does that have to do with anything?"

"'Tis a lull before a big blow," Aidan answered. "The wind calms. The sea goes flat. An inexperienced sailor is fooled that good weather is ahead, but a wise captain kens to furl the sails and batten the hatches."

"Aye," Niall added. "A bad storm is brewing."

"I think ye fash too much," Annie replied. "The

reason it was quiet yesterday is because the women who read our signs not only demanded answers from their husbands, but word would spread quickly to other wives who would question their husbands as well."

Aidan gave her an incredulous look. "And ye think that is good?"

"Aye. I ken that some women do nae agree with our club's purpose, but our ranks close when we are mistreated."

Niall grimaced. "Men close ranks too."

"But nae against their own wives."

"I will accede that point," Aidan answered, "but it does nae mean the union workers will nae rise against ye."

"Nae if they want to stay in the wives' good graces," Annie retorted.

"There are ways for a man to stay in his wife's good grace," Niall said.

"Like how?"

A corner of Niall's mouth quirked up. "If ye are sure ye want to ken, I will be happy to...*explain*. Later."

Annie had a sneaking suspicion that Niall's *explanation* might not just be words. Thankfully, Aidan cleared his throat and changed the subject.

"Since both of ye think I need an escort, I am surprised Owen did nae join ye."

"MacLean is spending the day sniffing out trouble," Niall replied. "If he scents problems rising, he will tell us."

"Ye make him sound like a dog."

"A wolf, more like," Aidan said.

Annie was glad when they reached the warehouse. "The two of ye can join him now, since wolves hunt in packs."

"I will spend the morning scouting, but on my own." Niall grinned at Annie. "'Tis only one lobo to a pack, lass."

Annie shook her head. Apparently the competition between the two of them had not ended. She turned to Aidan. "Are ye going to be a lone wolf too?"

"Perhaps later," Aidan answered, "but for now, I would like a tour of the warehouse facilities."

Annie bit back a groan. She'd hoped that argument had been forgotten. She should have known better.

****

The morning did not get off to a good start. Kingsley was in the warehouse inspecting a shipment of barley barrels that had just come in and he didn't look particularly pleased when Annie introduced Aidan and asked that he be given a quick tour of the facilities. The foreman said that he was busy and another time would be better. Aidan had replied that he could help in stowing the shipment. Kingsley had been downright brusque in turning the offer down. Aidan replied he would simply wait, then, and proved his point by moving to one side and leaning against the wall. Kingsley glowered at him and Annie had the strange sense that each had made some sort of silent challenge to the other. Men. To avoid any further conflict, she'd offered to show Aidan around the warehouse herself.

Mr. Haines was in the office when they finished. So was Mr. James, the chairman from the Trades Hall. Both turned as Annie and Aidan walked in. Neither smiling. Was the day going to get worse?

"It seems you had a busy Sunday, Miss Ferguson," Mr. Haines said.

"Perhaps." Annie felt a twinge of uneasiness. Was Mr. James going to try and get her fired? "What exactly are ye referring to?"

"I suspect you know," Mr. James said, "but in case you have a poor memory—"

"I doona think there is anything wrong with Annie's memory," Aidan said. "Just speak plain and keep your tone respectful."

Annie groaned silently. Was she going to have to avert another confrontation?

Both men frowned. "Who are you?" Mr. Haines asked.

"This is Aidan MacDonald," Annie replied. "Niall's brother." Not that she would have needed to add that since they looked alike. She went on quickly. "He wanted to inspect the warehouse since he'll be in charge of kelp shipments arriving from Skye."

Mr. Haines gaze sharpened like it always did when he was appraising a potential new customer. Mr. James' expression remained dour. He looked at Annie.

"Your women's club gathered in front of the cathedral yesterday morning and caused trouble."

"We dinnae say a word."

"You did not have to," Mr. James replied. "Your signs did it for you."

Annie lifted her chin. "We only wanted to let the wives ken what happened at your meeting."

His face hardened. "You knew bloody well what you were doing. I've had nothing but complaints from the men since yesterday afternoon. Those wives gave their husbands bloody hell."

Aidan adjusted his stance. "I'll nae tell ye again to be respectful."

"Yes. Yes. Let us be courteous here," Mr. Haines interjected. "Perhaps the ladies didn't make the best choice in arranging that."

Annie's temper rose. "We had every right—"

"Allow me, lass." Aidan took a step forward and gave both men a steady look. "'Tis true that my brother and I wanted the ladies to stay home to avoid just this kind of trouble. That said, 'tis also true the women had a right to gather in front of the church. They did nae incite a riot. As Miss Ferguson said, they simply wanted the wives of the cowardly men involved in the totally disgusting melee Monday night to ken how they're husbands acted. Any man who was nae involved need nae fear a tongue-lashing."

Mr. James smirked. "You obviously do not know women very well."

Aidan shrugged. "I ken a woman expects her man to act with honor."

"Yes. Yes," Mr. Haines said again. "The whole thing was an unfortunate incident. We should put it behind us."

"Not until I have assurances that those..." Mr. James glanced at Aidan and then continued, "...*women* will not pull another stunt like this."

"I cannae promise ye that," Annie said. "I doona speak for the club."

"Very well then." Mr. James gathered his hat and coat to leave. "Let me put this another way. One more incident like that nonsense yesterday and we will—"

"Are ye threatening the lady?" Aidan asked, his voice deadly calm.

Mr. James seemed to recognize the danger. He stuck his hat on his head and flung open the door. "A threat? I would not think of it."

As the door slammed behind him, Annie was aware he didn't mean it. She shook off a feeling of unease and tried to ignore the fact that Aidan looked concerned too. Even though he had defended her, she had no doubt she'd be getting a lecture from him and another one from Niall when he heard about this.

The day just seemed to be getting worse.

****

Archibald Haines slipped into an empty chair at a table in Walker's Hotel on Buchanan Street. He'd almost been late to this evening's meeting, thanks to having to handle complaints from irate tradesmen whose goods were stored in his warehouse. He'd also spent a great part of the afternoon reassuring his partner, Oliver Nolan, that they would not lose business over those idiotic women's Sunday episode.

As the day wore on, Archibald had considered simply firing Annie Ferguson but then decided against it. There hadn't been a single error in the accounting ledgers since she'd started work, which was something he couldn't say about his former manager. More importantly, though, she did not have any clue that opium and gold were being exchanged in the false bottoms of the barley and tobacco barrels that crisscrossed the Atlantic. She signed invoices and bills-of-lading based on physical inventory. Someone with more experience might question why such an abundance of barley and tobacco was being exchanged in relation to other goods like woolens and linens. Better to keep an unsuspecting novice in charge.

He was so close to accumulating enough money to purchase one of the former tobacco lords' mansions and retaking his rightful place in society. He'd no longer have to take a hand in daily operations of a warehouse either. He could sell his half to his business partner and work strictly with investments, as a gentleman would.

Duncan Tate, the owner of one of the local woolen mills, stood up and the room quieted. "I'm glad to see so many of you here tonight."

Which was the man's way of calling their meeting to order. Tate was the official chairperson for their unofficial delegation. The men present tonight were members of the Committee for Organizing a Provisional Government. The topics they discussed would center on mundane issues of raising wages and improving the economy which had slumped more than two years ago with the end of the French and American wars. Privately, their group meant to rid Scotland totally of English control. That topic would be spoken of carefully in code as more and more power was consolidated and procedures slowly put into place. They weren't quite ready for a coup yet.

Which reminded Haines that he needed to check on some of his investments to assure that he had a place at the top of the new aristocracy when it took power. He wished Gordon Munroe would come back from wherever he had gone. If the man would return to his bookkeeping job at Henderson Shipping, those two pesky MacDonalds would have no reason to stay in Glasgow.

The fewer people scrutinizing his business, the better.

****

Kingsley watched from the shadows across the street as Haines, along with nearly a score of other men, exited Walker's Hotel shortly after nine o'clock. He mentally checked off each one, although he knew the same men met bi-monthly at the same time. Still, he couldn't afford to assume anything. If someone new had been added to the group or someone had stopped attending, Kingsley needed those names.

The prime minister expected accurate information.

Pity that Kingsley hadn't been able to infiltrate the inner circle of these men. They'd been friendly enough in the outer public room and seemed to agree when he mentioned the need for economic reform that they claimed their committee was trying to do. But the fact that he hadn't been invited to attend the private meetings made him all the more suspicious that more was going on than just reform. The Scots had a long history of rebelling against the English, and their last battle, at Culloden, had been more than seventy years ago. The French ousting Napoleon and the Americans revolting were simply fuel for the ever-smoldering ashes of Scottish independence to be reignited.

But he could make an example of one man and perhaps slow the movement down—or, even better, identify someone already in the circle who might become a turncoat. In Kingsley's experience, once a man realized he stood to lose everything—property, money, position, family—he could often be *persuaded* to talk. All Kingsley had to do was dig up the right information on the weakest link in this chain.

After discovering the false bottom filled with opium powder in the exported barley barrels at the warehouse and the gold at the bottom of the returning imported tobacco barrels, Kingsley passed the information to London, along with a request to trace the source of the opium, if it could be found. He might not be able to prove treason yet, but evading import taxes on opium would provide gaol time. The idea that Newgate prison might claim other "guests" from Glasgow could get one of the men to talk.

And Kingsley was very close to making that happen.

Chapter Thirteen

"Why cannae any of ye understand how important this job is to me?" Annie glared at Niall, Aidan, and Owen. Aidan had joined them since a room had been vacated in the boardinghouse. Now all three were sitting at the dining table, stone-faced as Puritans about to execute judgment.

"'Tis nae that we doona understand," Aidan replied with the patient tone one might use on a balkish bairn. "'Tis the risk of danger ye put yourself in."

"Aidan said James wanted to threaten ye," Niall added.

If Aidan had been within reachable distance from where she sat, she would have kicked him. Niall was critical enough of her job. She didn't need his brother giving him any more ammunition.

"But he dinnae," Annie replied. "He thought better of it."

"Only because my brother was there." Niall set his jaw. "Did ye think on what might have happened otherwise?"

Annie gave an exasperated sigh. "*Nothing* would have happened. Mr. Haines would have intervened."

"How do ye ken?" Niall asked.

"I just *do*." She folded her arms.

Niall made a growling sound. "Stubborn lass."

"Obstinate man," Annie shot back.

148

Owen looked from one to the other and shook his head. "If I might make an observation?" They both frowned at him, but he ignored the looks. "I do not think Annie is in any danger at the office—"

"Aha!" Annie glowered at Niall. "There. Ye see? Owen agrees with me."

"Only to a point," Owen said quickly before Niall could reply. "I think the danger lies when you move about on the streets."

"There!" Niall gave her a smug smile. "*Ye* see?"

Annie drew her brows together. "I doona—"

"Perhaps it would be best if we hear what Owen has to say," Aidan interjected.

"Yes. Hear me out," Owen said. "Haines strikes me as the sort who does not want trouble. He has Kingsley to handle the inventory and supervise the warehousemen. Haines can deal with customer disputes. As long as Annie sticks to processing the paperwork, she should be all right."

Annie opened her mouth to protest, but Owen held up his hand.

"Wait. I understand you do not want to be held back, but it is the best compromise at this time. If you cause too much disruption, he will simply dismiss you."

Annie started to retort, then snapped her mouth shut. She knew very well her position was tenuous. She refused to look at Niall. He was probably smirking.

"I agree that Annie will be safe at work," Aidan said. "I doona care much for Kingsley, but 'twas easy to see he was in charge of the men who work there. My concern is for what ye have left unsaid. What about the streets?"

"That is another matter." Owen grimaced. "I spent the morning at the Merchants House and Trades Hall, speaking with owners and proprietors of the textile mills, and the afternoon in taverns listening to talk. Men are not happy with what took place Sunday, even if they were not directly involved."

"We had a right to stand in front of the church." Annie lifted her chin. "We also have a right to expect to earn decent wages."

"Perhaps you do," Owen replied, "but the men are angry about it."

"And ye have seen what angry men do," Niall said to Annie. "Ye need to stay off the streets."

Annie scowled. "Doona tell me what to do."

"'Tis for your own good, lass."

She rolled her eyes. "There ye go, insulting me again."

Niall shook his head. "I am nae insulting ye."

"Ye *are*. Ye think I doona ken what is good for me?"

"I dinna say that." A muscle twitched in his jaw. "How many times do ye need to be accosted to understand the danger ye put yourself in?"

"How…many…" Annie started to sputter. "I am nae daft—"

"Nae. Ye are just stubborn."

"Ye are arrogant."

"Enough," Aidan said. "Sparring like bairns will nae solve the problem." He looked at Owen and then Niall. "We all need to keep our eyes and ears open for more discord." He turned back to Annie. "Meanwhile, at least one of us will be your escort whenever ye leave the house. Niall is right. 'Tis for your own safety. It matters nae how smart ye are, lass. A woman is nae match for a man's fist. Ye do ken that?"

As much as she hated to admit it, Aidan—and

Niall—were both right. Reluctantly, she nodded. "All right. I will agree to an escort." Annie focused on Niall. "But nae more hovering over me once I get to the office. I want Mr. Haines to respect me. Agreed?"

Niall looked as if he wanted to disagree, but instead he nodded. "Agreed. Ye drive a hard bargain, lass."

Annie shrugged. "'Tis because I am stubborn."

Niall's eyes widened and then he grinned. "That, too."

****

When Annie got to the office the next morning—Niall had left her at the door like he promised—she found Kingsley sitting at the desk, looking over the ledgers. She hung her coat on the rack and walked over to him. "What are ye looking for?"

"Nothing in particular. The warehouse has received several shipments as well as sent some out, and I haven't had a chance to double-check the accuracy of the entries." Kingsley closed the book and smiled at Annie. "Not that I find many errors. You are very accurate."

"Thank ye. I doona want Mr. Haines to be disappointed in my work."

"Neither do I, which is why two pairs of eyes are definitely better than one. We want to make sure nothing has been missed." Kingsley stood. "I think Mr. Haines said he was expecting another load of tobacco to come in, so I'd better go clear some space in the warehouse."

"He's expecting more barley to come in too, so be sure ye keep the area clear where he likes to store it." She frowned slightly. "I thought the barley had all been harvested already. I am nae sure where this is coming from."

Kingsley gestured to a sheaf of papers on the desk.

"What does the invoice say?"

Annie picked up the stack and thumbed through it. "From Galson, south of Kilmarnock. I guess some of the crofters are probably having a late season."

"That is what it sounds like."

"I wonder if the tobacco shipments will slow down when barley is done."

Kingsley gave her a sharp look. "Why do you say that?"

"Because the tobacco is coming from the port of Norfolk, Virginia, the same place the barley is shipped to." Annie rifled through the papers. "The invoices match one-for-one on shipments going out and shipments received."

"May I see those?" He held out his hand.

She turned the items over. "Aye."

"You are correct," Kingsley said after he'd separated several invoices and laid them side by side, "although the number of barrels varies."

"More tobacco comes in than barley goes out, but the prices reflect that." She looked at Kingsley, feeling a bit anxious. "I make sure I put the exact amount of money paid and the amount received."

"I am sure you do," he said reassuringly. "I did not mean to imply otherwise." He handed the papers back. "It is not surprising larger quantities of tobacco are being imported. After all, the tobacco trade made a number of Glasgow businessmen quite wealthy."

Annie nodded. "Virginia is much warmer than Scotland, and the planting season is longer."

Kingsley gestured to the watercolor on the wall. "Plus, those plantations are a lot larger than the plots the crofters tend."

Annie looked at the painting. "It looks like a beautiful place. I am sure Mr. Haines wishes he still owned part of it."

Kingsley gave her another sharp glance. "Did he indicate that he would?"

"Nae. At least, I doona think he did."

His gaze turned to the picture, his look thoughtful. Then he abruptly turned and went through the door to the warehouse.

Annie stared after him, perplexed. Then she shrugged and sat down at the desk. Sometimes men didn't make sense at all.

****

"Do ye think the turmoil over the Sunday protest has died down?" Niall asked Aidan several days later as they stood on the dock, supervising the loading of the barley barrels from the warehouse onto one of Henderson's ships bound for Virginia.

"Probably," Aidan replied. "It's been nigh unto two weeks. From what MacLean says, talk in the tavern is now centering on rising food costs due to the Corn Laws imposing a high tariff on grain imports."

Niall gestured toward the ship being loaded. "And yet, Haines manages to export barley, which keeps the prices higher too. A wee bit ironical, nae?"

Aidan nodded. "The landowners keep getting wealthier while the industrial and manufacturing workers are barely scraping by."

Watching as the last barrels were carried up the gangplank, Niall shook his head. "'Tis surprising the trade unions are nae calling for Haines' head."

"Unlikely. The tradesmen are too fond of their tobacco to lose one of its best distributors." Aidan said.

"Besides, he keeps the prices low for storing their wool and linen."

"Aye, he is shrewd in that." Niall turned his attention from the ship to Aidan. "Do ye really think Annie is safe working there?"

"Things seem to have quieted down," Aidan replied.

"Seem?" Niall frowned. "Do ye sense something is nae quite right?"

"I am nae Lachlan." Aidan shrugged. "I did nae see anything amiss when I was there."

"I wish I had nae agreed to leave Annie at the door in the mornings."

Aidan gave his brother a pensive look. "Ye are doing all ye can to protect her."

"I am nae sure," Niall responded. "I have an uneasy feel for all of this."

"We are all keeping our ears alert," Aidan said. "The lass has agreed to nae wander about without one of us as escort."

"Unless she decides to sneak out again." Niall frowned again. "'Twould be just like Annie to think the danger is past and she can do as she wishes."

"I agree that Annie is a bit headstrong—"

"A bit?" Niall asked incredulously. "I have nae met a more stubborn, willful woman."

Aidan smiled. "So ye've said. But she does nae strike me as someone who will go back on her word. At any rate, 'tis nae much more we can do. As long as Annie does nae stir up the workers again, she should be fine."

His brother was probably right. *If* Annie didn't stir up the workers again…but that was the real question. How long would she be content to remain docile?

It wasn't exactly a word that described Annie

Ferguson.

****

Annie hummed a little ditty to herself as she entered the office on a Thursday morning. A little more than two weeks had passed since the club's protest in front of the cathedral and tension seemed to have died down. Or, at least, Niall was not constantly bringing the subject up.

He hadn't insisted on accompanying her inside the office either, although she wasn't sure if that was because she'd agreed to an escort or because he and Aidan had begun appearing on the docks to check any stock leaving the warehouse bound for one of the Henderson ships. Niall had said he was only showing his brother the whole scope of the shipping business to aid in the opening of the Skye office, but sometimes she wondered if he wasn't counting inventory just as a back-up for her. Good lord! Kingsley was already doing that. Did men think women couldn't count?

But Annie pushed the irritating thought aside. She wasn't going to let anything spoil her good mood. It was a brilliant autumn day with colorful foliage still clinging to the trees. The sky was cerulean blue with only a few puffy, cotton clouds. The sun promised to warm the cool, crisp air to make the afternoon perfect. There was only one shipment of tobacco coming in this morning, and maybe once she'd taken care of the paperwork, Mr. Haines would let her leave. She'd been wanting to finish reading *Sense and Sensibility* by an anonymous author, because parts of it reminded her of herself. Nestling on a bench in George Square would be the perfect place to do it.

She hung up her coat and turned at the sound of the door opening, then smiled at her boss. "Good morning.

Ye are just the person I wanted to see."

He nodded his acknowledgment. "What did you wish to see me about?"

"'Tis going to be a fine day. I was wondering if I might have the afternoon off, once the tobacco is stacked and accounted for."

"Hmmm." Haines gave her an inquisitive look. "You are not planning to meet Kingsley some place, are you?"

Annie felt her mouth gape in surprise and closed it. Then she drew her brows together. "Nae. Why would ye think such a thing?"

"Do not take offense," Mr. Haines answered. "Kingsley sent a messenger around this morning that he would not be coming in today. Something about eating spoiled fish at dinner last night."

"If the man ate bad fish, why would I be wanting to see him in the first place?" Annie asked.

Haines sighed. "Never mind. I was attempting a jest."

"Oh." Annie felt a little foolish. "In that case, I will supervise the storing of the tobacco. The ship docked last night, so the wagons should be arriving any minute."

"No need to involve yourself since I am here."

Did Mr. Haines think she couldn't do the job? "I doona mind. 'Tis a part of my job to ken everything that is in the warehouse."

"Well, if you wish, you can assist me then." He tilted his head to listen. "I think I hear horses out back. That should be the shipment."

Annie gathered her invoices and followed Mr. Haines into the warehouse. Two large wagons were loaded down with a dozen barrels each. That matched her paperwork.

"Careful with handling those!" Mr. Haines said as one of the dock loaders rolled a barrel off the back of the wagon. "I do not want the wood cracking."

"Aye," the man grunted and shouldered the barrel. "Where do ye want it?"

"Right over here," Annie called and gestured to the spot that Mr. Haines preferred. The worker bent his knees and dropped the barrel with a thunk that made Mr. Haines glare at him. He ignored the look and went back for another barrel while Annie maneuvered the barrel into place by rocking it from side to side.

"Careful with that!" Mr. Haines called. "If the bottom breaks, the tobacco will get wet."

"Aye. I'll be careful," Annie replied, although she wondered how any of the barrels could get wet, cracked or not. They were specifically stored in the driest spot in the whole warehouse.

When all the barrels were stacked, the head dock loader handed Annie the bill of lading, which she signed and handed back. She and Mr. Haines went back into the office where she made an entry in the ledger and then closed it. "I think everything is taken care of here. May I leave?"

Mr. Haines raised an eyebrow and smiled. "You certainly seem to be in a hurry to go today."

Even though he hadn't again mentioned *meeting* someone, the unspoken implication was there. What kind of a woman did he think she was? She grimaced since the honest answer to the question would destroy her reputation. She drew a deep breath. Her secret was safe, but it would not do to have Mr. Haines think poorly of her. "I just wanted to spend the day outdoors. 'Tis too pretty to waste such fine weather."

Haines nodded. "You can leave in a few minutes. I just want to secure the warehouse first."

He had just gone out when the front door opened again. Two men she didn't recognize came inside. Neither one was dressed formally, although the taller of the two wore a morning coat and long trousers. The other had on breeches with knee-high boots and a heavy woolen fisherman's knit sweater.

"I am Miss Ferguson, the office manager," Annie said. "Can I help ye?"

"Aye," the taller one answered. "I am David MacQuarrie, magistrate. This is Tevis Shaw, a revenue man." Mr. MacQuarrie looked around. "Is Archibald Haines here?"

"Aye. He is in the warehouse," Annie answered. "I will get him for ye."

"Just take us there instead."

Annie nodded. "Follow me, then."

Mr. Haines turned as she led the men inside. He must have recognized at least one of the men because his eyes widened. "What do you want?"

The magistrate removed several pieces of paper from his vest and held one out. "I am authorized to inspect the shipment you just received."

"Why?" Haines asked, not taking the paper. "It is only tobacco from Virginia."

"That may well be," the magistrate answered. "My orders are to inspect it."

Mr. Haines grabbed the paper. He read it quickly, his lips tightening into a straight line. "Very well. Pick a barrel and I will open it for you."

Tevis Shaw pointed to a barrel in the middle of the

stack. Mr. Haines looked as though he wanted to argue, but then motioned for several of the warehouse workers to start removing the top barrels. They were clearly curious. Annie was too, but as much as she wanted to ask what was going on, she managed to keep silent.

Soon large, flat tobacco leaves were strewn over the floor. Both the magistrate and the revenue man peered inside.

"There. The barrel is empty," Mr. Haines said. "Are you satisfied?"

The magistrate stepped back, but the revenue man didn't. Instead, he picked up a crow bar and started poking around, tapping the sides and bottom.

"Now see here," Mr. Haines said. "If you crack the sides, the barrel will be worthless."

Instead of answering, the man hooked one of the boards and pulled, causing a loud splintering noise.

"Stop that!" Mr. Haines shouted and moved forward, only to be restrained by the magistrate while the revenue man tipped the barrel over.

Gold coins splattered and rolled across the floor.

Annie stared at them. What in the world...? She looked quickly at Mr. Haines.

He was staring at the money too. "How did those get there?"

"Why don't you tell us?" the magistrate asked.

"What do you mean?" An indignant expression crossed Mr. Haines' face. "You cannot think I knew anything about this!"

MacQuarrie looked at him speculatively. "I do not think it likely someone would put gold in a false barrel bottom unless it was intended for the receiver." He glanced at the paperwork he still held. "According to this, you purchase barley and trade it for tobacco, which you then have processed by local cigar shops."

Haines narrowed his eyes. "There is nothing wrong with that."

"I did not say there was," MacQuarrie answered.

"It is all perfectly legal. I pay my export and import taxes." Haines gestured. "Ask your revenue man there."

Tevis Shaw stopped pulling tobacco out of a second barrel. "Our records show taxes paid on the barley and tobacco. What they do not show is tax paid on opium smuggled into this country illegally."

Annie felt her mouth drop open. Opium? Here? In the warehouse?

Mr. Haines tugged on his lapels and lifted his chin. "I have absolutely no idea what you are talking about."

Tevis hooked the bottom of the second barrel with the crowbar and tipped it over, splattering more gold coins on the floor and then straightened. "I believe the opium you did not pay tax on was not only smuggled into this country, but also smuggled out to the States."

"Believe what you want," Mr. Haines huffed. "It is nothing more than a theory." "It is a bit more than that." MacQuarrie shuffled the papers in his hand and held one up. "A signed confession from the man who admitted to smuggling opium to you."

Mr. Haines paled, then pulled in a breath. "Nonsense. Everyone knows the English have no love of Scots. You probably tortured the poor man."

MacQuarrie shook his head. "We did not need to. Apparently, you did not pay as well as our agent who questioned him."

"Bribery," Haines declared. "A false confession that does not prove anything."

"Perhaps not by itself," the magistrate replied, "but we also put an agent on an earlier ship that delivered the barley to Virginia. The Americans inspected the barrels on their end and found the powder. Our man returned last Friday with the results." MacQuarrie folded the papers and put them back inside his vest. "I am taking you into custody, Archibald Haines."

Sweat broke out on Mr. Haines face. "*No!*" He turned and sprinted to the back door, knocking several warehouse workers aside.

Tevis looked up from the third barrel he was starting to empty. "Are you not going after him?"

"I have men covering both exits," MacQuarrie answered. "As soon as he's shackled, some of them will come inside to help you with emptying the rest of this shipment. Meanwhile…" He looked at the workers who stood around, gawking openly at him. "I suggest the rest of you leave."

No one waited to be told twice. They practically tripped over each other trying to get out. Still stunned, Annie watched them leave and turned to the magistrate. "I doona think any of them kenned anything about…this."

MacQuarrie shrugged. "I am more interested in finding out what *you* know about all this, Miss Ferguson."

Chapter Fourteen

"I kenned something was nae right," Niall said that evening after supper when Annie's mother had ushered them into her small, private parlor at the back of the boardinghouse. "I kenned it."

"Which you have said more than a dozen times since we brought Annie home," Owen said.

Niall glowered at him. "We? If I had nae stopped by to bring Annie lunch, she might be sitting in gaol at this verra minute."

"I stopped by right after you got there," Owen answered.

"Perhaps it was divine providence that ye *both* arrived when ye did. Angels sent from God," Annie interjected before their argument could escalate. Again. She inwardly shuddered at how close to the truth they were. The magistrate was planning to escort her to the courthouse, but Niall and Owen had managed to convince him she wasn't going anywhere and could be questioned at any time. Then they'd bickered between themselves all the way home.

At least, that had saved her from a lecture, although looking around the small room at them and Aidan and her mother, she was pretty sure a scolding would be forthcoming.

"I would imagine this is the only time in his life that my brother has been referred to as angelic," Aidan said in a rather dry tone. "More oft, our mother thought he was a more fitting companion for Lucifer."

Niall shrugged. "She said that about all of us."

"Depending on which one of ye was in trouble?" Annie asked, hoping to divert the conversation.

"Aye," Niall answered and fixed her with a dark look. "But the one in trouble right now is ye."

So much for hoping to avoid the chastisement. Annie sighed. "I dinnae ken anything about this."

Her mother moved over to the sofa and sat down beside Annie and patted her hand. "Of course ye did nae."

"'Tis the point, though," Niall said. "This smuggling was going on right under Annie's nose and she did nae ken it."

Aidan looked pensive. "I wonder how long it *had* been going on."

"Did the magistrate say anything about how long Haines was under watch?" Owen asked.

Annie shook her head. "I am sure that will all be investigated, but the paperwork Mr. MacQuarrie had was from a shipment sent several weeks ago."

"Before or after ye started working there?" Aidan asked.

"Only two loads of barley went to the States since I began working in the office." Annie tried to remember the dates and then felt most of the blood drain from her face. "Oh, dear God."

"What is it?" Niall leaned forward in his chair. "What is wrong?"

She put her hands to her cold cheeks. "The shipment the agent was on went out ten days after I started working there."

"That does nae mean ye kenned anything about the opium," Niall said.

"Nae, but I signed my name confirming the contents of the barrels."

"You would have no way of knowing about the false bottoms," Owen said, "since they were full when they arrived in the warehouse."

Aidan nodded. "That's true."

"Aye, but..." Annie paused as another memory jarred her. "But there were empty barrels brought in. I counted them. I moved them."

"That still does nae implicate ye," Niall said.

"But it might. I could be accused of kenning the false bottoms were there or even kenning about the opium."

"Highly unlikely," Aidan replied.

"I hope ye are right. I doona want..." She stopped as another thought abruptly hit her. "But ye could be implicated too."

The men frowned and spoke in unison. "How?"

"Ye—especially Niall—have spent a lot of time at the office—"

"Escorting ye to and from," Niall said. "'Tis only proper."

"But ye also spent time in the warehouse," Annie answered. "Ye wanted to check on Kingsley as well as all the workers, remember? And Aidan and Owen both requested being shown around too."

"Only to see where my kelp shipments would be held," Owen said.

"Aye, but all that looking around could be misinterpreted."

Aidan shook his head. "I doona think anyone is

going to question two prospective clients for wanting to inspect the warehouse."

"Perhaps nae…" Annie's voice trailed off as one more fact invaded her memory. She felt what little blood left in her head leave.

Niall left his chair to kneel at her side. "Ye have gone white as a Highland blizzard. Are ye ill?"

"I…I just remembered…those empty barrels I inventoried came back filled with barley. The shipment went out a few days after our protest." Annie fought off a wave of dizziness and then whispered, "It left on one of the boats belonging to Henderson Shipping."

****

"Ye do ken this is completely daft?" Niall asked Annie as they left the boardinghouse just past dawn the next morning.

"Ye are calling me stupid again," Annie picked up her pace to leave him behind—with no luck even though she was practically running.

"I am nae calling ye stupid," Niall replied, easily keeping up with her. "I am calling the *idea* of ye going to work today stupid."

"Someone has to go in," Annie slowed down so she could speak without panting. "Mr. Haines is in custody. Kingsley may still be ill. I want to be there when the workers come in."

'Did it nae occur to ye that anything ye do in the office right now might be suspect?"

Annie frowned. "Last night all of ye seemed to think there would be nae blame placed."

"I have had time to think. While we all ken ye had nothing to do with the smuggling operation, going to the office today when no one is there might make

MacQuarrie think otherwise."

"Ye escorting me might make him think the same of ye, since ye are in charge of Henderson Shipping and the last load of barley is on one of those ships." Annie paused. "Mayhap ye should go back."

"I am nae leaving ye alone."

"'Tis nae reason to give MacQuarrie cause to implicate Robert's shipping line," Annie insisted.

"It might be too late, since the ship has sailed," Niall answered. "Aidan is dispatching a rider this morning with a letter to Robert explaining the whole situation. He would expect us to stand by ye."

"Which is all the more reason I must go in today. I want to check the ledger to be certain everything is in order and nae mistake was made."

"Nae! 'Tis the last thing ye should do."

"I only intend to look over the numbers," Annie replied. "Ye remember how I counted nineteen barrels and ye and Mr. Kingsley counted twenty? I doona want a simple error to cast suspicion."

Niall clenched his jaw. Did the woman nae realize the danger *she* was in? "If there is a mistake and ye make any changes, it will be seen as tampering. Especially since ye decided to go in early this morning."

Annie scowled. "The workers will nae ken what to do if everything is locked up when they get there."

"Ye are a stubborn lass."

"And headstrong, obstinate and willful," Annie said. "Ye might as well add mulish and pig-headed to your list."

In spite of the frustration he was feeling with her, Niall had to grin. "I would nae compare ye to a mule or a pig."

"Humph."

"I would more likely compare ye to Boudicca."

Annie stopped walking to stare at him. "The Celtic warrior queen? Why?"

"She managed to hold off the Roman legions." Niall's grin widened. "I suspect ye could probably hold off all of Glasgow."

She started walking again. "I suppose that is a compliment."

"'Tis." Niall glanced at her, his smile gone. "But ye doona like compliments. Why is that?"

Annie shook her head, not looking at him. "I never said that."

"Actually, ye said ye put nae stock in flowery words. Is it so hard to believe me when I tell ye I think ye are strong?"

She colored, still not looking at him. "Thank ye, then. There. I can acknowledge it. Now can we change the subject?"

Niall didn't want to, but he knew better than to press the subject since it made her more prickly than ever. Some man must really have insulted her. He'd like to find the bastard. "Well, we are almost there," he said as they rounded a corner and the warehouse came into sight. "It looks as though there is a notice on the door."

"Oh, nae!" Annie started to run, nearly tripping on the steps as she reached the building.

Niall caught her, his hands nearly encircling her entire waist, reminding him that in spite of her bravado, she was physically fragile. Not that she would take *that* as a compliment. He dropped his hands once she got her balance, even though he had a strong urge just to pull her closer for protection. Annie would not appreciate that either.

"It says the office is closed until further notification." Annie turned to Niall. "There are goods stored in there that need to be moved. Today is the day the workers collect their wages, as well. What am I going to do?"

"What *we* are going to do is go home," Niall answered.

"But the workers—"

"Will just have to wait. That order is signed by the magistrate." Niall took Annie's arm. "There is nothing we can do right now." She reluctantly allowed him to lead her down the steps, but she was unusually quiet. Niall just hoped she wasn't plotting something. "Hopefully, we will have some answers by Monday."

****

Standing in the shadows, Kingsley watched through the office window as MacDonald and the Ferguson woman left. He sheathed the knife he'd been holding and breathed a sigh of relief. Murder was always messy. Not just the blood splattered all over his clothes, but the need to cover his trail as well. Kingsley was well aware of the rules. If he got caught, the prime minister would hardly vouch for him.

But he needn't concern himself about that today. So far, everything had gone smoothly. The anonymous letters delivered to the magistrate and the excise man contained enough information to warrant the investigation, but not enough to betray the sender. The danger of discovery had passed, at least for the moment. Dawn had broken. Within the hour, MacQuarrie's men would be back to search every corner of the warehouse, but Kingsley would be long gone by then.

He took a small, black leather notebook from the satchel he carried and smiled as he thumbed through it one final time, noting the entry dates of gold received and the investments made. Once Haines was convicted, that money would be turned over to the Crown. Kingsley had originally thought perhaps Haines would have hidden the little book behind a false compartment in the desk. That search had turned up nothing, so while Haines had been at the Monday night meeting at Walker's Hotel, Kingsley had picked the lock to the flat where the man lived and found it stashed behind books on a shelf. How predictable. But then, most criminals were.

Kingsley moved to the desk and pulled open the bottom drawer. He pushed the notebook toward the back and covered it loosely with papers. Not visible, but it would be found when MacQuarrie's men searched the place.

Closing the drawer, he walked into the warehouse and looked around. Tobacco leaves lay strewn everywhere along with cracked and splintered barrels from yesterday's raid. The gold, of course, had been taken away. Kingsley didn't have time to open the boxes and crates that had not yet been searched, but the bolts of woolens were wrapped only in linen cloth to keep them clean. Reaching into his satchel again, he withdrew two dozen sealed packets of opium powder—the smuggler who had been questioned had been most generous in turning over the stuff—and started sliding the small sacks between layers of wool. Even though there was enough evidence from the barley shipments to brand Haines a criminal, Kingsley liked to hedge his bets. He was nothing if not thorough. Lord Liverpool might not be able to hang the label of treason on Haines, but this incident would send a strong message to those contemplating rebellion.

Kingsley looked around the warehouse to make sure he had left nothing behind to indicate he had been here. Then he turned and slipped out the door, latching it behind him.

His work at Haines Consolidated was done. It was time to move on to another target.

****

"'Tis a lot of unrest about town," Owen said Saturday evening as the group had once again convened in the private parlor after dinner. "Every place I went, I heard nothing but talk of what's happened."

"I heard the same on the quay today," Niall said. "The warehouse workers did nae lose any time spreading the word to the dockhands that everything has been torn apart inside the building and that they did nae get paid Friday."

"I kenned they would be angry." Annie sighed. "I probably should have ignored the sign and gone into the office—"

"Nae!" Niall nearly growled the word. They'd argued all the way home yesterday, but not a word of what he said had sunk in, apparently. "Do ye want to be sitting in gaol as well?"

Annie frowned, looking as though she were about to start the argument all over again when Aidan interrupted.

"'Tis to be expected the workers are angry, but right now, ye can do nothing to help them." He turned to Owen. "What sort of unrest are *ye* referring to?"

"And where did ye hear it?" Niall asked.

"Various places," Owen answered. "I had lunch at Walker's Hotel. The overall tone of the conversations was surprise that Haines had been smuggling."

"That is an understatement," Annie said wryly. "I still can nae believe Mr. Haines was doing such a thing."

"Smuggling is nae that uncommon. The wars with France and the States have caused tariffs to rise excessively. People are not happy with the English government and do not want to pay the high taxes on goods they need." Owen shrugged. "Men are out of work too, so smuggling provides an income. They get a percent of the goods and the other people avoid the revenue man."

"Well, Mr. Haines did nae avoid Tevis Shaw," Annie said. "I wonder how he found out."

Owen nodded. "That is the question Kingsley brought up."

"Kingsley?" Annie asked. "Where did ye see him?"

"At Walker's."

"I guess he is nae longer sick then."

"He did not seem to be, although he said he could have kicked himself for not being there to help Haines when the magistrate arrived."

Annie shook her head. "There was nae much he could have done."

"Probably not," Owen agreed, "but he was also upset that he has, more than likely, lost his job."

"He is nae the only one." Niall looked at Owen. "Where else did ye go?"

"Well, the Trades Hall and Merchants House were closed since it is Saturday," Owen answered, "but the taverns were full of tradesmen."

"What did they say?" Aidan asked.

"I cannot repeat the language." Owen glanced at Annie and her mother. "But they are all angry as well.

The main concern is when the warehouse will reopen."

"Or *if* it will reopen," Aidan said.

Annie stared at him. "What do ye mean, *if*? There are goods stored and ships due in."

"Aye, but if MacQuarrie and Shaw find any other goods being used in smuggling, those goods will be confiscated."

"Mr. Haines could nae have used all the stock for smuggling purposes," Annie said.

"We doona ken that," Niall said.

Aidan gave him a sharp look. "Do ye think any of our kelp bales have been involved?"

"I doona ken," Niall answered. "Robert's only used this warehouse a short time. Since I have been here, I've inspected our bales. I dinnae see anything, but then, we did nae suspect anything wrong with the barley barrels either."

"But your kelp?" Annie asked.

"I hope nae," Niall answered, "but who kens what has been used?"

"But…" Annie paused and her eyes grew round. "The weavers' union just delivered near a hundred bolts of woolens to be sent to France. If those doona get delivered, the mills will nae pay the weavers."

Silence met that remark. Niall looked at the grim expressions of his brother and MacLean. All three of them had realized that possibility after listening to the talk on the streets. He just wished Annie hadn't figured it out.

"'Tis nae need to fash," he said, although he knew he sounded like a hypocrite. "We cannae do anything until Monday when the magistrate's office will be open."

Annie wasn't about to be pacified though. With a

deliberately willful look in her eye, she raised her chin. "And what if Mr. MacQuarrie keeps the office closed? Or confiscates everything in it? What will the workers and the weavers do then?"

****

"Ye are going to wear tracks on my carpet, pacing like ye do," Annie's mother said to her Monday morning as they awaited word about the warehouse opening.

Annie sank into a parlor chair, then popped back up. "I cannae sit still. I should have gone with the men."

"Nae," her mother replied. "Niall was right. We doona ken what the decision will be or the reaction to it."

"I would have been safe with three Highlanders escorting me," Annie said stubbornly.

"Even armed as they are, they cannae take on several scores of angry men."

"But why would they be angry with me?" Annie asked. "'Tis nae my fault the warehouse is closed."

Mrs. Ferguson shook her head. "An angry man does nae think clearly and is nae ruled by logic. Ye put together a crowd of angry men and they become a mob that doesn't listen to reason. 'Tis why the witches were burned."

Annie blinked. "Are ye talking about what happened one hundred and fifty years ago? 'Twas madness!"

"Aye, it was madness," her mother replied, "but it did nae stop those poor women to be put to death here in Scotland and also in the States."

"Well, we are more civilized now."

Before her mother could answer, Niall came into the room. From the grim look on his face, Annie knew the news wasn't good. "The warehouse is remaining closed?"

He nodded and went to stand by the window. "Everything has been confiscated as well."

"But why? 'Twas only the barley barrels that were used."

"It seems nae just them," Niall said. "MacQuarrie's men found additional opium hidden in the bolts of woolens—"

"That cannae be! I checked those bolts myself when they came in," Annie said.

A muscle twitched in Niall's jaw. "Aye. One of the weavers brought that up."

"That clears the weavers, then," Annie said.

Niall hesitated. "But it does nae clear ye."

Annie frowned. "What do ye mean?"

"Someone put that opium inside the bolts. Haines swore he hadn't been in the warehouse since the woolens were delivered."

"He is nae lying about that," Annie said. "The wool came in Wednesday afternoon. I was already in the office Thursday morning when Mr. Haines arrived "

"That does nae help ye," Niall said, his face growing dark. "And Kingsley? He was ill Thursday morning. Was he at the warehouse Wednesday after the wool came in?"

"Aye. He counted the bolts."

Niall brightened. "Was he still in the warehouse when I came for ye?"

Annie thought a moment. "Nae. He said something about his horse having thrown a shoe that morning and he wanted to get to the farrier's."

"Damnation." He glanced out the window and then turned back. "I need for ye to pack a bag. I am taking ye away from here."

"Why? I have naught to hide."

"I ken that, but 'tis nae the point. Ye had the opportunity to—"

"But I didnae! I—"

"For once, doona argue with me." Niall gave her an exasperated look. "The men were getting riled up when I left. 'Tis *why* I left. If they turn into a mob…"

"Niall is right," Mrs. Ferguson said. "Ye will be safer away from here until tempers cool down."

"But I—"

"Will ye at least listen to your mother if ye will nae listen to me?" Niall glanced out the window again. "I expect Aidan or MacLean to be here any minute with more news. I'm going to go saddle two horses. When I come back in, I want ye ready to leave."

He didn't wait for an answer. Annie stared after him and then looked at her mother. "Do ye really think this is that serious?"

"I saw a riot once in Edinburgh. It was nae pretty. I would rather have ye safe." Her mother bit her lip. "I trust the Highlander."

Annie hesitated a moment, then nodded and went upstairs to gather her things. She changed into breeches and a linen shirt and pulled on a man's jacket. It was an outfit she'd used several times when she and other members of her club wanted to travel incognito on the streets. She stuffed a couple of dresses and some necessary articles into her portmanteau. Just as she finished pinning up her hair, she heard a commotion outside. Her window looked into the alley and she couldn't tell what was making the noise. Grabbing her bag and a cap, she went down the steps to find Owen in fast conversation with Niall while Aidan stood at the front door.

"What is happening?" Annie asked, trying to peer around Aidan.

"'Tis nae time to explain," Niall said. "There is a mob on the way."

"But—"

Owen turned to her, his burr evident. "'Tis talk of lynching. This place is nae fortress. We can hold them off for only so long. Ye need to go."

"It may be too late," Aidan said from the doorway and pulled his sword. "The men are here."

Owen drew his sword and joined him.

"The back door! Quickly!" Annie's mother said, but Niall was already heading that way. "I'll latch it behind ye."

Annie and Niall were halfway to the horses when two men slipped into the alley, blocking their path. She saw two silver flashes as Niall's knives hurled through the air and found their marks. Both men dropped. Annie froze at the sight of blood gushing from the wounds.

"Nae now, lass." Niall turned her with a gentle push. "Get to the horses. I'm going to retrieve my blades."

He had just sheathed them and turned around when three more men came into the alley and jumped him. Dropping her portmanteau, Annie mounted her mare and took the reins of Niall's gelding. The sounds of fists thudding against bones and flesh amid grunts and groans was sickening. From the tangle of men—three down and two still fighting Niall—she could not tell who was winning. But she had to do something.

Remembering Niall had compared her to Boudicca, she pulled down her cap and let out what she hoped was a war cry, charging toward them with the horses.

Chapter Fifteen

At the sound of horses' hooves pounding in the narrow alley, the men looked up momentarily, giving Niall the seconds he needed to land a fist in one man's face and cause him to fall back on the other. They both staggered. Annie looked like a wild barbarian bearing down on them and Niall hoped she had control of the horses. He stepped to one side and then grabbed the saddle, feeling a searing, sharp pain to his thigh as he vaulted onto his horse.

More men came running around the corner of the boardinghouse. Although his sword hung from his saddle, he didn't draw it, since fighting in such close quarters would be useless. They needed to get away.

The alley finally opened onto a street. Men were already pouring into the street, no doubt alerted by the noise of the horses. Annie looked back, inadvertently pulling her reins, and her mare slowed.

"Go!" Niall yelled. If the men closed in on them, Annie would be pulled down. That she was a woman wouldn't matter in their current crazed state. He'd seen mob mentality before. It was akin to the feeding frenzy of sharks when the fishermen threw chum back into the water. "Go!" he shouted again as a rock came flying way too close to their heads. "Go!"

Annie's eyes widened as she evidently understood the danger. She kicked her horse's flanks, leaning low as another rock came hurtling by. A third rock hit Niall's shoulder, but he ignored it as he did the slash from the knife to his thigh when he'd mounted. Red stained his breeches, but at least it wasn't flowing freely. Tending it would have to wait.

They thundered down Argyle Street, causing carriages to swerve and the drivers to swear at them, then on to Trongate and past the Tolbooth, scattering pedestrians along the way. It wasn't until they veered onto Gallowgate on the way out of town that Niall finally called to Annie to slow down.

"Are we clear?" she asked as he came alongside, keeping them to a trot.

"Nae yet," Niall answered, "but I doona risk injury to the horses by galloping further on cobblestone. Besides, the ruckus we raise will leave a trail for any who are following us."

Annie's eyes widened again. "Do ye think they will?"

"I doona ken. The men were all on foot, which means they'd have to get to mounts. But I doubt any heads will cool so soon." Niall gave a quick glance behind him to the presently quiet road. "We may have a quarter hour's lead on them."

"Where will we go?" Annie asked.

"For now, we just need to get into the country where we can hide."

"And then?"

"And then, we head north," Niall answered.

"How far north? Will I be safe? I doona feel—"

"Doona fash. I am taking ye where ye will be safe."

Annie looked unconvinced. "And where is that?"

"Arisaig," Niall replied. "My home."

****

The gloaming had settled in by the time Niall finally called a halt to their travel for the day. The horses were tired and had taken to plodding along. Annie was exhausted from the hours of riding, and she thought Niall was looking a little peaked too. The empty shepherd's shack he chosen to stop at didn't look like it would offer many creature comforts, but at the moment, Annie didn't care. Even a bed on rock-hard ground would feel good after hours spent in the saddle.

"'Tis nae an inn," Niall said as he helped her down, "but 'tis dry shelter and there is a burn nearby for water."

"I doona need an inn, but I wish I had nae dropped my portmanteau. My mother had put bread and cheese in it."

"Doona fash," Niall replied, "Shepherds oft leave supplies for the next one to use."

"I will go in and check."

Niall nodded. "I will tend to the horses and bring some water."

"Do ye want me to help with the horses first?"

"Nae. Just check on the food supply."

Annie noticed that his mouth looked tight and a bit white at the corners. Maybe he was really thinking there would be no food at all or maybe he was just really hungry. Standing there and pondering wasn't going to help. She hurried inside.

Niall was right about the shelter being sturdy. Even though it was nearly dark, Annie could see no openings in the overhead thatch or the mud and wattle walls, and the dirt floor was dry. The only furniture in the small room was a rough-hewn table and two straight-back chairs. A tin basin, along with a candlestick and tinder box, sat on top of a cabinet on one side of the room. Annie took a pile of wool blankets from the table and placed them on the chair and then lit the candle, carried it to the table, and finished her visual tour.

A good-sized hearth took up most of the space on the other side of the tiny enclosure. Annie eyed the kettle hanging from a thin pole laid across two Y-shaped iron yokes. A stew pot meant there might be food after all. She went to the cabinet and opened the doors and breathed a sigh of relief. Along with tin plates and bowls, there was a mortar and pestle and a small sack of oats. A half-full jar of honey sat next to it. There was also a partial wheel of cheese wrapped in oilskin, and when she undid it, the cheese had only a few mold spots, which meant it hadn't been there all that long. It would be a meager supper, but it would feel like a meal fit for kings.

Annie poured some oats into the mortar and ground them, then placed the mashed contents in a bowl to add the water that Niall would bring. Once she was satisfied she had enough to fill both their stomachs, she cleaned the hearth of ashes from a half-burned log, then went outside to look for kindling. Niall must have taken the horses behind the shack since there was no sign of them. She wasn't sure how far the burn was, either, although she remembered hearing it for a short way while they cut through a forest trail. Hopefully, she could have a fire going by the time he came back.

Going back inside, she laid the twigs and small branches she had gathered around the log. One of her jobs at the boardinghouse had been to lay the fires, so it didn't take much time to strike the tinder box and get a small flame started. Once that was done, she looked around to see if there was anything else to do and then frowned. Total darkness had fallen. Wherever that burn was, Niall should have been back by now.

Had they been followed after all? She didn't think it possible since Niall had left the main road as soon as they cleared Glasgow. They'd cut through fields and forests and across several burns and avoided country roads. She didn't think even bloodhounds would have been able to track them. So where was Niall?

She moved to the door, reached for the dagger Niall had insisted she keep strapped to her leg, and cautiously stepped back outside. Only the silence of the country filled her ears. Day creatures had settled in and night creatures were not yet about. Annie began walking around to the back of the shack. If one of the horses was missing, perhaps Niall had ridden off in search of food.

Both horses nickered as she came around the corner. Annie frowned again. If the horses were here…

Then she heard the moan. Squinting in the darkness—why hadn't she brought the candle?—she moved forward and then nearly tripped over something. She bent lower and then gasped as her eyes adjusted.

Niall lay on the ground, a red stain running down his left leg.

*****

Something warm and soft and gentle stroked his forehead. A woman's hand? Niall murmured incoherently. God's teeth! The lady had the most uncomfortable bed he had ever slept in. Still, she smelled good. His arm flailed out, finding silken hair. His hand instinctively cupped her head and he drew her down on top of him.

"Stop it! Let me go!"

Hmmm. Those weren't the right words. The lady

wanted him…

"I said, *let me go!*"

Niall groaned. His leg felt like it was on fire, but this very soft, curvy woman fit against him perfectly. He never was one to say no…

"Are ye daft? Did ye hit your head?"

That was definitely not the tone of a woman encouraging him. Niall opened his eyes woozily. "Annie?"

"Aye!" She scrambled off him as soon as his hold relaxed. "What do ye think ye are doing?"

Niall wasn't really sure. He remembered taking the horses to the burn for water, then bringing them back. One minute he'd been tending the animals, getting them settled, and the next he was lying on the ground, looking up at a very irate Annie Ferguson. He bit back another moan as pain seared through his thigh again.

"I was stabbed."

Instantly, her look changed to one of concern. "Here? By the cottage?" She picked up the dagger she'd dropped and looked around.

"Nae." Niall forced himself to a sitting position. "It happened while we were leaving."

Annie stared at him. "Ye rode all day with a wound? Why did ye nae say something?"

Niall shook his head. "What good would it have done? We had to get away."

"We should have stopped sooner."

"It was more important to put mileage between us and the weavers."

"Stubborn man." Annie put her hand to his forehead. "Ye are fevered. I need to get ye inside."

"I can walk." Niall forced himself to stand, then

grimaced as pain shot through his leg when he put weight on it.

"Let me help." Annie pulled his arm around her shoulders and put hers around his waist. "Ye can lean on me."

Normally his pride would have made him refuse to look weak, but at the moment he wasn't in a position to argue. The air was turning chill, which wouldn't help his fever, and he had no idea if the wound had already begun to fester. He nodded silently. At Annie's surprised look that he didn't argue, he knew he was in worse shape than he thought. That he'd passed out was a sign of fatigue. At least, he hoped it was only that.

"I need to take the saddlebag in."

"I'll come back for it," Annie said. "And I'll fetch water."

"Nae need." He pointed with his free hand. "'Tis water in the bucket." At least he wasn't completely useless this evening.

They limped around toward the door. Niall was trying to be careful not to put too much weight on Annie's shoulders, but each step was becoming increasingly harder. He didn't think he'd ever been so glad to see the inside of a room. Annie pulled one of the chairs close to the fire and he sank gratefully onto it.

She moved the other one for him to prop his leg up and then looked at the stained breeches. She hesitated, her expression speculative. "I…I am going to need to look at the wound."

Niall thought she blushed, but it could have been the heat from the flames in the hearth. The thought of her unlacing his breeches to expose his thigh sent warmth through his body that didn't have anything to do with his fever. Slowly, he placed a hand on the waistband, his eyes not leaving her face. "These will need to be removed."

This time she *did* blush. "I ken that." Annie went over to the pile of blankets and brought one back to hand to him. "Ye can undress beneath this. I will go get the water." She didn't wait for him to answer as she rushed to the door.

"I've got my kilt in the saddlebag," he called after her, not sure that she heard. "And whisky."

By the time she returned, he'd completed the painful process of removing the breeches. Dried blood had made the fabric stick to his skin and pulling it off had caused the wound to bleed again. Annie's eyes widened as she saw the fresh blood. Setting down the saddlebags and bucket, she hurried over.

"Ye need stitching."

"'Tis nae that serious." The gash was deeper than Niall wanted to admit, but there was no point in worrying Annie when there was no needle and thread to be had. "A tight binding will do."

She looked doubtful. "I will heat some water, then, to clean it first."

Niall shook his head. "I will lose more blood waiting for the water. Just hand me the whisky."

"Aye." Annie opened the saddle bag and pulled out the bottle. "Ye could probably use a drink."

"I could, but 'tis nae what I had in mind." Niall pulled the stopper and poured the alcohol into the wound, clenching his teeth to keep from cursing when it stung. He picked up his breeches to tear at a leg. "This will have to do as a bandage."

"Wait," Annie said. "I can do better than that." She

pulled the tails of her shirt out. "Linen makes a tighter binding." She tried to rip the bottom, then frowned. "Damnation." She looked quickly at him. "Sorry."

"Nae need to apologize, lass."

"The blasted thing will nae tear." Annie looked at his wound again and quickly removed her coat, then began unlacing the shirt. She glanced at him. "Close your eyes."

He obeyed, although it took every bit of his willpower, especially when he heard rustling and knew she would be bare to him if he looked. And, despite his condition, he wanted to look. To see those luscious breasts unfettered... Niall raised the whisky bottle to his mouth and took a long swig.

"Ye can open your eyes."

He did, hoping against reason she would still be half-naked, but she had the coat on and buttoned. Niall took another swallow of whisky.

Annie had managed to tear out one of the sleeves and she leaned over him now, placing a hand on either side of his thigh to push and hold the edges of his wound together. "Ye need to begin wrapping"

He did, all the time aware of the scent of her skin wafting up to him. The man's jacket she wore was too big and gaped, allowing him to see the cleavage of her breasts. Hellfire, but he wanted to see the whole of them. Cup the creamy, lush rounds in his palms. He was probably near delusion to even be considering such thoughts. He tried to bite back a moan.

Annie took the strip of linen with which he'd done one successful wrap around his thigh, and she continued the job. "I ken it hurts."

What was really hurting right now was a part of him

that he hoped she wouldn't notice as it grew under the blanket he'd draped over himself. It wasn't helping his situation that her hands were dangerously close to it. That unruly head wasn't acting any better than the one he was trying to think with. It wanted touching. To feel her soft hand on him, her cool fingers stroking him… Niall bit back another moan and lifted the bottle again.

Annie looked up as she finished wrapping and tucked the end of the strip inside the top binding. "Ye are looking very flushed. Are ye sure ye should be drinking so much?"

The reason his face was hot had nothing to do with the whisky, but he could hardly tell her that. Not that he was in any condition to act on his lecherous thoughts, but he doubted Annie would welcome knowing about them. The lady had been nearly killed this morning and she was counting on him to get her to safety. For that matter, to keep her safe tonight as well. He couldn't do that if he were drunk. Niall put the bottle down. "Ye are right."

"Good. Then ye have left enough for me." Annie picked up the bottle. "I will see to supper in a minute, but first I need a wee bit of fortification."

Niall raised an eyebrow as he watched Annie take a long swallow. When she didn't choke on it, he managed a grin in spite of the pain. Annie Ferguson was quite a woman.

Chapter Sixteen

Annie woke the next morning to bright sunshine streaming in the small window. Niall still slept. After their meal last night, she had laid several of the blankets on the floor in front of the hearth and brought in a few logs to keep the fire going throughout the night. It hadn't taken much argument—for once—to get Niall bedded down with his wounded leg closest to the warmth of the hearth.

She pushed her own blanket aside to check on his fever. It wasn't much of a reach, although she didn't recall lying down quite so close to him. She must have rolled in her sleep. His skin felt warm, but not as hot as it had last night.

Niall opened his eyes at her touch. His expression was momentarily confused and then cleared. "How long have I been sleeping? Did we lose a day?"

"Nae," Annie answered. "'Tis still early."

He sat up, wincing when he moved his leg. "We need to be on our way."

"I doona ken if ye should be riding. Can we nae stay here for another day until the wound has a chance to begin closing?" Annie asked. "We are hidden from view."

Niall shook his head. "We are maybe fifteen miles from the city. And the smoke from the chimney can give us away. 'Tis too great a risk to stay."

"What if your wound opens?"

"I'll put a second binding on it. Once we get past Loch Lomond, we can look for a physician to stitch it."

"But your fever is nae completely gone either," Annie said.

"'Tis better for now. We need to take advantage of that." Niall braced his hand on one of the chairs and pushed himself to his feet. The great plaid he'd wrapped himself in last night fell in surprisingly neat pleats down his hips and thighs. He arched an eyebrow as he saw Annie watching him.

She quickly turned away, busying herself with stacking the blankets. "There's some cheese and cold oat mash left. I can reheat—"

"'Tis nae time for that. We will take it with us." Niall eyed the jacket she'd slept in. "Ye need a shirt. I have an extra one in my saddlebag."

"It will be too big," Annie answered.

"Ye can just stuff the extra material inside your jacket," Niall said. "'Twill round ye out so ye doona look like a girl."

Annie frowned as she put the blankets back on the table. "Ye doona want me to look like a girl?"

"'Tis nae me. If there are search parties coming out, they will be looking—and asking—about a man and a woman travelling together. If ye look more like a boy, it will confuse them."

He had a point. She was not as curvy as a lot of women, so stuffing her jacket could make her look like a pudgy boy, especially with keeping her hair completely under the cap. "Do ye think it will work?"

"It cannae hurt," Niall answered. "Besides, the disguise will protect your reputation from harm if people think ye are a lad."

Her reputation. Publicly, it was intact. How ironic that she had allowed herself to be ruined by a man who didn't care and have Niall be concerned about preserving her reputation when he hadn't attempted to ruin her at all. "I agree."

He nodded and removed the shirt from the saddlebag and handed it to her. "I will go saddle the horses."

"Ye should wait and let me help."

He walked to the door and opened it. "'Tis my thigh that is wounded, nae my arms."

"I dinnae mean ye were nae strong. I just doona want your leg to start bleeding again."

"I will be careful." Then he was gone.

Annie rolled her eyes. Why were men so sensitive about such things? She'd saddled her own horse many times. What she couldn't do was stitch his wound if it opened. Stubborn Highlander.

She caught his scent as she shook out the shirt and held it up to her nose. Slightly woodsy and a hint of spice clung to it. The material was finely woven linen and felt soft against her skin. Then she realized it was the dress shirt that he wore with his full tartan. A part of his clan identity. She inhaled his scent again. Niall.

****

Niall sucked in a lungful of cool, crisp air. He'd gotten out of the shack just in time before he did something stupid like wait for her to put his shirt on. He could have held off on tending to the horses, could have stayed, could have closed his eyes while she took off the jacket. He could have controlled his wayward thoughts. He hoped. He'd managed quite well in doing so, these past weeks. But that was when Annie Ferguson wore a dress. Having her legs—not to mention a very comely arse—so well-defined in breeches was driving him to a fevered state that had nothing to do with his wound.

The first time he'd awakened last night he'd found Annie lying a few feet from him. Even with a blanket covering her as she lay fully clothed, he'd had the oddest sensation of what it would feel like to wake up next to her in a nice, soft bed. And without the clothes. Each time he awoke, he'd had to resist the urge to pull her close, put her head on his shoulder, and cradle her through the night. But no woman, trustfully sleeping in peace and innocence, deserved to be taken advantage of. He'd contented himself with moving as close as he could without physically touching her.

Niall winced as the cold air made the injury throb. Annie was right that the wound hadn't closed. Hopefully, they could make it to Loch Lomond and a doctor before it began to fester.

By the time he got the horses saddled, a painfully slow process since he didn't want to risk having the bleeding start again, Annie had repacked the saddlebags and was waiting for him. He noticed she'd buttoned his shirt right to the collar that tucked under her chin and that the extra material scrunched under the jacket did obscure her feminine shape, which was a godsend to his unruly thoughts. Her hair had been pushed into the cap as well. Not a strand of red could be seen. Niall frowned.

"Your hair is nae red."

"I put soot on what could be seen." Annie shrugged. "I figured anyone looking for us would be sure to include I have red hair."

"Smart lass."

"I hope so. It feels filthy."

Niall smiled. "Perhaps tonight ye can have a bath."

"That would be heaven," Annie replied.

"Then we had best get started. 'Tis a long day ahead." Niall helped her mount, then turned to his own horse. He felt a tugging at the edges of the wound when he raised his foot to the stirrup, followed by a tearing as he added weight to his leg. Niall clenched his jaw at the sharp pain, then moved the gelding to the left of Annie so she wouldn't see the blood he felt trickling down.

Since he wanted to avoid being seen as much as possible, they stayed just inside the forest line that paralleled the main road north, but that also meant they needed to keep the horses to a walk most of the day. They stopped several times to water and rest the animals and he had the chance to wash the blood off his leg before Annie saw it, but each time he remounted, he could feel the wound stretching. Thankfully, Annie had packed the remains from last night's meal, so they didn't have to stop at a village to eat.

By the time they reached a coaching inn near Crianlarich, dusk had fallen. Niall was tired, but he knew Annie must be near exhaustion. They'd ridden a good twelve hours and she hadn't spoken more than a few words the past five miles or so.

"We will stop here for the night," he said.

"But 'tis nae village here nor doctor," Annie said. "Ye need to have your leg tended to."

"It will have to wait until morning," Niall answered. "Darkness will have fallen before we reach Crianlarich. Highwaymen could be about and I'll nae risk ye travelling."

"Ye taught me to handle a dagger."

"Only in self defense if ye have to. I'll nae put ye in danger on the roads at night."

"But—"

"Besides," Niall interrupted, "I doona want to push the horses farther."

Annie frowned and then nodded. "Ye are right about that. The animals are as tired as we are."

"Aye. This will be as good a place to stop as any."

"Do ye think it safe?" Annie asked, looking down the road that led to Glasgow.

"I doubt any searchers would come this far north," Niall replied, "especially if they've been asking if we were seen and the answers have been nae. They will probably go east toward Edinburgh instead."

"I hope ye are right," Annie said. "In truth, I have been thinking about that hot bath for half the day."

Niall nodded as they stopped the horses in front of the inn and he helped her down. "It should nae be long before that wish is granted." He hoisted the saddlebag over his shoulder and handed the horses' reins to a stable boy, along with some coin for extra oats, and hoped Annie didn't notice his limp as they went inside.

The innkeeper, a short, bald-headed man of middle age, looked up from the counter. He studied Niall's tartan. "MacDonald, is it?" His gaze traveled to the sword hanging at Niall's side and the knife sheathed on his sporran belt. "This be Campbell country. I doona want any trouble."

"Neither do I," Niall answered. "We are just passing through and need rooms for the night."

"Only one room left."

Niall heard Annie's sharp intake of breath. Under any other circumstance, he would let her have the room, but she was supposed to be a lad. Giving her the room would seem strange to the innkeeper and Niall didn't want to raise any suspicions. "We will take it."

The older man arched a brow. "Plenty of room for your boy in the stables."

Annie started to speak, but Niall cut her off with a sharp glance and she coughed instead. He knew she wasn't happy with the way things were progressing. At least, the disguise was working. But it also created a dilemma. He couldn't let her stay in the stables where she would be in danger of being discovered, but it would also seem strange if he ordered a bath if they were sharing a room. He couldn't even say she was his brother since they looked nothing alike and she was dressed in English clothes. Niall gave the clerk a conspiratorial smile. "The lad tends to get himself into trouble when left to his own devices, if ye ken what I mean. I've found while traveling 'tis best to keep an eye on Alan."

This time a noise which sounded like a muted growl came from Annie.

"Aye," the innkeeper answered, "the young ones are always randy."

"That they are." Niall didn't dare look at Annie. "The lasses will be safe if the lad stays with me."

The innkeeper nodded and handed him a key. "Second floor. Last door on the right. I'll have my wife bring up water."

"Could ye have some stew brought up as well?" Niall asked. "We've had a hard day's ride. The lad is about to fall asleep standing up."

Annie cleared her throat rather loudly.

Niall ignored the sound and remembered, just in time, not to step aside for Annie to precede him. She seemed to understand since she followed him up the stairs without a word.

Her silence was short-lived. As soon as the door closed behind them, she folded her arms across her chest. "Falling asleep standing up?" Her hands went to her waist. "I get in trouble left to my own devices?"

Niall grinned at her indignation. "Well, ye can nae deny that part is true. Do ye want me to count the times in the past weeks?"

"Nae." Annie frowned. "Did ye have to add that the *lasses* will be safe from me?"

"Ye are supposed to be a *lad*, remember?"

"But I am nae—"

"Ye doona need to remind me." Niall sobered. "Even dressed as ye are, I am all too aware that ye are nae a lad."

Annie gave him a startled glance, then shifted her gaze to the bed and quickly looked away from it. Niall followed her look. The bed, while not big, could certainly accommodate two, especially if they nestled… He turned his attention away. Now was not the time to think about sharing a nice, soft bed with Annie.

"Ye can have the bed. I will sleep on the floor."

Her expression turned to consternation. "But the floor is hard."

Niall shrugged. "I've had worse."

Before Annie could respond, a knock sounded on the door, followed by the innkeeper's wife opening it. A younger maid stood behind her holding a tray with a tureen that smelled deliciously of mutton stew.

"I've brought ye water to wash," the older woman said, placing a pitcher and a bar of soap next to a tin basin already on the chest of drawers. She gestured toward the young maid. "Elsa has stew and ale as well."

"Put it here," Niall said, removing his saddlebag from the small table. "It smells wonderful."

"Thank ye," the girl said and cast a sideways glance at Annie. "I can take ye downstairs to where the men servants wash." She smiled prettily when Annie blinked at her. "'Tis nae trouble at all."

Niall quickly squelched a grin, since Annie eyes were flashing blue fire at him. Maybe the disguise was working a little too well. "'Tis nae need to put ye through that trouble," Niall said to Elsa. "Alan can use my water when I am through."

Elsa looked disappointed, but before she could say anything else, the innkeeper's wife took hold of her arm and hustled her out the door. Niall could hear the woman scolding the girl as they went down the hall.

"Thank ye," Annie said when the sounds faded away. "That…has never happened to me before."

"'Tis good to hear." Niall couldn't help smiling. "I had nae given it much thought, but ye do make a rather handsome lad. I will have to make sure we doona stop in any taverns where the wenches are a bit more aggressive."

Annie drew her brows down. "Will ye stop teasing me?"

He sobered. "I am sorry that ye will nae have that hot bath ye wanted. 'Twould look a bit awkward if I ordered one and then left the room while the water was still hot."

Annie nodded and then sniffed appreciatively. "I think I care more about hot food than a hot bath at the moment."

"I agree." Niall moved to the table to hold out a chair

for her and then winked. "I doona do this for just any lad, mind." Annie gave him an exasperated look which only made him chuckle as she took the seat.

She picked up the ladle and spooned stew into the two slightly chipped bowls on the tray while Niall poured ale into tin cups. He sat, lifting his. "A toast."

Annie looked surprised as she lifted her cup as well. "To what?"

He touched his rim to hers. "To a successful escape."

"Aye." Annie took a sip of ale. "I have ye to thank for that. If that mob had caught me—"

"Doona think on it," Niall replied and changed the subject. "Let us just enjoy the first real meal we've had in two days."

She nodded again and they both set to devouring the delicious stew and fresh bread with soft butter. Having a full belly restored his strength and he was almost able to ignore the pain in his thigh as he finished his ale. Even so, it was hard not to wince when he pushed back from the table and stood.

"I'll take a short walk while ye wash at the basin."

Annie gathered the dishes and put them back on the tray. "Perhaps ye can take this back downstairs?"

Niall had intended only to linger down the hall and not use the stairs until morning, but he nodded. Annie probably didn't want Elsa showing up again. "I will."

He made his way downstairs and had a tankard of ale in the public room, hoping that would give Annie enough time to freshen up. He had no idea how long she needed. Some women seemed to require hours, but then Annie wasn't preparing to attend a ball, just go to bed.

Bed. Niall pushed away the thought of the soft bed

upstairs that was large enough for both of them. He hardly relished sleeping on the hard floor, although he had spoken truth when he said he'd had worst. But the last thing Annie needed was to feel threatened by him after they'd narrowly made their escape from the angry horde in Glasgow. Maybe he should have another tankard of ale and when he went upstairs she'd already be asleep.

No such luck. When he opened the door to their room some twenty minutes later, Annie was sitting up in bed, braced against the headboard, the woolen blanket pulled to her waist. She was still wearing his shirt, but he noticed the breeches were neatly folded over a chair, which meant her legs would be bare under the covers. He bit back a groan. It was going to be a long night.

"I was wondering what happened to ye," Annie said.

Niall shrugged. "I did nae ken how much time ye would need."

"Nae much," Annie replied. "I left ye some fresh water to wash with."

"Thank ye." Niall pulled off his boots and began to unwrap his great plaid. As he did, he noticed that even though Annie had turned her head, she was watching him out of the corner of her eye. He smiled in spite of himself. Would she turn away when he removed his tunic as well?

He let the tartan drop and reached for the hem of the long shirt. He had it half the way over his head when he heard a rustle and then a thud as Annie's feet hit the floor. For a moment, he thought she was fleeing the room. He pulled the long shirt back over his head to see her standing there, staring at him. Or rather, his thigh. It took another moment for him to realize she looked horrified, not fascinated. He glanced down and then frowned.

Dried blood stained the bandage and the skin around it was an angry-looking red.

"Sit." Annie pulled up a chair and practically pushed him into it. Then she started unwrapping the dirty linen to expose the cut. She made a clucking sound. "The wound looks like it has festered."

"It has nae festered," Niall said. "'Tis just nae closed yet."

Annie gave him a look as though he were a half-wit. Which maybe he was since the sight of her bare legs was making it impossible for him to think clearly. "The doctor in Crianlarich can tend it tomorrow."

"If the infection spreads…" She didn't finish the sentence but hurried to the saddlebag, burrowing through it like a squirrel for his flask and the rest of the shirt she'd torn apart the night before. "I doona ken why ye did nae tell me of this condition earlier," she fussed as she poured whisky into the wound and then started wrapping a clean bandage around his leg. "Stubborn man."

Niall clenched his jaw at the sting of the liquor, then forced a smile. "I did nae ken ye wanted to see my thigh."

Annie gave him another infuriated look, although she blushed a little. He glanced down to where her hands still rested on his leg. The softness of her touch so close to his manhood made his cock stir with interest under his tunic. He shifted to squelch the movement, but it was too late. Annie's face flamed. She whisked her hands away as though she'd just touched hot iron. Which was rather the way his shaft was feeling.

"If ye will hand me one of the blankets, I will just settle in here by the fire," he said.

Annie shook her head. "Ye are nae lying on a hard floor in that condition."

Niall felt his eyes widen before he realized she was talking about the condition of his leg and not his cock. "'Tis only one bed, lass. I will nae have ye sleeping on the floor."

If possible, her face turned redder. "I ken that."

Niall paused. "Ye would share the bed with me?"

She looked over his shoulder at the wall and then nodded. "I trust ye will nae take advantage of the situation."

He pressed his hand down—hard—on his groin. "Ye doona have to fash about that. I am so tired I will be asleep before my head touches the pillow."

That seemed to reassure her, although Niall doubted he'd get any sleep at all. He watched as she sat down on the edge of the bed to swing her lovely, bare legs under the covers and then scoot toward the wall until she was backed up against it.

Snuffing out the candle, Niall lay down on the edge of the mattress, trying his best to ignore where their bodies made contact in the narrow bed. He put his arms under his head and stared into the darkness. It was going to be a long night.

The floor might have been a better choice, after all.

Chapter Seventeen

Annie pulled the covers closer, wondering why it suddenly felt so cold. Sleepily, she opened one eye. Dawn was breaking and Niall was pouring water into the basin on the dresser.

That explained the sudden coolness. His body heat had kept her warm and snug as they shared the bed. She half-closed her eyes, still not quite fully awake, rather liking the scent Niall had left on the pillow...and the fact that, except for his small clothes, Niall stood naked as he washed.

He certainly was well-made. She'd known his shoulders were broad, but seeing them bare and the broad expanse of muscles flexing across his back as he moved his arms was sheer beauty. His back tapered to a narrow waist and tight buttocks beneath the linen cloth he wore. She already knew how well-muscled his thighs were...

Niall glanced over his shoulder toward her. "Are ye awake?"

Dear Lord. Annie pinched her eyes shut. Had he sensed her gawking at him? Or worse, *seen* her looking? She wanted to pull the covers over her head, but she forced her eyes open.

"Aye. 'Tis barely morn though."

"I would like to get an early start."

As the grogginess left her brain, she realized that was probably a good idea. She had no desire to encounter

Elsa—or any other maids who thought she was a handsome lad. If her disguise was uncovered, she would be truly ruined since she had spent the night with a man. Equally bad, should someone still be following them, they could be more easily identified.

Annie swung her legs over the edge of the bed and shivered. The fire had died down and the room was chilly. Niall didn't seem affected as he took a towel and began drying himself. She tried not to stare at his expansive chest with its dark dusting of hair that trailed a fine line down his flat, hard belly to disappear into the loin cloth that hung low on his hips. She forced herself to avert her eyes and then remembered his bandage.

"How is your leg?" she asked as she got out of bed and pulled on the breeches she'd left folded over a chair.

Niall pulled his tunic over his head. "'Tis fine."

"Have ye looked at it?"

"Nae."

Annie shook her head. "Then how can ye say 'tis fine? Perhaps we should check it."

"Nae," he said again, putting more emphasis on the word as he wrapped his plaid around his waist. "'Tis *fine*."

From his tone, it didn't sound as if his leg was *fine*, but Annie wasn't sure if Niall was hiding pain or if he just didn't want her touching his thigh again. And perhaps he had the right of it. She'd seen the reaction of his manhood last night when she'd wrapped the bandage. She knew that when a man hardened, it became painful. At least, that was what Broderick had told her, along with the fact that if a woman teased a man, she was responsible for that aroused state. Niall had not touched her last night, but she didn't want to cause him any more discomfort.

"We will have the doctor at Crianlarich look at it, then. 'Tis nae far, is it?"

"A little less than an hour," Niall replied. "'Tis another reason I want to leave early. Taking time to stitch the wound will already delay us."

"It needs to be done." Annie eyed him suspiciously. "Ye are nae thinking of skipping the visit, are ye?"

Niall grimaced as he pulled on his boots. "Nae. I will admit that it hurts like the devil has placed a hot anvil on it."

Annie bit her lip. For Niall to *admit* that the wound hurt was amazing in itself, but that it felt that bad was disconcerting. Even though he'd claimed last night the injury was not festering, she was pretty sure it was. The sooner the leg was properly cleaned and stitched, the better.

"It will take me only a minute or two more to be ready."

Niall nodded as he went to the door. "I'll get the horses saddled and see if I can get some bread and cheese to break our fast."

Annie hurried with her ablutions after Niall left, then stuffed what remained of the shirt they'd been using for bandages into the saddlebag. Hopefully, they wouldn't be needing it anymore once the doctor got the wound closed and a proper wrapping put on. She pinned her hair up and pulled her cap down low, making sure no red showed, and then went downstairs.

Niall sat on the bench by the door waiting for her, beside him a small sack which probably contained their food. He winced slightly as he stood, and Annie noticed, for the first time, that he favored his injured leg as they walked outside to the horses. And, also for the first time, instead of vaulting onto the gelding's back, Niall led the animal to a mounting block. Annie frowned. Niall would never do such a thing unless he was in dire pain.

Thankfully, the doctor wasn't that far away.

****

"What do ye mean, the doctor is nae here?" Annie stared at the middle-aged woman who'd opened the door to the doctor's cottage. "We saw the shingle out front. Is this nae the right house?"

"'Tis. I am his wife." The woman pulled her woolen wrapper closer to avoid the morning chill. "He is nae here."

"When do ye expect him back?" Niall asked, his lips white at the corners.

The woman shook her head. "I doona ken. 'Tis an outbreak of typhus at Killin, northeast of here. My husband left two days ago to tend to it."

Annie heard Niall stifle a groan and felt like she'd just swallowed lead. What were they going to do now? The physician probably wouldn't be back for several days. Even if he came back earlier, would he be carrying the disease? Typhus was highly contagious. News of an epidemic in Ireland just last year had travelled to Glasgow. Another epidemic had occurred in London's Newgate prison just this year and spread to the city. A travelling cooper had brought the news. In addition to fever—which Niall probably already had—the disease caused delirium and coma. Annie's mother had burned the bed sheets the man had used and scrubbed every inch of the room with lye soap after he'd left.

"Do ye have any clean bandages that we can have?" Annie asked. "And maybe a salve?"

The woman looked at her suspiciously. "Just what is wrong with ye?"

"'Tis nae me—"

"My wife is making much ado over a slight scratch I received with a ruffian who insulted her yesterday," Niall said quickly, "but I would appreciate a clean bandage if ye have it. I have coin, of course."

The woman opened the door wider. "Come in, then."

She left them to sit on a wood bench just inside the door while she went to get the supplies. Annie turned to him as soon as she disappeared. "I am your wife now?"

"'Tis better that she think us married, lass."

Annie frowned. "I thought I was supposed to be a lad."

"That would have been better." Niall looked at her cap. "But half your hair is down."

Annie's hands went up and found the offending tresses. "Bloody hell!"

Niall managed a smile. "Ye are acquiring quite a vocabulary." Then he put out a hand to stop her from pushing the hair back under the cap. "Leave it be for now. We doona wish to raise any questions."

"I'm sure the woman already has some," Annie replied, "or do women in the country often wear breeches?"

"'Tis nae unheard of," Niall said. "The doctor's wife already saw we had two horses. 'Tis easier to ride astride in breeches. The farther ye go into the Highlands, the more what is practical applies."

"Ye doona think she will wonder though?"

"She might." Niall shrugged. "What would make her more suspicious is for you to have your hair tucked back up and looking like a lad when she comes back with the bandaging."

A young girl of perhaps three-and-ten appeared in the hall. "My mother bids ye come with me."

"Where are we going?" Annie asked.

The girl gave her a look as though she were daft. "To my da's office so my mother can tend the wound."

Niall shook his head. "'Tis nae necessary—"

"Aye, *'tis*," Annie hissed at him. "Ye did nae let me check this morning for festering."

He sighed and stood. Annie noticed his limp was worse as they followed the girl down the short hall to a room toward the back of the house.

He was shown a seat and the girl shooed from the room by her mother before she turned back to him. "Where is this wound?"

"My thigh." Niall folded back his plaid to reveal the bandage and then held out his hand. "I can do this myself."

"Aye. Men always think they can take care of themselves." The doctor's wife swatted his hand as she started unwrapping the old bandage. "Which usually just makes more work for the woman." She tsked as the linen came undone. "By all the saints! This is nae a scratch. And 'tis infected."

"I kenned it!" Annie said and came closer, then stifled a gasp. The wound was now a deep, ugly red with purple mottling around the edges, and Niall's leg had swelled as well. "God's teeth!"

"Aye. 'Tis bad," the doctor's wife said. "I can put some moldy bread on it to keep the infection down, but ye should stay here and let me send someone for my husband."

"How long would that take?" Annie asked.

"He could probably be here by tomorrow afternoon, if he can get away."

"If he can get away?"

The woman looked uncertain. "Usually when he travels to an outbreak, he waits a few days to return home to make sure he doesn't bring the disease with him."

"That makes sense," Niall said, "but 'tis better we travel on and find a physician in another town."

"The nearest would be Fort William," she answered, "but 'tis a two-day ride. Three or maybe more, in your condition."

Niall grimaced. "'Tis a better choice than waiting for your husband to return home."

"Ye do have a point. I will do what I can with a poultice and clean bandage."

After the doctor's wife left to retrieve the bread from the kitchen, Annie gave Niall a worried look. "Two days or more to Fort William? And how far from there to Arisaig?"

Niall shrugged. "Probably another two days."

"Ye can nae ride for four days wounded! I think ye should stay here," Annie said. "I can go with whoever is sent to Killin. I will persuade the doctor to come back one way or another."

"I have nae doubt that ye would." Niall tried to smile. "But ye heard what his wife said. We cannae risk spreading the typhus. 'Tis too deadly."

"People die from infected wounds, too," Annie said. "Ye can nae ride for four days with that festering."

"Ye are probably right."

"Good." Annie gave a relieved sigh. "Then we will stay here."

"Nae."

Annie stared at him. "What do ye mean, nae? Has the fever taken hold of ye?"

Niall shook his head. "We will cross to Oban. We can get there by nightfall."

"And then what?"

"We catch a boat north on Loch Linnhe."

Annie frowned. "That is nae going to get us to Arisaig."

"True. But it will get us close to Loch Shiel," Niall answered. "Bridget's brother Ian MacLeod has a holding there."

"And he will welcome ye?"

"Of course. Even if Alasdair were nae Ian's brother by marriage—which makes him mine in a way—we are in the Highlands now. 'Tis an unwritten code of hospitality that rules."

"'Tis still a long way to go." Annie was not totally convinced. "I think we should wait here."

"Nae. We will nae wait." Niall said as the doctor's wife reentered the room with the bread. "We will go."

"Bossy man," Annie muttered under her breath. Why wouldn't he listen to her before he let infection kill him?

****

As the schooner pulled away from the dock in Oban's harbor early the next morning, Annie was still full of misgivings. They'd arrived after dark last night and the town's small apothecary had already closed for the day, its only doctor well into his cups at a local pub. Annie hadn't argued with Niall about the futility of getting his thigh looked at. It was more important they book passage and get to Ian MacLeod's holding as soon as possible.

They'd been lucky to find a ship setting sail so quickly for Fort William, especially one which had room for their horses in the hold, probably because Captain Vance knew Ian MacLeod of Glenfinnan. While that might have helped them secure passage, Annie had misgivings about the vessel, too, since everything on it from the timbers of the hull to the deck and masts creaked and groaned as though any minute the whole thing would splinter apart.

She clung to the starboard rail as the ship made its way out of the bay below the cliff on which stood an ancient castle. It looked as abandoned as she felt. The sails suddenly flapped loudly as the vessel began its turn to the north. Annie grabbed the rail tighter as the deck seemed to lurch beneath her feet and everything tilted in her direction. The sea was closing in and for a panicky moment Annie wondered if the boat was going to tip over. Then a strong arm circled her waist and a large hand covered one of hers. "Doona fash. The boat is only listing," Niall said as he moved a step closer so she could brace herself against him. "'Twill right itself as soon as the sails get adjusted."

Annie wasn't sure about that either. Not only was the boat leaning far to the right, it also seemed to be speeding ahead, slicing through the water, as though the hounds of hell were on its stern. When she said as much to Niall, he chuckled.

"Ye have nae sailed before?"

"Nae." Annie tried not to look at how close the rail was to the sea. "And I doubt I'll do it again."

"Ye'll get used to it," Niall answered. "Just wait a minute or two."

To her surprise, the boat did straighten until she was able to stand with her weight evenly distributed on both feet instead of looking like a fencer without a sword.

But then, the ship started rocking from side to side and she tightened her hold on the rail again. "Is this motion going to continue for the whole trip?"

"That depends on the wind," Niall said. "Right now, 'tis behind us since the island of Kerrera creates a narrow channel. Once we get into open waters of the Firth of Lorn, 'twill be a different direction."

"That will stop the rolling motion?" Annie asked.

"Aye. She'll either heel again or pitch, depending." Niall gave Annie a sharp look. "Are ye feeling ill?"

She shook her head, not wanting to admit how queasy her stomach was.

He squinted. "Ye are beginning to look a bit green at the gills, lass."

"I…" Annie swallowed hard. "I will be fine."

Niall looked unconvinced. "The best thing for ye to do until ye get your legs is to look at the shoreline. It keeps ye from feeling dizzy."

Annie swallowed again and looked at the passing scenery and the mountains farther inland. The steadiness of the land did seem to help. She turned to Niall and changed the subject. "What are ye doing up here? The doctor's wife said ye should nae be standing on your leg."

"She is nae here to see me."

"'Tis nae the point, is it?" Annie gave an exasperated sigh. "The more ye move around, the more ye aggravate the wound."

"I will manage," Niall said and then winced as a sudden lurch of the ship caused him to shift his weight unexpectedly.

"Aye, ye will manage. Now ye are the one looking green…" She stopped as Niall grimaced again. "…or I should say white. Ye look about to faint."

"I…doona…faint…" Niall said haltingly.

"We need to get ye to your berth." Annie changed positions and brought Niall's arm over her shoulder so she could help him walk toward the stern of the ship and the companionway that led below. "And I will hear nae argument from ye."

"Ye…are…a…stubborn…" Niall didn't finish the sentence as his legs buckled and he slid onto the deck.

Captain Vance seemed to appear from nowhere. He motioned to two deckhands to assist. "Take Mr. MacDonald to my cabin." The captain turned to Annie. "Do you know what is wrong with him?"

"Aye. 'Tis a knife wound to his leg."

He sucked in a breath. "Why the devil—pardon me—did he not say something?"

Annie shook her head. "Because he is too proud to admit he was hurt."

"Neptune's bullocks!" This time the captain didn't bother to apologize for his language. He turned and barked an order to a sailor standing nearby. "Get the quartermaster. Tell him to come to my cabin." As the man hurried away, Captain Vance turned back to Annie. "We do not have a surgeon on this ship, but our quartermaster has some medical skill. We will see what he says."

Annie followed the captain below. The quartermaster soon clattered down the ladder, carrying a leather bag, and pushed past her to enter the captain's quarters. Since the cabin was too small to accommodate more people, Annie took a seat on one of the empty berths. The smells from the hold, which included chickens and sheep as well as their horses, nearly choked her and, without benefit of the horizon, the continued roll of the ship was making her queasy again, but she ignored both. The only person who mattered was Niall. She looked at the closed door. What was taking so long?

Finally...*finally*...after what seemed like an eon of time, the captain and the quartermaster emerged. Both looked grim and Annie felt an icy fear clench her stomach.

"How is he?"

The quartermaster shook his head. "Mr. MacDonald's entire leg is infected. He will be lucky to still be alive by morning."

Chapter Eighteen

Annie stood at the small porthole of the captain's cabin and stared out at the dark water. A sliver of new moon barely cast light on the sea, causing the swells to look like giant, black monsters undulating toward her to crash with the pounding force of cannon against the hull. The first hour they'd been in open water, she had been sure the boat was going to splinter apart, even though the quartermaster had assured her the ship had crossed the Atlantic in much worse conditions. There wasn't even a storm forecast this night.

There might not be a storm brewing on the water, but there was one raging in her heart. Annie leaned her forehead against the cool brass fitting and closed her eyes. Niall was lying at death's door because of her. He had saved her from falling into the hands of an angry mob and gotten stabbed in the process. He hadn't had adequate medical care because he refused to stop too close to Glasgow. He'd insisted they keep moving, all the while aggravating the injury and causing it to become worse. He hadn't let on how much pain he was in.

Or had she just been too stupid to see?

Annie opened her eyes again to look into the never-ending black night. The captain had said they should reach the end of the loch by midmorning and then it was just a few miles to Ian MacLeod's. Captain Vance had assured her that he'd transported the MacLeods before and that Ian kept a carriage at the coaching inn by the small dock since it was often quicker to travel to Loch Linnhe and catch a boat than to go through Loch Shiel.

She just hoped the carriage wouldn't become a funeral coach.

Niall emitted a low moan and Annie spun around. His eyes remained closed, which meant he was probably still in the semi-coma he'd been in since the sailors carried him down. Reaching for the washcloth lying in a basin of water, she wrung it out and sat on the edge of the narrow cot. Even sitting on the side opposite his infected leg, she could feel the fever heat radiate from him. Annie dabbed his forehead and cheeks with the cool cloth, then dipped it in the basin again and wiped his throat and chest where his tunic lay open. The shirt was drenched with sweat and clung to his skin, revealing the powerfully-muscled chest and arms. She hoped that strength would get him through the night.

He wouldn't be in this condition if it hadn't been for her.

Annie put the washcloth back in the basin and picked up Niall's hand. It felt as hot as though he'd been holding it over an open fire. She intertwined her fingers with his. "Ye are a willful man, Niall MacDonald. Now use that will to stay alive." She felt a teardrop run down her cheek. "Will ye stay alive? Please?" Another tear rolled down. "Please? Please stay alive."

Niall didn't open his eyes and he didn't answer. Annie was about to reach for the cloth again when she felt a slight squeeze on her fingers. It was so feeble, she wondered if she'd imagined it. Then it came again, light as a cat's paw.

Annie squeezed back. "Niall? Can ye hear me?"

When there was no response, she sighed. She had hoped he'd heard her, but the movement might have been involuntary. People tossed and turned in their sleep, after all. But then…maybe the fragile pressure to her fingers *hadn't* been involuntary. Maybe Niall *had* heard her. Maybe if she kept talking, she could hold that link. Let her strength flow through that connection. Maybe, just maybe, she could keep him alive.

She settled on the bed, holding Niall's hand in both of hers. "Ye said I was a stubborn lass, Niall MacDonald. Verra well. Now I will show ye just how stubborn I can be. Ye cannae die. Do ye hear me? Ye cannae die."

Niall's fingers moved ever so slightly and Annie began talking. She talked throughout the night, telling him of all the things he had to live for, asking questions about his family even though she knew he would not answer, and eventually, near dawn, even telling Niall of her childhood, stopping only when she reached the part about Broderick.

Having exhausted conversation, but encouraged by the occasional twitch of Niall's hand in hers, she began to sing. Off-key and flat, no doubt, but she didn't care. Her voice grew hoarse over the next hours, the sound more like a croaking frog, but still she continued, but that didn't matter if her voice could keep Niall in the world of the living. *Please, Lord. He cannae die!*

****

Annie startled when she heard the cabin door open. She blinked her eyes open to find herself looking up at the quartermaster looming in the entrance. She tilted her head, rubbing it against something hard, and realized she had fallen asleep slumped over Niall. Annie sat up quickly. She wasn't supposed to fall asleep! Her gaze flew to Niall. *Dear Lord…* She heaved a sigh of relief when she saw Niall's chest rise and fall.

"He still breathes," the quartermaster said as he stepped inside. "Perhaps the infection hasn't spread throughout his body, then."

"Is it morning?" Annie croaked, her voice scratchy and barely audible.

"Aye." The quartermaster moved to Niall's other side and lifted the blanket to unwrap the bandage on his leg. "Hmmm."

The man's face was as impassive as a faro player's. The grogginess left Annie's mind as her senses kicked in. She tried to peer over the sheet, but it was held too high. "What does that mean?"

"It means he is not worse."

Annie placed her hand on Niall's forehead. "But his fever still burns."

"I didn't say he was better."

"Doona talk in riddles," Annie said. "Speak plainly."

The quartermaster arched a brow. "I thought I was. It is a good sign that your husband has held his own overnight."

Annie didn't correct his assumption that she was Niall's wife. When they'd boarded the boat yesterday her cap had flown off and her hair had tumbled down. No one seemed particularly surprised that she was a woman wearing breeches, but then this was a working ship. And Niall had acted very protective. Her breathing hitched. Niall had always acted protective with her, but she hadn't appreciated it.

"How long before we dock?"

"Less than a half hour. I came down to see if we

would be needing…" He stopped. "Well, I will let the captain know to send someone for the MacLeod carriage."

Annie looked at Niall and then up. "Should we try to wake him?"

"Better not to agitate him. If he wakes, the pain will be bad and I gave him all the laudanum we had last night." The quartermaster secured the bandage and dropped the blanket. "I will send some men down once the carriage gets here."

Annie picked up Niall's plaid after the man left and shook out the long length. She knew how it was supposed to look since she'd seen Niall wear it a dozen times, but how did he get everything to fall into neat pleats around his hips and have material left over for a sash? She folded and unfolded it several times, trying to figure it out before she gave up and went to the saddlebag to pull out the stained and torn breeches that Niall had worn when he'd gotten stabbed. At least she knew how they fit.

Annie pulled back the blanket and felt her breath hitch again at the redness and swelling. The wound itself was covered with the bandage, but she could imagine it only looked worse. Carefully, trying not to disturb Niall, she slipped his feet through and tugged the breeches slowly upward. Lifting his hips to slide the pants under him was difficult since his body was dead weight, but she managed it. Then she hesitated. The codpiece needed lacing, but did she dare touch him *there*? Annie paused for a moment more, then shook her head. She was being silly. Niall was not conscious and would never know. Pushing his tunic out of the way, she started threading the laces through the eyelets. She was halfway through when she felt his manhood stir. Her gaze flew to his face. Niall's eyes remained closed and nothing had changed in his expression. His breathing remained even, yet… She felt it move again and quickly dropped her hands. Apparently that part of a man worked independently of his brain. Annie tugged Niall's tunic down. The breeches would have to remain half-laced.

By the time the ship docked and two sailors came down to carry Niall up on deck, she'd managed to get his boots on and wrapped his plaid around him in a shawl-like fashion. At least the wool would keep him from getting chilled, something he didn't need with the fever he was running.

Captain Vance met her as she came up the companionway. "I've informed the driver to take you straight to MacLeod," he said, "and I dispatched my boatswain to ride to Glenfinnan for a physician."

"Thank ye."

The captain nodded. "God's speed."

"Aye. God's speed," Annie said.

They were going to need it.

****

The carriage that awaited them was not much bigger than a curricle, although it did have four wheels and two horses. The benches, while well-padded and upholstered in soft leather, were too short for Niall's length, so the sailors placed him on the floor. Annie put the saddlebag under his head for a pillow and bent his knees so he would fit. He mumbled something and Annie thought she saw his eyelids move before he went still again. She wondered why anyone would choose to keep such a small carriage for transport. It seemed even smaller when Captain Vance hitched their two horses behind it.

217

Her unspoken question was answered a short time later as they left the shoreline and started to climb. She looked out the window to see only sky. Leaning forward she looked down and then quickly jerked back, pulling the drape closed. Merciful heavens! They were on a road that was only a narrow ledge with a sheer drop to what looked like a ravine far below. The sight—short as it was—gave a whole new meaning to the term *high* lands. The horses continued to climb, the wheels of the carriage now catching on ruts and protruding rocks and causing it to tilt dangerously. Annie slid down to the floor beside Niall and propped his leg over her lap. He opened his eyes briefly, not focused, before he closed them again. That he was beginning to wake gave her some hope. She prayed his fight to stay alive wouldn't be lost to a carriage tumbling off a mountainside.

Every lurch—of what now seemed to be an oversize vehicle for the road—brought Annie's heart into her mouth. The carriage finally rolled to a stop, although the driver did not jump down. Annie's heart jumped again. Had they actually arrived at Ian's or was there a rockslide ahead and they weren't able to turn around in such a tight space? Why wasn't the driver doing something?

Annie eased herself back onto the seat and slowly pushed the drape aside from the window. They had arrived at someplace, but she wasn't sure *where*. The carriage waited in front of a tall, stone curtain wall while a massive iron-grated gate was being raised. A portcullis? Annie leaned her head outside the window and gasped. Inside the courtyard stood a medieval castle, complete with merlons and embrasures along its roof.

A guard appeared on the curtain wall and waved them through. As the carriage rolled toward the four-storied keep, its massive double oak doors opened and a large, broad-shouldered man in a tartan appeared on the steps, looking every inch a barbarian warlord with his long, ebony hair and eyes nearly the same color. One hand rested on the pommel of his sword. His face could have been chiseled out of the granite hills they'd just climbed.

What in the world had she and Niall gotten themselves into?

Chapter Nineteen

The unsmiling man strode toward them, although a look of surprise flitted across his face as he noticed Annie looking out the window. She quickly pulled her head back in. Dear Lord! If that was Ian MacLeod, he certainly didn't look welcoming. What would they do if he turned them away?

"Why are ye bringing a woman here?" he asked the driver. "And in my own carriage?"

Before the driver could answer, Annie pushed open the door and jumped down. The black-haired man frowned and looked down at her. Good heavens, he was tall. She lifted her chin. "I am nae important. I have a wounded man in here."

The frown deepened. "We are hardly a way-stop. Why bring him here?"

"For heaven's sake, does it matter?" a female voice asked behind him.

Annie started as a young woman, with chestnut hair that had an odd blonde streak through it, appeared beside the man. A resigned look replaced the frown. "I thought I told ye to stay inside, Jillian, until I kenned it was safe for ye to come out."

"I believe you did say that, Ian." The woman turned to look at Annie. "My husband is quite overly protective of me. How badly is your friend hurt?"

Her accent was English, but Annie felt an immediate

empathy for her. "His leg is infected from a stab wound four days ago—"

"Four days! Why did ye nae take him to a physician?" Ian asked, giving her a look that said in no uncertain terms she must be completely daft. "I ask again. Why bring the man here?"

"'Tis where he wanted to come and Captain Vance has already sent for the physician from Glenfinnan," Annie replied. "Niall said ye were Alasdair's brother by marriage—"

"Alasdair? Niall? Ye have a MacDonald in there?" Ian pushed past her without waiting for a response and jerked the door wide and then cursed. "God Almighty! He is near death."

Jillian gestured toward two soldiers standing nearby. "Come here and assist."

"Just have them get the door," Ian said as he pulled Niall halfway out of the carriage, then stooped to bring Niall over his shoulder. With a grunt, he stood and began walking toward the house.

Annie stared after him. Niall was a solidly built man and not short, yet Ian MacLeod did not seem to be bothered by the weight. Jillian caught her look and smiled. "As laird of this branch of MacLeods, my husband also insists on being the strongest."

"Laird? I thought the English outlawed that claim," Annie said as she and Jillian followed Ian inside.

"Oh, they have." Jillian smiled again. "But one thing I have learned since marrying Ian is that Highlanders do not much care what the English think."

"But ye are English?"

Jillian nodded. "It is a long story and one which you will probably have time to hear while your...*husband*?...heals."

"He is nae my husband." Annie felt her face warm at Jillian's inquiring look. "'Tis a long story too."

"Then it can wait," Jillian answered as two identical-looking girls no more than four-and-ten rushed into the foyer, trying to shout over each other.

"Who is the stranger?"

"Why is he here?"

"Was that why the carriage—"

"Hush," Jillian said and looked at Annie. "Our nieces, Kaitlin and Kaylin. They are a rather long story, too." She turned back to them. "I want one of you to go upstairs and get the faerie stone, then go to the glade in the forest and wait for the crone. Bring her here."

"We will both do it!" one of them said as they rushed off.

"And no loitering!" Jillian called after them.

"The faerie stone?" Annie asked as they followed the twins up the stairs at a somewhat slower pace. "I ken of rumors that Clan MacLeod keeps the remnants of a faerie flag at Dunvegan castle on Skye, but I have nae heard of a stone."

Jillian nodded. "The flag is part of the ancestral legend, but the stone was given to me by a young girl at the local market two years ago. It is brown with a golden streak through it, much like my hair. The child said a faerie lived inside and I could call on her for help if I needed it."

"And ye think she spoke true? That the stone has powers?" Annie tried to keep the skepticism out of her voice, but Jillian probably heard it, because she raised one shoulder in a half-shrug.

"I can only tell you that when Bridget and I went

back to look for the girl, she was nowhere to be found and no one else had seen her." Jillian hesitated and then went on. "And, a few weeks later, when my life was in danger, a young woman appeared out of what seemed nowhere and intervened." Jillian stopped in front of a door on the second floor. "But enough on me. It is your…um, Niall…that is in danger now. The Crone of the Hills is a healer."

Jillian opened the door and stepped aside to let Annie enter. She looked around in amazement. In the few minutes it had taken for them to get up here, servants were bustling about. One maid stoked the fire in the hearth while another poured water into a kettle and set it in front of the fire to heat. A third ripped strips of linen into bandages while a fourth dipped a washcloth into a basin and pressed it to Niall's forehead and then down his neck and on to his shoulders as he lay in the bed, a crisp white sheet pulled halfway up his bare chest. All of his clothing, including the bloodied breeches, lay neatly folded in a stack at the foot of the bed. Annie frowned, wondering which one of the maids had undressed Niall. They were all young.

Ian stood in the middle of the room, an apparent pillar of stone in the midst of all the movement. The servants were evidently well-trained—not a surprise if they considered Ian their laird—because he didn't say a word but commanded with a glance.

He did look somewhat relieved, though, when Jillian came in to take charge. "I will go and get the crone."

"I have already sent the twins for her," Jillian said, looking around the room with a practiced eye.

"The twins? Are ye sure that was a good idea? The healer has nae liking for the noise they make. She might well hide instead."

Jillian shook her head. "She will come when she sees the stone."

Ian grimaced. "Let us hope they doona lose it first."

"They will not lose it."

Annie didn't know how Jillian could be so sure, but she moved away from the conversation and went to stand by Niall's side. She held out her hand to the maid who was semi-bathing Niall. "I will do that."

The girl glanced in Jillian's direction before giving over the cloth with a grumpy look. Annie ignored it and dipped the cloth again before sitting on the edge of the bed to apply it.

Niall's eyes were still closed, but she thought his breathing was stronger. That, along with the two times his eyes had fluttered open, made her think he might be coming out of his laudanum-induced coma. She desperately wanted him to, but then wondered if the pain would be unbearable if he did. If he started thrashing around, it would only make the infection spread.

Annie lifted the sheet slightly to check Niall's leg. Ian had left the bandage on so all she could see was the redness around it. The swelling hadn't gone down, but she didn't think it had gotten worse either.

She hoped the doctor wouldn't be long in coming, although she didn't know how long it would take for him to climb the mountain. Would he make it before nightfall or would he wait until morning? Annie bit her lip as she applied the damp cloth again. It seemed all they did was wait.

As if reading her mind, Jillian came to her side as Ian left the room. "It should not be long. Once the crone sees the stone, she will hurry."

"Ye put a lot of faith in that stone," Annie said, hoping she didn't sound too cynical. Magical stones and local healers whose reputations were often more folklore than fact didn't exactly set her mind at ease. But then she remembered the conversation she'd had with Mrs. O'Connor at the convent home regarding the Fae. *Maybe one day ye will believe*, she had said.

"Perhaps, but superstitions run strong in the Highlands. What Ian said is true. The healer has no liking for all the chattering the twins do. It is one reason I sent them." Jillian winked conspiratorially. "To hurry her along."

Annie smiled, in spite of the grave situation. She liked Jillian even if Ian did seem a bit imposing. "Where did your husband go?"

"He is going to send a messenger to Arisaig to let Niall's family know he is here."

"'Tis a good idea. Could ye send a post to his other brother in Glasgow—as well as my mother—to let them ken where we are?" Annie said and then paused. "Niall was going to take me to Arisaig to be safe."

Jillian gave her a curious look and then shooed the maids out of the room. She waited until the door had closed behind them. "Safe from what?"

"My life might have been in danger," Annie said.

Jillian studied her a moment. "Are you in trouble with the local authorities?"

"Nae. At least, I doona think so," Annie answered as she thought about how complicated the whole situation was.

"I am only asking because if I do not, my husband certainly will," Jillian said quietly.

Ian MacLeod would no doubt command to know not

only how the stabbing had happened, but why it had happened. He and Jillian had the right to know if they were protecting fugitives. Annie swallowed hard. They certainly wouldn't put Niall out since he was wounded and kin by marriage, but she was not related to them in any way. Ian looked formidable enough to toss her out and let her fend for herself.

Before she could begin to speak, Ian returned. The room suddenly seemed smaller with him in it.

"Annie was about to tell me what happened in Glasgow," Jillian said.

Ian folded his arms across his chest. "And I was about to ask. 'Tis why I came up here."

Annie swallowed again and told them what had transpired, from the time she got her position as manager of the warehouse to the magistrate raiding the place and finding the smuggled opium. Ian listened impassively until she came to the part of the weavers becoming angry and forming an unruly mob bent on finding her. Then his face darkened.

"What kind of men hunt down a woman?"

"They blamed me for their losing their money from the wool being confiscated," Annie replied. She might as well tell him everything. "I was the one who signed the paperwork, so they held me responsible."

"Nae matter. They wanted to harm ye."

"Aye. Owen and Aidan heard talk of lynching—"

"Lynching?" Jillian broke in, her eyes wide. "God's merciful heavens!"

"Go on," Ian said, his voice cold and hard as steel. "I'll ken the whole story."

"Well, they got to my mother's boardinghouse with only a few minutes to spare. Niall and I went out the back door, but some of the men had already rounded the corner and blocked the alley. We—Niall—had to fight his way out." Annie paused and looked at the bed where Niall lay far too still. "He risked his life to save me."

"He is a Highlander. What else would he do?"

Annie frowned slightly and looked back at Ian. His tone was nonchalant as if the men of the Highlands risking their lives for women was a common occurrence. Was it? She had grown up in the city and knew next to nothing about the wilds this far north. Owen and Aidan had also been protective in defending the Progress Club women. Maybe that was part of an unspoken code they all seemed to follow. Maybe Niall would have taken the same action for any woman in peril. Maybe all these feelings she'd begun having for Niall since their escape were just one-sided on her part. He had certainly never said he cared for her in any special way. Unless, of course, she counted being called stubborn, which was hardly a compliment.

"Still, I will be forever grateful to him." And she would. Niall had saved her life, but she needed to remember what Ian had just said. Niall had followed the Highlander Code and done what he considered was his duty.

Their conversation was interrupted by the door banging open as the twins burst in. "I brought the crone," one of them said.

"*We* brought her," the other one corrected.

"Will ye both quit your blethering?" A small, hunched-over woman, with a shawl covering her head as well as most of her face, hobbled in behind them. "'Tis the stone that spoke to me, nae the likes of ye."

Although they did not look particularly chastised,

the twins lapsed into silence. Jillian gestured them to leave and then turned to the healer. "Thank you for coming."

"Aye." She pushed the shawl off her head to reveal long, white hair. "'Tis me duty to the MacLeod."

"Niall is a MacDonald," Annie blurted and then blinked as the old woman looked at her. Although her face was weathered and wrinkled, her eyes were surprisingly sharp and as black as Ian's.

"'Twas the MacLeod who summoned me, nae?" The healer moved to the bed, folded back the sheet and removed the bandage from Niall's leg, then tsked sharply. "How long has the wound been festering?"

"I am nae sure," Annie answered. "I ken at least two or three days. Maybe four."

The crone gave her the same look that Ian had when she'd said the same words. "We stopped at Crianlarich to treat the wound, but the doctor was away—"

"'Tis nae matter now." The old woman looked at the pile of bandages the maid had left and then at the kettle in front of the hearth that had steam rising from it. "Bring me some of that hot water."

Annie moved quickly to take an empty pewter bowl the maids had left by the bandages and dipped it into the kettle, then carried it over to the bed. The crone set the small cloth sack she carried on the bedside table and took out a vial which she opened and poured a few drops into the water. Instantly, a pungent odor filled the air and a cloud of mist rose to envelop her and Niall. Nodding to herself, the old woman reached into the bag again and took out a mortar and pestle, along with some dried leaves and what looked like small twigs.

As she began to grind them into a fine powder, the

mist thickened, fog-like tendrils curling around the bed. The crone's appearance seemed to change as she worked. Her back straightened, she grew taller, and the lines and wrinkles on her face faded away as her hair darkened to brown with a golden streak running through it.

Annie squinted through the now-dense haze. Perhaps Jillian's talk of the faerie stone having a gold streak was making her imagine the shift in the crone's appearance or maybe it was the strong, intoxicating scent in the air that was making her somewhat dizzy. Her eyes stung and she closed them for a moment.

When she opened them, the healer was finishing wrapping a fresh bandage around Niall's thigh. How could the woman have finished so quickly? Less than a minute ago, she was grinding herbs... Annie blinked several times. The room was back to normal. The mist was gone and only a faint smell lingered in the air.

The old woman was back too, her hair completely white. She put her mortar and pestle back in her sack and nodded to Jillian. "I am leaving a bag of the sphagnum moss for ye to dress the wound with daily until it heals."

"Then Niall will survive?" Jillian asked.

The crone nodded. "Aye. 'Tis nae his time."

"I doona ken how to thank ye," Annie said.

The crone set her dark gaze on her. "'Tis him ye need to thank."

"Aye," Annie said, although she wondered how the woman knew that Niall had gotten the wound saving her life. Maybe Ian had told her before she came upstairs.

"I will walk you to the door," Jillian said.

"Nae need. I ken the way out," the healer said.

Jillian smiled. "I suppose you do. I am sure Ian will

be waiting to escort you back."

"Better him than those two young ones," the crone said as she stepped into the hall. "It will take me hours to get the creatures of the forest calmed down."

Annie waited until the woman had gone and then she turned to Jillian. "I doona ken how she worked so fast, but that was some spectacle."

Jillian frowned. "What do you mean?"

Annie gestured toward the bed where Niall now lay sleeping peacefully. "How the mist rose from the water and looked like fog around the bed. It was so thick I could hardly make anything out."

"Fog? Mist? In this room?" Jillian's frown deepened. "I did not see anything."

Chapter Twenty

The physician arrived shortly after the crone left. "I got here as soon as I could, my lady," he said as he was ushered into the parlor where Jillian and Annie were finishing a tray of sandwiches since they'd missed the noon meal. "It took a bit longer than I expected since I could not use my regular carriage on the steep hills and my horse was not used to climbing such."

Annie could sympathize with the horse, although from the doctor's rather shaky voice she wondered if he might have been the one more concerned with the steep hills. Not that she blamed him. She recalled all too vividly looking out the window to the sheer drop of the ravine below.

Jillian nodded. "The road is difficult."

"I hope his lordship will understand."

"I am sure he will," she answered. "At the moment, he is not here, but he should return soon. Meanwhile, let me take you to our patient."

Annie followed them upstairs. Mrs. Cameron, the middle-aged housekeeper, rose from the chair near the bed as they entered the room.

"Mr. MacDonald has been sleeping quietly. I think the fever may have broken."

"Thank God!" Annie said as she rushed over to lay the back of her hand on Niall's forehead. "I think ye are right."

"Hmph. I will be the judge of that," the doctor said as he walked toward them and moved the sheet back. His brows drew together. "Someone has already tended the wound?"

"Yes, we have a healing woman who lives nearby," Jillian said. "An old lady who keeps a herbal garden in the forest. She applied a poultice."

Annie gave Jillian a curious glance. Was that all the Crone of the Hills was? An old lady with a herbal garden? Could the change in appearance that Annie thought she saw, along with mist that didn't exist, been a result of those herbs put in the water? Jillian had acknowledged that she'd seen steam rise momentarily, but that was all.

"Hmph," the doctor said again.

"We were not sure if you would be able to get here today, since it is treacherous going," Jillian added. "Mr. MacDonald was in serious condition. Ian thought it not wise to wait when we had a healer close."

The physician looked like he wanted to argue the point, but he nodded, evidently realizing that disagreeing with a laird's viewpoint was not prudent. "Of course, Mr. MacLeod made the right decision."

A short time later, after the doctor grudgingly admitted there was nothing more he could do, they descended the steps to find Ian had just returned.

"I believe your guest is on the mend, your lordship," the physician said.

"'Tis good to hear," Ian replied. "And I thank ye for coming so quickly."

The doctor smiled. "Think nothing of it. I am most happy to attend to his lordship and lady anytime."

As Ian walked the man to his horse, Annie turned to

Jillian. "I was nae aware that your husband should be addressed as 'his lordship.' I am sorry to have blundered."

Jillian shook her head. "You did not make a mistake. Actually, Ian hates being called that."

Annie raised an eyebrow. "Then why does he nae stop it?"

"Well, the physician was trained in London, and there it is customary to address the aristocracy as such."

"Aye. I ken that." Annie felt confused. "But your husband is a Scottish laird."

Jillian nodded. "True, but he is also an English earl."

"*What*? An *earl*?"

"The Earl of Cantford, to be exact," Jillian replied. "His great-grandfather fought with King George and was rewarded with a title and land in England which bordered my own. That is how I met him."

"Your land? Ye mean ye hold the title to it?" Annie asked. "I dinnae think women could do so, although I definitely think we *should* be able to."

"Well, these were special circumstances and not pleasant." Jillian's expression darkened as though she were remembering. "The marquis' nephew, who would have been the heir, was..." She hesitated, her breath hitching. "...mentally unfit. I was awarded the title."

Annie blinked. "Then ye are a marchioness? In your own right?"

"Yes."

"Then... Excuse my asking, but why are ye *here*? In Scotland, I mean?"

"I fell in love with the Highlands when Ian brought me here." Jillian smiled. "Besides, can you see my husband acting the part of an English gentleman?"

No, Annie clearly could not grasp that image. Ian MacLeod looked more like he belonged on a horse, leading a wild charge down a hill, waving a sword and sounding a battle cry. She smiled too. "So ye have an overseer tending the land?"

"Ian's brother Jamie, who does not care much more for English life than Ian does." Jillian's smile broadened. "But he is more or less stuck since my sister Mari is his wife and she prefers England."

"He must love her verra much to make such a sacrifice."

Jillian nodded. "They are crazy about each other, although you might not know it, given that they argue at the drop of a hat."

Annie felt a little nudge of guilt. She and Niall did much the same. Not that *arguing* signified *caring*.

"Neither of them likes admitting they are wrong either," Jillian added.

That sounded like her and Niall too. While stubbornness probably wasn't a great trait, it was still nice to know other women didn't back down either. And—even better—given the right circumstances, a woman could *own* land. In her *own* right.

Hopefully, Jillian would be willing to explain how that had come about, at some time. It was information Annie could use when it was safe to return to Glasgow.

Meanwhile, the priority right now was to get Niall well.

****

Niall opened his eyes slowly, letting his sight get accustomed to the dim light of the room. He became aware that he was lying in a very soft bed of feathers, covered in a crisp sheet that smelled of fresh air and sunshine. Niall felt no pain. The last thing he remembered was the anguish of something akin to a red-hot knife searing through his leg. Was he dead? He faintly recalled a female voice singing softly to him and looked up, half-expecting to see a ceiling fresco of angels. Instead, he saw high timber beams and walls of stone. An earthly room, then.

A warm fire blazed in the hearth across from the bed. Dark blue velvet drapes were closed against a window that was probably also shuttered to keep the cool air out. A small table and chair stood near the window. On the opposite wall, a tapestry depicting a hunting scene hung over a solidly built dresser. Earthly things. No sign of an angel who had sung to him.

A creak in the far corner caught his attention. He turned as a middle-aged lady rose from a rocking chair. Had she sung to him, willing him to live? She didn't look like an angel, but then, what did he know about angels? He only knew that melodic voice had kept him clinging to life.

"Ye are finally awake!" The woman came closer. "'Tis glad Ian and Jillian will be to hear of it."

Ian. Reality returned to Niall with a jolt. He had been taking Annie Ferguson to safety at Arisaig, but his stab wound had forced him to change his plans. "I am at the MacLeod holding, then?"

"Aye. I am Mrs. Cameron, the housekeeper. Ye arrived two days ago."

"Two days! I have been unconscious for two days?" Niall struggled to sit. "Did a young lady come with me? She has red hair—"

"Rest easy, lad," Mrs. Cameron said as she provided a strong hand to help position him against the headboard.

"If 'tis Annie ye are asking about, she is here, safe and sound."

Niall breathed a sigh of relief. "Thank God. I was escorting her—"

"Nae need to explain. Save your strength." The housekeeper straightened. "I'll go down to get ye some broth."

"I appreciate that, but can ye bring something I can set my teeth into?" Niall asked. "I feel as though I haven't eaten in weeks."

"Broth is what ye need," Mrs. Cameron said in a tone that brooked no argument. "'Tis the best thing to start with. Ye doona want your stomach rebelling, since it's been without food."

Niall gave her a smile that he used to use on his mother to wheedle another fruit scone when he was a child. "But I am hungry."

"A good sign." Mrs Cameron paused and then relented. "All right. I'll put a wee piece of bread on the tray as well." She moved to the door. "Would ye like me to send Annie up? Jillian insisted she have a bit of rest since she's hardly left this room, but 'twas an hour ago."

"Doona disturb her, then," Niall said. "But if nae too much trouble, I would like some hot water to clean up with."

The housekeeper nodded. "I'll have some lads fetch it straightaway."

After she left, Niall pushed back the cover and swung his legs over the bed. The injured thigh had a clean bandage wrapped around it and the swelling had gone down. Whoever the healer was, she had done a good job. He stood slowly, hating that he felt wobbly as a newborn foal. A slight wave of dizziness washed over him, but that was probably from hunger. He forced himself to move, willing his strength to return with each step. By the time Mrs. Cameron reappeared with the food, he had made it to the table and chair.

"Do ye think ye should be sitting up so soon?" she asked as she put the tray down.

"Aye. Lyin' abed does nae help," Niall answered.

"And breakin' your skull open because ye are too weak to stand does nae help either." The housekeeper tilted her head to one side to study him. "But I suppose I might as well be talking to the wind."

"I am sure your broth will give me enough strength nae to fall on my face." Niall gave her another smile. "It smells delicious."

She colored slightly. "I had the cook put in a few extra herbs."

"I appreciate that," Niall answered. "It should hit the spot, then."

"Aye, well. 'Tis nae much." Mrs. Cameron sounded a bit flustered. "I'll just go and find out what is keeping the lads with your hot water."

"Thank ye," Niall said again and tore into the bread before she was hardly out the door. He hadn't been exaggerating when he said the broth smelled delicious. Right now, it tasted as good as anything on a feast table. He was already beginning to feel his strength build. It took a good half hour to finish bathing and washing his hair with the water the kitchen lads finally brought up, but by the time he did he felt like a new man.

He needed to thank Ian for the hospitality and the healer as well, but the first thing he needed to do was make sure Annie was safe and well.

Opening the door, he nearly ran into her.

****

Annie lowered the hand she'd raised to knock on his door and stared at him standing there dressed in breeches and a tunic that was half-open. His face had returned to its normal color. His hair was slicked back from washing and his gray eyes were clear.

The transformation from him lying still as death and white as the linen sheet was nothing short of amazing. She closed her eyes momentarily, hoping she wasn't having a distorted vision like she'd had with the healer. But when she opened them, he was still standing there, looking hale.

"Mrs. Cameron told me ye had awakened."

Niall stepped back and motioned her inside. "Aye, about an hour ago."

"Someone should have come and gotten me."

"I told Mrs. Cameron to let ye rest," Niall said, "and I needed a bit of time to put myself to rights."

Annie nodded. "Ye have nae been conscious for nigh three days."

"The last thing I remember is standing on the deck of a ship." Niall sat down on the edge of the bed. "Mrs. Cameron told me we have reached the MacLeod, but how did it happen?"

Annie took the housekeeper's chair and filled Niall in on what had taken place and how they'd feared for his life until the crone had come with her healing herbs. Annie left out the part that she thought she'd seen the old woman transform into a young girl. Niall would think she was the one fevered if she told that story. "What is most important is that the healer's poultice seems to have drawn the poison out."

"I hope I can thank her. Is she still here?"

"Nae. Jillian said she lives in a cottage in the hills."

"Then perhaps I can ride over there tomorrow," Niall said.

"Tomorrow?" Annie asked, not quite sure she heard correctly. "Saint Peter was all but holding the pearly gates open for ye only an hour ago."

Niall smiled. "Are ye sure 'twas Saint Peter and nae Lucifer?"

"'Tis nae jest," Annie answered, although now that he mentioned it, the black stubble that shaded his jaw did make him resemble a dark angel somewhat... She pushed the errant thought aside. "Ye are in nae condition to ride anywhere."

One eyebrow rose. "Are ye questioning my stamina?"

"Your..." Annie felt herself blush as she remembered how his manhood had reacted to her bandaging his thigh on the ship. "I... Oh." How stupid could she be? Niall was asking if she was questioning his ability to ride. A horse. Tomorrow. He was not asking whether she questioned his virility. Which she didn't. She already knew... At that thought, her face heated even more. Maybe she had taken a fever too. Why else would her mind be racing in such a direction? She attempted to answer once more. "Nae, but I am questioning your sanity."

His brow went higher. "My sanity?"

"Aye. Your leg is nae healed."

"It does nae pain me."

Was the man daft? "Just because it does nae hurt, that does nae mean 'tis well enough to ride."

Niall shrugged. "'Tis well enough for a short ride to thank the healer."

"Nae."

"Aye."

Annie glowered at him. "Ye are being obstinate."

"I think ye have used that term before." Niall grinned at her. "Would ye like to add a few more, so we can spar?"

Annie didn't return his smile. "Ye nearly *died*, Niall."

He sobered. "And I nearly failed ye as well."

"Failed me? Ye dinnae fail me."

"'Twas my responsibility to protect ye and get ye to safety."

Responsibility. That word again. Ian had basically said the same thing. Niall's *obstinacy* had made him keep going with a festering wound because he felt *obligated* to whisk her away from danger. Highlanders followed a code of honor. That was all. Annie straightened her shoulders and raised her chin, and looked past Niall at the wall. "Ye have gotten me to safety, and I thank ye. Your duty to me is done."

He frowned. "My duty?"

"Aye. Ye felt responsible to save me. Ye just said so." Annie studied the wall over Niall's shoulder. "Ye would have done the same for anyone. Ian said 'tis what Highlanders do."

"Did he, now?"

"Aye. 'Tis noble of ye."

"I was nae thinking of being noble when I took you away."

Annie looked down at her folded hands. "It does nae matter."

Niall leaned forward from the edge of the bed and put a hand under her chin, tilting it up so she had to look at him. "Do ye really think I would have risked my life for just anyone?"

"Ian said—"

"Ian does nae ken me," Niall said, his eyes growing dark. "Come here."

Annie gave him a startled look. "What?"

"Come here." Niall took hold of her arm and pulled her toward him, his other hand sliding along her jaw to cradle her head and then bent his head to brush a kiss across her mouth and then another, letting it linger slightly. Annie moaned, her lips parting for him. His arms slipped around her waist, pressing her closer while his tongue swept across her open mouth.

"They're kissing!"

Annie jumped back at the sound and turned to find the twins standing in the open doorway and giggling. The door Niall had left open probably because he was a gentleman.

Niall seemed unfazed, although the glower he gave the twins made them stop giggling as he released Annie. "Is there a reason the two of ye are standing there?"

They looked at each other as if suddenly struck mute, then one of them finally found her voice. "Aunt Jillian wanted to ken if ye wanted a tray sent up for dinner."

"Nae. Tell your aunt I will come down."

The girls turned, practically tripping over each other, trying to get away. Annie turned to Niall. "Perhaps I should have a tray sent up. I am nae sure I can face those two at dinner."

Niall gave her an amused look. "Ye doona mind facing a crowd of angry union workers who pelt ye with rotten fruit, yet ye are afraid what two bairns might say?"

"They are nearly fully grown, nae bairns," Annie answered. "I doubt Jillian—or Ian—will appreciate their witnessing what they just did."

"'Twas just a kiss, lass."

The words stung somehow. Maybe it had been no more than a kiss, but the feeling of Niall's lips on hers, his mouth covering hers, had been incredible… "But it does nae set a good example, especially from a guest who is a stranger."

"I suspect neither of them will say anything for fear of a tongue-lashing for being caught eavesdropping," Niall replied, "but perhaps we should make our way downstairs so there will be nae more speculation."

"Aye, 'tis a good idea," Annie answered as she quickly walked to the door.

'Twas just a kiss. That's what Niall had said. *'Twas just a kiss.* She needed to remember that.

****

Annie postponed going down to break her fast the next morning for as long as she dared before someone would be sent up to check on her. She wanted to make sure others were up and about, so she wouldn't be left alone with Niall. Last night's dinner had been a disaster.

Caitlin and Caylin had been seated at the table when they'd entered the dining room. Although they didn't say anything, they would shift their gazes from her to Niall and one or the other would start to giggle. The giggle would abruptly end when Niall fixed the scamp with a look. It happened often enough that Ian began to follow the interchange as well. She hoped he hadn't questioned the girls later.

The morning room where breakfast was served, near the kitchens, was empty when Annie got there, although there were still some covered dishes on the sideboard. Sunshine streamed in from the eastern window, lighting the pale yellow walls with its warmth, and she could hear servants going about their duties for the day. Annie wondered just what time it was. Perhaps she'd delayed a bit too long. She hurriedly helped herself to some porridge that smelled delightfully of cinnamon and spooned clotted cream on a freshly baked scone and sat down to eat quickly. Avoiding being alone with Niall to squelch any notions someone might have was one thing. Appearing lazy and laggardly was quite another. She'd just finished her meal when she heard the shout.

"Riders coming!"

Annie went outside to see a guard posted on the curtain wall by the gate. She'd almost forgotten, with all that had happened yesterday, that they had arrived at an actual medieval castle. Apparently, one that kept up the practice of medieval times. She almost expected the portcullis to be lowered, but it remained up.

"Riders approaching!" the guard called again, although there was no need since the pounding hooves of a number of horses could be heard.

Annie walked down the front steps into the bailey and stared out through the gate. She couldn't ascertain how many horses since a massive cloud of dust encircled the group, but from the thundering noise it must be quite a few. She looked up again, wondering if archers would actually appear between the embrasures, but no one joined the single guard.

The massive oak doors opened behind her and she turned to see Ian and Niall standing there. "Are we in danger?"

Ian shrugged. "That is always a possibility when two

clans meet."

Two clans? They were going to *fight*? Why was he just standing there looking nonchalant? "Should we be doing something?"

"Well, ye might want to get back on the steps so ye doona get trampled," Ian said as the lead horses came galloping over the bridgeway and through the gate.

Annie turned back to stare at what looked like a small army pushing through and in the next instant felt a powerful arm encircle her waist, lifting her none too gracefully and letting her feet and arms dangle in the air. Ian reached the steps in four long strides and deposited her beside Niall.

"The lass does nae listen well."

Niall grinned. "Ye have that right."

Annie frowned at both of them. "'Tis nae like they are going to gallop right to the door."

"Doona be too sure," Niall said. "Those are my brothers."

Niall's *brothers*? Annie whipped her head around. Now that the horses had reached the cobblestone of the bailey, the dust had settled and she could get a better look. There were five massive men in tartans, with long, flowing manes. Three had black hair like Niall's and two—who looked like twins—had auburn. Three younger lads wearing caps were behind them, along with a portly gentleman clad in hat and coat. The seven men dismounted almost in precision and strode forward. As they approached, Annie could see they all had light-colored eyes, although some were blue or green, not gray like Niall's. Still, there was no mistaking the whole group of them were related. They split apart to make way for the gentleman and the lads.

"Mother?" Niall asked and limped down the steps to the person removing the hat, showing a tidy bun of dark hair streaked with gray. He swept her into a hard hug. "When Ian told me he sent a rider, I expected ye would follow in the carriage."

His mother stepped back and fixed him with a look that was surprisingly like the one he'd used on Caitlin and Caylin. "Do ye think I am going to crawl across the country at a snail's pace when my son could be dying?"

"Aye." A younger, higher-pitched voice said. The speaker pulled off a cap, allowing riotous red curls to tumble down around her shoulders. "Just because we are female does nae mean we cannae keep up!"

"Margaret—" Before Niall could say more, the girl hurled herself at him, throwing her arms around his neck, her feet leaving the ground. His injured leg buckled and he stumbled back, but managed to keep his balance.

"Ye *eejit*!" one of the young lads said, pulling his sister off.

She spun on him. "Doona call me that, Rauri!"

"Well, ye *are* daft to try and knock over Niall when he is hurt," the other lad said.

"Ye shut your mouth too, Ewan," Margaret snapped, her face nearing the color of her hair. "I was nae trying to fell Niall—"

"I am fine," Niall interrupted. "Doona fash."

"But she's still an *eejit*," Rauri said.

"And daft," Ewan added.

Their mother held up a hand. "Enough."

They subsided into silence, but the looks the three gave each told Annie their conversation would continue once out of earshot of their mother.

"See what ye are missing?" one of the men said to

Niall.

"'Tis nae wonder Alasdair made off for London and Aidan followed ye to Glasgow," another said. "'Tis the only way to get a bit of peace and quiet."

The brothers all laughed and Margaret looked furious, although she held her tongue. Annie had a sudden empathy for the girl. She looked to be a few years older than Caitlin and Caylin, but quite a bit younger than herself. It couldn't be easy dealing with ten brothers. Especially if they were all as obstinate as Niall, who shouldn't be putting a lot of weight on his leg for a long period of time. Not that telling him that—again— would do any good. She stepped forward.

"Margaret? I am Annie Ferguson." Seven pairs of male eyes suddenly focused their attention on her. Laughter turned to inquisitive expressions as they studied her. She suddenly was acutely aware that the dress Jillian had brought up to her last night was a bit too snug in the bodice.

"And who are ye, Annie Ferguson?" one of the men who had golden eyes the color of a wolf's asked. "There are nae Fergusons for miles around."

"I am from Glasgow."

The wolf-like look intensified, as though he were closing in on prey. "Glasgow? Did ye come with Niall, then?"

"Aye, she did, Lachlan," Niall said and came to stand by her side. "The lass was in danger."

"Probably from ye," a brother with bright blue eyes said.

"Back off, Braden." Niall practically growled the words.

Knowing smirks appeared on the other brothers'

faces. Annie didn't like the direction this conversation was taking. She wasn't about to let these men get any ideas. She certainly didn't want Ian thinking her of loose morals, especially if he'd talked to the twins after dinner last night. "Niall is my guardian," she blurted out.

"Your *guardian*?" another, whose hazel eyes were only a little less wolfish than his brother's, questioned, while all of them laughed. He turned to Niall. "I have nae heard ye ever called that before. Is it a word the lasses use in Glasgow to—"

"Shut your mouth, Gavin."

"I think ye are making our brother mad," one of the auburn-haired twins said.

"'Tis a pity we cannae have a good brawl about it," the other one added.

Niall glared at both of them. "Ye will have your brawl as soon as my leg mends in a day or two."

"A day or two?" Annie put her hands on her hips. "Ye are nae going to be brawling in a day or two."

"Ah! A feisty one!" Braden said. "'Tis the type ye like, is it nae?"

Gavin nodded. "I will wager there is an interesting story to be told here."

"Aye. Do tell." Lachlan moved a step closer and Annie had the distinct impression she really was his prey.

Niall looked about ready to get into fisticuffs regardless of his wound. Annie remembered something her father had once told her about picking her battles. This was not going to be one of them. She held out her hand to Margaret.

"Would ye like to come with me inside?"

Margaret grinned at her, a knowing look in her eyes. "Aye, I would."

****

Niall watched his sister and Annie leave with mixed emotions. Part of him was glad Annie had been wise enough to extricate herself from the web of interrogation his brothers were weaving around her, but the other part of him wasn't sure that pairing off with Margaret was any better. From the conspiratorial exchange of glances, Annie and his sister were probably well on their way to becoming allies, which did not bode well.

"So, who is she?" Lachlan asked.

He should have known he wouldn't escape the grilling so easily. Niall turned to his brothers. All of them stared at him intently, arms crossed, which meant they weren't going to go anywhere until he answered them. Even his mother and the two younger lads looked expectant.

He gave them a brief accounting of what had happened to Annie, finishing with what, he hoped, would put an end to the questioning. "I had to get her out of Glasgow. Any of ye would have done the same."

"'Tis one thing to get the lass away from danger." Lachlan raised a brow. "'Tis another to bring her home with ye."

Rauri poked Ewan and laughed. "Like a rescued kitten."

Gavin gave the younger boys a look. "I doona think Niall considers the lass a kitten."

"I doona ken," Cory, one of the twins, said. "Kittens have sharp claws—"

"And that one looks like she does, too," Carr, the other twin, finished the sentence. "If I were Niall, I would take care nae to get scratched."

Niall turned on them. "If I were *ye*—both of ye—I

would take care what words I choose to speak. 'Twas Annie who stayed by my side while I lay fevered on the ship. 'Twas Annie who talked me back from near death. 'Twas Annie who got me *here*—"

"Ye owe her much, son," his mother said. "If she needs a safe haven, she is welcome at our home in Arisaig for however long she needs it."

"A generous offer, but one that has already been made." Ian stepped down from the steps. "We have ample room here. Jillian has already taken to her and I've learned to trust my wife's instincts."

"And avoid her wrath, mayhap?" Braden asked, his blue eyes twinkling.

Ian grimaced. "That too. Perhaps we should all go inside before she has reason to chastise my hospitality."

"A good idea," Niall said and offered his arm to his mother, walking ahead of his brothers to the door.

He might have eliminated the incessant questions he'd seen lingering in their eyes for now, but he knew it was only postponement before they started asking all sorts of personal questions about Annie.

Questions he wasn't sure he was ready to answer.

Chapter Twenty-One

The MacDonalds left five days later, thundering out
the gate at a full gallop, the same way they'd arrived. The
castle, even with servants bustling about their daily
work, suddenly seemed silent as a tomb. Even the twins'
constant shenanigans felt subdued. It was almost as
though Niall's brothers were their own vortex of energy,
zapping everything in their path.

Annie looked up from the book she'd been
attempting to read when she heard footsteps outside the
parlor. Almost as though she'd conjured him, Niall
appeared in the doorway, dressed casually in breeches
and boots with a riding coat over a linen shirt open at the
throat. For a moment she felt something almost like
panic at his attire. Was he planning to ride after his
family, after all? They'd decided—or rather Ian and
Jillian had—that Niall and Annie would remain here for
another week or two.

"Are ye planning to go somewhere?"

Niall nodded. "I thought I would ride into the woods
and finally thank the old crone who saved my life."

Annie started to say he really shouldn't be riding,
but stopped herself. It had been a week and she doubted
Niall would accept any more excuses for not getting on
a horse. It had been a minor miracle that he'd refrained
from brawling during the past several days, since his
brothers seemed to enjoy provoking each other. Annie

suspected their continual badgering of each other was just a reason to trade punches that often had them rolling in the dirt. If she lived a century, she'd never understand why men liked to fight.

"Are the twins going to show ye where the cottage is?"

"Nae." Niall smiled. "Jillian said the crone has a tendency to disappear when she's disturbed. Ian gave me directions."

"Is it far?"

"Perhaps a mile. Would ye like to go with me?"

"Aye." Annie closed her book and set it down. Fresh air, especially on a day that was unseasonably warm and filled with sunshine, was probably just what she needed. A ride through the countryside, even a short one, sounded wonderful. And she'd learned that protocol was much more relaxed in the Highlands. Even when Ian's twin nieces had gone riding with Niall's twin brothers, no one had accompanied them. There would be no need for a chaperone for a short afternoon ride…or even a riding habit. "I'll go change into my breeches."

"I'll get the horses saddled, then."

Ten minutes later they were on their way. Thankfully, the forest lay behind the castle and they did not have to use the treacherous shale path that led down to the loch. It took less than half an hour to reach the tree line. The fragrant scent of pine filled the air while patches of brown leaves still clung to oak branches overhead. Bracken crackled beneath the horses' hooves as they went deeper into the shadowed recesses of the forest.

"Ye are sure ye ken the way?" Annie asked as the vegetation and trees grew more dense.

"Ian said to follow the deer trail."

"What deer trail?"

Niall pointed down. "That one."

Annie peered over her saddle. She could faintly make out what looked like trampled dirt a few inches wide. "I doona think a deer would fit on that."

Niall laughed. "A deer could stick to that trail at a dead run."

"I hope we doona meet one," Annie replied.

"Doona fash, city lass."

"Are ye making fun of me?"

Niall flashed her a grin. "I would never do that."

"Hmph." Annie decided she didn't want to argue the point, but simply enjoy the ride. The path was too narrow to ride alongside anyhow, so she was content to let her mare amble behind Niall's horse.

The forest, once they'd ceased talking, held its own conversation, she realized. The wind had a melody, rustling the leaves on the trees, whistling through the open spaces, while murmuring more quietly through the branches of pine. An eagle soared overhead, releasing a high-pitched shriek as it dove for prey. Blue jays and magpies chattered away. Annie heard something scurry through the bracken and hoped it wasn't going to be dinner for the eagle.

They broke through the forestry into a little, circular glade with a small, white-washed thatched cottage precisely in its center. A child was bent over near the door, tending some herbs. She straightened as the horses approached and when she turned, Annie gasped.

No child, only a young woman who was short. But that wasn't what made Annie stare. The girl's long, brown hair had a golden streak through it exactly like the one on the girl Annie *thought* she'd seen while the old crone attended Niall. She grabbed her saddle. What on earth was happening?

The girl smiled at Niall, her tilted eyes the same color green as the pines. "Ye are here to see my grandmother, I suspect?"

Niall dismounted. "Aye, if she is the one who saved my life at the MacLeod holding a week ago."

"Wait here. I will get her." She stepped into the house and shut the door.

He turned to Annie. "Let me help ye down."

"Nae. I…" She couldn't very well say she wasn't sure her legs would support her while she was trying to make sense of everything. She felt slightly dizzy. "I will wait where I am."

A minute later, the door opened again and the healer came out. Annie breathed a slight sigh of relief. At least this old woman looked like the crone who'd come to the castle.

She gave Niall a toothless smile. "I see ye survived."

"Aye. I wanted to come and thank ye personally," Niall said, "and ask if somehow I can repay ye for saving my life. Do ye need anything for your cottage? Food? Clothing? Wood cut? Just say the word—"

"'Tis nae necessary," the crone replied. "My granddaughter sees to all those needs."

"Does your granddaughter ever accompany ye when ye heal?" Annie hoped her voice didn't sound shaky.

The woman gave her a sharp look, her dark eyes growing even darker. "Why do ye ask?"

"I…" Suddenly, Annie felt really foolish. How could she say, "*Because I thought I saw her exchange places with you,*" and not sound completely insane

253

herself? "I…just wondered. She was gathering some herbs when we arrived."

"Aye, that she does, but 'tis I who make the rounds to heal."

Niall gave Annie a curious look, then turned back to the crone. "Well, if ye think of anything I can do for ye, please send word. I will be at the MacLeod home for another week or two."

"I will remember that," the old woman said.

"Well, thank ye again," Niall said as he mounted his horse. "I am forever beholden to ye."

As they headed their horses toward the deer trail, Annie couldn't resist turning around once more, but the crone had gone inside and there was no sign of the granddaughter.

"Is something troubling ye?" Niall asked. "Ye look worried."

"I…" There was no explanation for what she thought she'd seen. She didn't understand it, and Niall certainly wouldn't. "Nae. I just doona want ye to overstrain your wound."

It wasn't really a lie, after all. She clicked her tongue at her mare and moved ahead of him so he wouldn't ask any more questions.

****

Inside the cottage, the crone watched them leave through a curtained window. She slowly straightened and ran her hands over her white hair, turning it back to brown and gold and then smoothed the wrinkles from her face.

Strange that the red-haired woman had actually seen her the night she'd healed Niall. Care would need to be taken for the next two weeks while the woman was still here, since it bode trouble for mortals to discover her. The faerie uttered a spell and cast it silently on the wind. *Forget…*

Only MacLeods should be able to see the descendant of the Faerie Queen.

****

The sooner they could leave the forest, the better. Even the woods seemed to agree for there was only silence, save for the tread of the horses' hooves. No birds chirped and nothing stirred. Not even the wind. The air itself felt heavy, as though Annie sat under a blanket as she rode. What she needed was blue skies and sunshine.

The whole experience at the cottage had unsettled her more than she wanted to admit. Annie had almost talked herself into believing the experience in Niall's bedroom had been because she was tired to the point of exhaustion. That she'd only imagined the transforming of facial features because of the effects of the herbal mist. Not that she was given to flights of fancy, but still it was a more or less rational conclusion.

But seeing a young woman in the middle of the forest that looked *identical*? Annie wished the girl had reappeared while they were there so she could have studied her more. Maybe it had been the hair with its strange streak of gold that had made Annie think the girl resembled the other one. Maybe they didn't really look the same after all—Annie frowned, feeling confused.

She shook her head. There was no sense pursuing this line of thought unless she wanted to drive herself mad. Since her mount seemed to have no trouble following the twists and turns of the trail without any direction, she looked back over her shoulder to check on Niall. At that moment, a red deer bounded across the path and her mare reared, causing Annie to lose her balance. She landed on her backside with a hard thump as her horse cantered away.

"Are ye hurt?" Niall asked as he slipped from his saddle and knelt beside her.

"I doona think so," Annie said, feeling embarrassed that she had been so lost in fanciful thoughts that she'd not kept a tighter rein. She started to get up, but Niall put a hand on her shoulder.

"Doona move just yet. Let me see if anything is broken." He placed his hands on her ribcage and Annie's breath hitched. He looked up quickly. "Does that hurt?"

She shook her head, not quite trusting her voice. Where his hands encircled her was awfully close to her breasts. His thumbs practically grazed the undersides. And, for some unexplainable reason, the fact that he was *not* touching them made her nipples peak. Hopefully, her jacket hid her response to him. "I…am fine."

"I doona think ye have cracked any ribs, but I want to make sure."

As Niall's fingers gently slid down toward her waist, something clenched low in her belly. When he traced lightly over her hips, wet heat began to pool between her legs, followed by a throbbing at her core as his hands settled on her thighs. Her breath hitched again and Annie fought for a gulp of air, trying to ignore the sensations that racked her body. If Niall's examination continued much longer, she'd be whimpering and wiggling like a puppy, in need of a whole lot more touching…

"O*uch*!" The pleasure she'd been feeling turned sharply to pain as Niall picked up one foot and started to rotate her ankle.

He stopped immediately. "Ye must have twisted it

when ye fell."

"Is it broken?"

"'Tis hard to say without removing your boot, and I'd rather keep it on for support until we get home."

Annie smiled ruefully as the pain subsided somewhat. "My horse is probably already there."

"Nae matter." Niall put one arm under her knees and the other about her shoulders and stood, lifting her as though she weighed no more than a sack of feathers, and started toward his horse.

"Your leg!" Annie said. "Ye should nae be putting so much weight on it."

"My leg is fine. 'Tis yours I am concerned with," he answered and then placed her on the saddle while he vaulted up behind her. "The sooner we get ye tended to, the better."

He edged forward, lifting her slightly until her legs dangled over one of his thighs and her bottom was settled firmly against the other. It was surprisingly comfortable even though she was seated sideways across the horse. Niall's arms went around her, cocooning her warmly inside his embrace, filling her nose with his scent. It wasn't until the gelding started trotting that Annie became aware of something hard bumping against her hip in rhythm to the gait. All of the earlier awareness of him came rushing back like a kindled fire. Heat rippled through her, igniting all her vulnerable spots.

Annie didn't dare look at Niall. She knew from her experience with Broderick that men's bodies hardened when physically close to a female. She didn't want Niall to see in her face what she was feeling right now. Instead, she closed her eyes and laid her head against his chest, feigning sleep.

Which was probably an even bigger mistake. Lord, but Niall felt good.

****

"How do ye like the stallion?" Ian asked as he and Niall were returning from a good gallop across the nearby glen. "Gunnar is Jillian's favorite."

Niall petted the sleek neck of the Andalusian. "'Tis a fine animal." The stallion was well-trained, but spirited. Passing through the village, he'd picked up the scent of a mare and given Niall a bit of a challenge, one that Niall had met gladly, since he could identify with the randiness of the horse. He felt the same way.

This was the fifth day since Annie's fall and their ride home together. He could still recall—in achingly vivid detail—each time his hard cock had pounded against Annie's hip. It had taken every ounce of his considerable willpower not to pull her on top of him so he could at least get partial relief. Thank God the ride was only a mile because he didn't know how much longer they could have kept pretending... Annie for "sleeping" so she could ignore his unwelcome assault or him for trying to act as though he weren't ready to explode like a green lad.

"The bairns sometimes keep Jillian busier than she likes," Ian said. "The horse needed exercising and he does nae take to many people."

"Glad to help," Niall replied and wondered if the stallion hadn't perhaps felt an affinity for his own needy predicament.

It had come as a surprise to him that the herd of beautiful Spanish horses had been Jillian's dowry and that she was the one who bred them. Evidently there were English women as well as Scottish ones who didn't follow traditional roles. Annie had all but crowed like a rooster when she'd learned of it. She'd already asked Jillian about books on breeding and how active she was with the actual sale of the colts and fillies.

As they rode through the gate into the bailey, Niall looked for Annie. Luckily, the ankle had only been sprained and she'd been up and about for the last two days. Usually she was outside with the twins, but today the courtyard was empty. He and Ian led their horses into the barn and rubbed them down before heading into the castle.

It was also eerily quiet. Ian's bairns were probably napping in the nursery upstairs, but usually the twins could be heard if not seen. Neither Jillian nor Annie met them in the entryway either, which was unusual. Ian exchanged a glance with Niall, about to make a comment when they heard the murmur of low voices coming from a room down the hall that Jillian had converted into a parlor.

Jillian and Annie were seated on the sofa, the twins occupying chairs on either side. A man Niall had not seen before sat stiff and upright in a chair across from them.

"Who are you?" Ian asked.

"Charles Curtis, from the magistrate's office in Glasgow." The man stood. "Mr. MacQuarrie sent me."

Niall felt the hair at his nape prickle. "MacQuarrie? What does he want?"

Annie held up a piece of paper Niall hadn't noticed she'd been holding.

"We have to return for questioning," she said.

Chapter Twenty-Two

"I still doona like the idea," Niall said later that evening when everyone was gathered in a room that served as a library. "Curtis could nae guarantee Annie's safety on return."

Annie looked down at the letter in her lap that she had folded and unfolded dozens of times. "The instruction is pretty clear."

Niall scowled and resumed the pacing he'd begun earlier. "The *command*, ye mean."

She sighed. "Does it matter which word we use? The letter says I must appear before the magistrate within a week or be considered a fugitive. I doona want to be placed in gaol."

"Ye can take my fastest carriage," Ian said from his place on the sofa next to Jillian.

"'Tis nae need for a carriage," Annie replied. She didn't even want to think about the perilous winding road down to the loch in anything with wheels. "We brought our horses and 'twill be faster to ride."

"Do ye want me to send some men with ye as guards?"

"'Tis nae need for that either," Niall said. "We will catch a ship to Oban and, from there, 'tis nae more than three days to Glasgow. We will stop well before dark each night, so nae need to fear brigands."

"I understand your need for haste in getting Annie

away from Glasgow." Jillian gave Niall an appraising look. "But have you thought of the repercussions if the two of you arrive without a chaperone of some type after several nights on the road?"

Annie drew her brows together. The flight from Glasgow had been so hurried, and with Niall wounded, she hadn't given much thought to propriety. Besides which, she had been disguised as a lad until they got on board the ship. She could dress that part again for the journey, but arriving in Glasgow with only Niall as an escort—and facing a different sort of interrogation from her mother's—did pose a problem.

"I wish I could accompany you," Jillian said and then held up a hand to quiet Ian as his face turned thunderous, "but with the bairns still small—"

"We can go!" Caitlin practically shouted.

"Aye! Let us go!" Caylin was only marginally less loud than her twin. "We've only been to Glasgow once!"

"And Glasgow is probably still recovering," Ian said.

Jillian shook her head. "You girls are too young to serve as chaperones."

"We are near five-and-ten," Caitlin muttered.

"Practically grown-ups," Caylin added.

"Nae. 'Tis the end of the discussion," Ian said.

"Aye. 'Tis the end of the talk," Niall stated. "I have already decided the best course to take."

"Which is?" Jillian asked.

"I will marry Annie before we leave," Niall answered. "Do ye have a priest that can be summoned?"

Annie stared at Niall, speechless.

Ian nodded. "Aye. I can have him here tomorrow."

"Wait." Annie finally found her voice. "What kind

of a daft idea is that?"

"'Tis an excellent idea," Ian said. "As your husband, Niall can legally protect ye."

"How…" Annie started to sputter as she completed her own thought. "Be-because I…I will be his property! Is that it?"

Niall frowned. "I dinnae mean it like that."

Annie turned on him. "But 'tis true. A woman is considered chattel, according to English law. Ye would own me."

"I cannae change the law—"

"If I might interrupt?" Jillian asked and looked at Annie. "'Tis nae so bad to be married—"

"'Tis *nae so bad*?" Ian glowered at her. "'Tis nae so *bad*?"

Jillian smiled at him, unfazed, and leaned over to plant a kiss on his cheek. "When you are bad, you always make it up to me, do you not?"

Two spots of color highlighted Ian's face, which would have been comical given that he usually looked more ready to do battle with a whole army, but Annie still couldn't get her thinking straight. Jillian turned back to her.

"I cannot speak for how Niall feels—and this is certainly not the place for that—but he is a good man who will treat you well and take care of you always. I am sure about that."

"Aye, I've proved myself on that point several times," Niall said and looked at Annie. "Have I nae?"

Annie nodded reluctantly and looked down at her hands. Niall had gotten her out of several dangerous situations, even if she didn't count the last one. But he had done so out of a sense of honor. That was not a reason to get married. If—and it was a huge *if*—she ever got married, it would be because the man loved her. She nearly gasped as the full impact of that thought struck her. She'd never considered herself a romantic—she'd only read parts of *Pride and Prejudice* and thought some of the sentiments rather silly—but yes, if she were going to allow herself to be owned according to English law, then by all that was holy, she'd have to be convinced the man actually loved her.

Annie glanced up at Niall and then past him to focus on an oil painting of Ben Nevis, majestic and towering, yet tranquil as well. Hardly what she was feeling. She couldn't deny that she was attracted to Niall and, if the ride home had been an indication, he was attracted to her too—at least that he wanted her body. But Broderick had wanted that as well. Coupling did not constitute love.

"I am truly grateful for all the times ye have been by my side when trouble called," Annie said. "Ye dinnae have to do that."

"I told ye weeks ago that I would be responsible for ye. That has nae changed." Niall shrugged. "We may argue, lass. 'Tis in our blood. But I will never harm ye. Ye have my word on that."

"I believe ye," Annie said as she stood, "but my answer is nae. I will nae marry ye."

****

Niall leaned on the rail of the ship as it approached its berth in Oban's harbor and shook his head. He'd been shaking it so much the past two days, it was a wonder his brain wasn't addled. Annie Ferguson had to be the most perverse, stubborn female he had ever met. Not only did she refuse a very practical proposal that would have kept her safe, she wouldn't even explain *why* she was so

263

adamantly mulish. Every time he'd tried to bring it up on the journey south, she'd simply smiled and thanked him for his offer and then added that she didn't wish to discuss it.

Well, he wanted to discuss it and, by God, he would before they reached Glasgow. He understood—he really did—that Annie didn't want to be dependent on a man. Margaret had much the same temperament, and from what Niall had observed about Bridget, she had an independent streak as well. Still, she had married Alasdair. And Niall didn't expect Annie to give up her Progress Club activities. He'd even told her so at least twice since they boarded the ship. He didn't expect her to sit inside a house all day working on needlepoint or watercolors.

Hell, he really didn't know what he expected. Or why he couldn't just let go of the idea. It wasn't as though he had been actively seeking a wife. Marriage was something he figured he'd put off for another five or even ten years. And he'd envisioned—more or less— that the lass would be biddable. Certainly a word that would never apply to Annie Ferguson. Marriage to her would be a constant uphill battle of challenges.

But maybe that was what he wanted and he just hadn't recognized it before. He couldn't recall a single animated or thought-provoking conversation he'd had with any female he'd bedded. Dialogue before coupling was intended to reach that goal. Talk afterwards consisted mostly of satisfied murmurings and not-so-subtle invitations from his bedmates for repeat performances, which he rarely did since he didn't want any female to get too attached. All those romps had been pleasant and he'd taken care not to leave any girl with a by-blow, but that's all the experiences had been. Enjoyable, if somewhat blurred, interludes. He suspected a first time with Annie would be seared into his brain like a brand from a hot iron.

There, perhaps, was the crux of it. Niall wanted Annie like he'd never wanted any other woman. As irritating as her tenacity could be, he enjoyed sparring with her. She was opinionated, but those opinions were well thought out. Annie didn't back down from an argument or from much else either. He admired her spirit and her spunk, even if it did cause him more than an occasional headache.

And he knew damn well he was lying to himself if he thought one time was all he would need. He wanted Annie in his bed every night, having hot passion explode between them, then lying with naked bodies entwined as they slept. He wanted to wake up to her every morning and start the day by sucking her nipples to hard peaks and then plunging between warm, wet thighs. His cock hardened.

"They are leading our horses down the plank," Annie said from behind him.

He swiveled, careful to make sure his coat was shielding his wayward shaft. He'd been so lost in thought he hadn't even realized they had docked. "Aye. We'll give the animals a few minutes to get used to solid ground again and then we'll be off." He looked up at the sun's location. "We can probably make Crianlarich by nightfall."

"A night at an inn would be wonderful," Annie replied. "Even though the captain gave me his cabin, I doubt I will ever get used to the movement of a ship."

Niall grinned. "At least ye did nae turn green around

the gills this time."

She nodded. "There is that. I will be glad, though, when we get to Glasgow."

He started to say, once more, that she would be better protected as his wife, but decided to hold his peace. Perhaps tonight, settled in front of a warm fire at the inn, a hearty meal, and a tankard or two of ale, Annie might be more amenable to listening to his proposal.

The cook gave him a small sack filled with the biscuits sailors called hardtack along with some surprisingly soft cheese and dried venison. Twenty minutes later, Niall turned their horses onto the path inland.

"Are ye sure we will make the village by nightfall?" Annie asked several hours later as the sun was past its zenith.

Niall glanced up at the sky. "'Twill be close."

"How close?"

"Perhaps by an hour or so. We may need to make camp tonight."

Annie gave a soft sigh. "I would rather ride an hour in the dark if it means having a soft bed and a good meal."

Niall would too. Lying on cold, hard ground bundled in all their clothing with no fire and only meager food offerings was not conducive to persuading Annie to see reason, but it would be safer. "Riding after dark is dangerous."

"'Tis a moon out for the horses to see the way, and the road is dry, nae rutted," Annie replied. "And we didnae hear of a single brigand in the area when we rode north."

That was true. If they could make the inn... "We'll

wait and see how close we are when the sun sets."

Annie nodded and they rode on in companionable silence, stopping once to rest the horses and give them a drink at a burn. Annie had even suggested they eat their meal while they rode in order to get to the inn. Still, dusk settled, and by Niall's estimation they were still a good ten miles from Crianlarich. As much as he didn't want to stop, he slowed his horse. "'Tis another two hours to the inn. We had better find a spot to stop."

"Nae! There is nae even a crofter's cottage about. I doona want to sleep outside," Annie said and then reached over to put her hand on his arm. "Please, Niall. Let's ride on."

Hell. He didn't think Annie had ever asked him for a favor before. How could he refuse? Niall looked down the road. The moonlight clearly lit a path, and Annie was right that there had been no reports about highwaymen in the area. He smiled to himself as another thought came. Maybe once they reached the inn, he could insist Annie have a hot bath before dinner and he could order a bottle of wine if the proprietor had one… Niall nodded. "Let us continue, then."

Annie looked happy enough to kiss him, and he was tempted to sidle his horse closer and reach over to draw her to him and do just that, but Annie had kicked her horse to a canter and was already several yards ahead of him.

"Wait!" he called as she rounded a bend and temporarily disappeared from sight. He muffled a curse as he nudged his own horse to a run. When he caught up to her, she was definitely going to get a lecture on not only galloping at night, but also on putting distance between them. Annie Ferguson had to be the most perverse, stubborn female he had ever met…

As he rounded the bend, large black forms suddenly emerged from both sides of the road, closing him in. Before he could draw his sword, something hard and solid struck him from behind and the last thing he remembered was falling from the saddle.

Chapter Twenty-Three

Annie stared at the dark figure on horseback blocking her path. She couldn't make out his face since a hood partially covered it, but the moonlight reflected off the steel blade he held in his hand. Brigand. She wheeled her horse swiftly, only to find another dark-cloaked rider behind her. He didn't make a sound as he grabbed her reins. Annie thought to reach for the knife in her boot, but the man was pressed too close to her leg to maneuver.

Where was Niall? She hadn't been that much ahead of him... At the sound of pounding hooves, she breathed a small sigh of relief. As soon as he distracted the two men, she could reach for her own blade.

But her hope was short-lived. There were several horses galloping toward her, one of which was riderless. As they came closer, she recognized Niall's gelding. Her stomach suddenly felt as though she'd swallowed lead.

"Is the guard dead?" the brigand holding the knife asked.

"Aye. He hit his head hard on a rock," one of the three others replied. "We threw the body into the ditch."

Annie's heart stuttered in her chest. Niall was dead? She felt the blood drain from her head and the world started to spin around her. She clutched her saddle and struggled to breathe. Niall couldn't be dead. No. No. *No*.

"Are ye sure there were nae more men behind him?"

asked the knife-holding brigand who seemed to be their leader.

"Aye. Nae one followed."

"'Tis strange to have only one escort for the lady."

"Well, this one was well-armed," the second rider replied. "Half a dozen knives and a sword, plus a musket in the saddlebag."

"And doona forget the coin." The third one held up a leather pouch. "'Tis enough to keep us in whisky and women for weeks."

The leader turned his hooded face toward Annie. "And what riches are ye carrying?"

"Besides the obvious," added one of the men, snickering.

"Aye, we can draw lots who will have her first." Another man looked inquiringly at the leader. "Unless ye want to be first, Calum."

"Stop your blethering," Calum snapped. "We are holding Lady Briana for ransom, nae ravishing." He sheathed his knife. "At least, nae yet. If the Campbell refuses to pay, ye can all rut her until she is raw."

Annie still felt dizzy, the conversation swarming around her like a cloud of midges, but slowly the words began to sink in. Apparently these men mistook her for someone of some importance to a Campbell. That might buy her a day or two of time before whoever this Campbell was refused to pay ransom for someone who had not disappeared. It also meant this band was not regular highwaymen out simply to rob. And rape. A cold shiver swept down her spine as she recalled that part of the conversation. The leader had told the men to hold off, but as soon as they realized they had the wrong person… Annie took a deep breath. She still had her knife. Now she needed to collect her wits.

"So what riches are ye carrying?" the leader asked again.

Annie swallowed and lifted her chin. "I do nae carry jewels or coin when I travel."

"I can check your saddlebag later." Calum's cloaked head moved up and down as he appraised her. "'Tis a rather clever disguise for ye to dress as a lad, but ye took a foolish risk with only one escort."

A lump rose in Annie's throat as she thought of Niall's body lying in a ditch. She felt the lightheadedness begin again and willed herself not to faint. "My…guard was well-armed."

"Aye, but nae match for five MacDougalls."

So that's who they were. Was this about a clan feud? Even though the English had implemented the Disarming Act over fifty years earlier, she knew Highlanders still remained loyal to their clans, but she wished she understood more about such things. A wild idea flitted through her mind. It might not work, but it was worth a try.

"Your men must have remained well-hidden for Campbell men nae to notice them."

The leader frowned. "What do ye mean?"

"Well, we did have several men travelling ahead of us to be sure the road was clear," Annie said, her mind racing. Surely there must have been other travelers on this road earlier. "Since we should have been in Crianlarich by now, they'll be coming back to search for me."

Calum tossed back his hood and she could see the hard lines of his face. His eyes glinted near black in the moonlight. "Ah. I dinnae think your uncle was so stupid as to let ye ride with one guard, although 'twas clever enough of the bastard to nae call attention to ye." He looked down the road in the direction they had come. "And does he have a rear guard following as well?"

Annie forced herself to smile and managed a shrug. "Perhaps."

The leader's brows drew together. "I doona like lasses with sassy mouths. If ye are nae careful, I may let my men have sport with ye in spite of a ransom."

"'Twould be a fittin' revenge for what Campbell men did to your sister," one of the riders said.

"Aye, it would," another added. "Perhaps just a wee taste of her now?"

"Not now." Calum turned his hard gaze on Annie. "Ye would be wise to watch your mouth."

Annie steeled her hands not to shake and hoped her voice didn't either. "I simply meant that my…uncle…did nae advise me of his plans."

"That sounds like him. Nae matter though." He pulled a small sack from beneath his cloak and shook it out. Before Annie could respond, he reached out and pulled it over her head, blinding her. "We will be well out of the way by the time they pass by."

****

Niall groaned and slowly opened his eyes. Or one eye, anyway. The other seemed to be pressed shut by something damp and hard. He lay still, trying to adjust his senses to where he was. An earthy, somewhat putrid smell filled the air and he realized that half his nose was buried in something slimy. He snorted and pushed himself up to find he was sitting in a grassy ditch still muddied from the last rain.

His head throbbed. Niall touched the egg-size bump

along the side of his head and stared at his hand, covered in half-dried blood. How long had he been out? And why? His memory cleared and he remembered the ambush.

Annie. Where was Annie?

He started to leap up and then fell back as dizziness swept over him. Damnation! Now was not the time to be weak. Niall gathered his strength and rose, more slowly this time. He had to wait a moment for his equilibrium to adjust itself and then looked in either direction. The road was deserted. He glanced up. The moon was low in the western sky and streaks of lavender heralded dawn in the east. He had been unconscious for several hours.

His horse was gone. The brigands obviously had stolen it, but had they abducted Annie as well? A slim sliver of hope that she'd managed to ride on to Cairnlarich shriveled when he thought of the time elapsed. If she had managed to escape, she'd have had time to reach the village and return with help. Was she lying somewhere up ahead in the ditch? Hurt? Or even dead? Fear washed over him like a cold bucketful of water as he forced himself to start walking, crisscrossing the road to check both sides, hoping he would not find her body. She couldn't be dead. *She. Just. Could. Not. Be. Dead.* Niall knew he was repeating the words in his head to reassure himself, but it was somehow comforting, nonetheless.

He wished he knew who had done this. Brigands who wore hooded cloaks were unusual, but who else would lie in wait along a well-travelled road? Niall cursed roundly at having continued on for the night. He knew damn well they made an easy target after darkness fell. He should have insisted that they stop and take shelter in a copse of trees, hidden from view. Had he not been so intent on reaching the inn and setting the mood to persuade Annie to see his reasoning was right, this wouldn't have happened.

Niall stopped when he saw the jumbled hoof prints about a half mile from where he'd been attacked. The dirt on top of the road was dry, but loose. He wasn't the expert tracker that his brother Braden was, but the sky was lightening and as Niall bent down, he counted different hoof imprints of at least six or seven horses. One horseshoe had a missing nail. He straightened. Only three men had accosted him, which meant two more had been waiting around the bend. That was strange too. Usually a band of brigands surrounded whomever they were robbing so no one could get away.

And usually, they didn't take victims with them. But he hadn't seen Annie lying in the ditch and her horse was gone. The trail led clearly off the road and toward the woods. Niall started along the path. Whoever the abductors were, they either were unskilled in covering their tracks or they didn't care if they were followed. If the latter were true, that probably meant there were a lot more of them lurking inside the forest.

Niall didn't have the talent for stealth that Gavin had, but he'd learned enough from his brother to know how to shadow. He moved from tree to tree cautiously since he his weapons had been stolen. He didn't know what odds he would be facing, but it didn't matter.

They had Annie.

****

Annie blinked in darkness almost as dense as the sack over her head had been. At least, her abductors had taken that off after she'd been pulled from her horse and half-carried, half-dragged across a rocky path full of gnarly tree roots. Perhaps it was just as well that two of the men had a firm grip on her, since her legs almost buckled when she dismounted. She didn't know how long they'd been riding—the hood had made her disoriented—but it seemed like hours.

She sat on hard-packed ground in a small enclosure that smelled damp, a cave of sorts, made of outcroppings of rocky ledges and boulders. She could hear the men's voices, so the entrance must not be far away, although she couldn't see it. She guessed it was still night.

She heard the scuffling of boots and then a lantern flared, the sudden brightness nearly blinding her in the cramped space. Annie shielded her eyes. A moment later, the wick dimmed and she dropped her hands.

Calum crouched down beside her, setting the lamp on the floor, and handed her a small sack which she recognized as the one the cook on the ship had given Niall.

"Your food," Calum said. "Ye should eat."

"I am nae hungry." Her stomach growled just then to give lie to the fact, but Annie didn't think she could swallow past the lump in her throat. This was food she should have been sharing with Niall. But Niall was... No. no. *no*. She couldn't bear the thought that he was truly gone.

"Suit yourself." Calum cupped a hand under her chin, forcing her to look up, and studied her. "Your hair is much redder than I expected."

He expected? Annie held herself still, although her mind was moving as fast as a hare being chased by a hound. Had he never seen her, then? That was a blessing.

"Ye are taller than I was told, as well."

275

Her stomach knotted, threatening to push itself up to join the lump in her throat. She had no idea who Briana was or what she looked like. Would Calum believe Annie was the Campbell girl? She desperately needed to convince him she was.

"Your source was nae verra accurate, then."

His eyes narrowed and he released her chin. "Ye need to curb that saucy mouth before ye truly vex me."

She looked away so he wouldn't see the apprehension that was probably showing in her face. How many times had her mother tried to instill the need to think before she blurted out words? Annie recalled all too well the threat Calum had made at her earlier remark. He didn't need to repeat it. She'd seen the lecherous looks on the other men's faces before the hood had been pulled over her head.

Annie felt a hysterical bubble of laughter rising. After Broderick had taken her virginity and she'd asked when they were getting married, he'd scoffed and said not to think she was that special. Put a bag over a woman's head and they were all the same…

The hysteric bubble turned into a choked sob which she quickly stifled. She dared not show fear in front of Calum MacDougall.

"I dinnae mean to offend ye. I just doona understand why I am here."

He stared at her. "How can ye nae ken?"

Oh, Lord. She suspected she knew what Briana's brother had done to Calum's sister, but what if she was wrong? Or it was even worse? She couldn't afford to blunder. "Since I am here, I would prefer to hear your version."

"My *version*?" Calum practically sneered at her.

"'Tis nae *version*. 'Tis *fact*."

Annie nodded. "Fact, then." He looked at her suspiciously and Annie held her breath, afraid he was going to realize he had abducted the wrong person, but he finally answered.

"Your fine, upstanding brother—a man with a wife and two bairns—got my sister with child. That fact is plain enough and getting plainer every day."

"But—"

"Doona try to defend your brother! My sister kens who took her virtue. I've heard enough lies from your father."

She wouldn't defend the man even if he was her brother. He was a worse cad than even Broderick had been. She had only started to say it wasn't her fault, although she doubted Calum cared. "I am sorry about your sister, but how can abducting me undo what's been done?"

"It cannae." Calum stood to leave. "But your ransom will pay for my sister to move to Edinburgh, once the babe is born, so she can begin a new life."

Dear God. The amount he was asking for must be huge. Not that the amount mattered, since Briana Campbell was safe and sound somewhere and her father would simply ignore a ransom note. That meant… Annie put the thought from her mind. As if he read her thoughts—hopefully, she hadn't spoken aloud—Calum smiled grimly.

"In case ye are wondering, if your father doesnae deliver the full amount, we will take the rest of the payment from ye."

Annie raised her chin, determined not to let him see her fear. "He will pay."

Calum stopped smiling. "For your sake, lass, I hope he does."

He had hardly cleared the door before Annie's body began to shake uncontrollably. She had no power to stop it. She fought the nausea that threatened, as well, and tried to think, but she felt as though she was floating in fog.

Eventually the shaking subsided and her head began to clear. She had to get out of here. Somehow. Annie looked toward the entrance, now visible in the dawn light. A pair of booted legs blocked the way. They'd posted a guard. She quickly surveyed her surroundings, which didn't take long. There was no other way out. She picked up two loose rocks from the floor and laid them beside her.

Had the MacDougall leader already sent one of his men to deliver the ransom note or would he have waited for dawn? How long did she have before the man returned and Calum would find out she wasn't Briana Campbell? Would he listen if Annie pleaded for mercy and spare her from rape? Annie doubted it, given his remarks that his men could rut her raw. In any case, it wasn't a risk she wanted to take.

There were five men in the party, plus one who had been waiting here for them when they arrived, so that made six.. Perhaps two would ride to deliver the ransom note. She hoped—prayed—the others wouldn't just sit in camp all day, but be patrolling or hunting or something. If they left just the one guard… Annie fingered the knife hilt in her boot. Niall had taught her to use it. She choked back a sob, realizing too late that she had grown to love him dearly. A tear trickled down her cheek, followed by another. She wiped them away with the back of her hand

and took a deep breath. Niall wasn't here, but she wouldn't disappoint him.

She picked up her rocks and moved closer to the entrance to wait for the right moment, as he had taught her.

Chapter Twenty-Four

At the sound of horses approaching, Niall crouched behind a thick pile of dried bracken. The forest had thinned out considerably, giving him fewer places to hide as he tracked Annie's abductors. It had also given way to a narrow, dirt road which probably explained why those men had not been that concerned about the trail they'd left earlier. Numerous hoofprints were jumbled together, making it harder to find the distinctive one with the missing nail in the horseshoe.

The sound grew louder as the horses came into sight past a small copse of trees. Two riders, wearing MacDougall tartans. Niall wondered what they were doing so far into Campbell lands. Being a MacDonald—and still not fond of Campbells—Niall had decided travelling would be safer for Annie if he wore conventional clothes. The riders had just passed him when one pulled a dark cloak from his saddlebag and flung it over his shoulders. It looked vaguely familiar. When the other rider did the same thing, Niall realized why. The men who'd accosted him had worn the same type of cloak.

Niall stared after them, staying hunched until they'd ridden a good distance and then he slowly stood. MacDougalls had taken Annie? Niall couldn't fathom why, but that was something that he could ponder on later. They had come from the south and Annie hadn't been with them, so the other three abductors must be holding her farther along. Niall just hoped there were only three of them and not half a clan waiting.

He checked the hoofprints of the horses that had just passed. Neither of them was missing a nail in the shoe, so he hoped he could continue to track that print. Niall proceeded slowly up the road, his ears alert for other riders. It was still early in the day for travelers to be about, but he didn't want to be spotted.

He'd gone not quite another mile when he noticed grass that had been trampled off to one side. He couldn't find the track of the missing horseshoe nail, but it looked as though a number of horses had left the road. Niall looked up. The terrain was steeper here, the trees somewhat sparse, replaced with boulders and shale overhangs that would provide cover. A rocky, rutted trail led upwards.

Niall began to follow it. There wasn't enough space between the rocks and scraggly bushes that grew out of crags to hide horses, but the deep crevices could certainly hide a man acting as a guard. He hated feeling so exposed, especially since he was unarmed. At least, the damp moss that covered the ground masked the sound of his boots, but he still needed to keep a sharp lookout.

Even so, he almost missed the slight noise off to his left. It sounded like boots shuffling. A soft thud followed. Niall dropped to his stomach and began to crawl, staying close to the side of large boulder. He peered around it cautiously.

The trail had ended abruptly at a flat, open area and Niall realized he must have climbed to the top of a ridge. A guard stood only feet away, leaning against a tree and looking across the clearing toward another man who was tending the horses. Niall recognized his gelding and Annie's mare. So he had found their hideout, but where was Annie?

Niall scanned the clearing again. There was no sign of her anywhere. Had they taken her someplace else? He frowned. But her mare was here and he hadn't passed any houses this last mile. He spotted another man standing in front of a darkened crevice. The ledge overhang looked like it could provide a small cave. Was Annie being held there?

Niall snaked his way backwards, praying he wouldn't dislodge some small rock and give himself away. If Annie was here, he'd soon free her. If not, three MacDougalls were about to tell him where she was.

He wedged himself behind the boulder and then slipped around to its other side. The tree the guard leaned against was directly in front of him now. Niall kept an eye on the man tending the horses and the one by the cave. Neither seemed to be looking in his direction. Niall loosened his belt, wrapping the ends around each of his hands and crept forward. Gavin was better at this maneuver than he was, but if all went well, the guard would go down without a sound.

Things didn't go well. Niall flipped the garrote over the guard's head, drawing back and twisting the leather tightly, but not before the man managed to croak out a yelp. The man near the horses turned, as did the cave's guard, and both started running toward him. Niall dropped the unconscious man and slid the man's knife from its sheath. The blade didn't balance like his own, but it would have to do. He assumed a battle position.

The two men were almost on him when he saw a blur in his peripheral vision. Annie burst out of the cave, screeching like a banshee and brandishing the knife he'd given her. His mind registered that she truly did look like Queen Boudicca at the same time he registered she'd just put herself in harm's way. The man who'd been guarding the cave turned and jumped toward her. Niall raised his arm, his purloined blade flipping over twice as it soared through the air and lodged in the man's back. He fell forward with a grunt and Niall turned to fend off the other attacker as Annie ran toward them.

"Get back!" he shouted. "Take your horse and ride."

"Nae without ye!"

"Doona be daft!" It only took that momentary distraction for the man's fist to find his jaw. Niall's head snapped back and he went down. Rolling, he managed to miss the other man's weight crashing down on him. "Slide me your knife, lass!"

For once she didn't argue. Annie slid her knife toward him and Niall regained his feet at the same time the attacker did. Armed now, Niall waited for his opponent to make his move. And then Annie screamed again.

"Behind ye, Niall! Behind ye!"

He whirled as a fourth man came running up the path into the clearing. Where the hell had he come from? There were only supposed to be three… Niall hurled the blade he held, this time catching the newcomer in the gut. He clutched his stomach and fell. Niall turned to finish what he had started and nearly tripped himself.

Annie had jumped on the guard's back. One hand was pulling hard on the man's hair while with the other, she was pummeling him with a rock she held. The guard was spinning in circles in an attempt to dislodge her, but she just clung tighter, a few choice words, ones Niall didn't think he'd ever heard a woman say, coming from her mouth. Her hair had come loose and swirled around her head like a halo of fire. Niall would have liked to admire the whole image, but the man was nearing a tree, obviously intent on knocking her against it. Niall leapt.

And found himself clutching thin air as the man fell. One of Annie's whacks with the rock had found its mark. Annie went down with him. Niall caught her, barely managing to pull her off before she hit the ground.

She stood there shaking. "If ye had nae come—"

"'Tis nae the time to talk," Niall replied, half-carrying her to their horses and lifting her onto the mare. Quickly, he grabbed the others' saddlebags before turning their horses loose. "Those men are nae dead. I suggest we ride."

For the second time in minutes, Annie didn't argue.

****

They were several miles down the road before Niall finally slowed the horses and gestured. "There is a village up ahead."

It really didn't look like much more than a few cottages and a building that might be a coach exchange. "Do ye think it safe to stop?" Annie asked.

"Nae. We will go around. The MacDougalls will be following us as soon as they patch up their wounds and catch their mounts. If nae one spots us, they may think we went in a different direction."

"'Tis a good plan." Annie looked around. "But there is nae other road."

Niall grinned. "We follow the sheep, then."

"Sheep?" Annie gave him a worried look, wondering if the fighting had done something to his brain. "There are nae sheep in sight."

"True." He pointed to the ground. "But their droppings leave a trail."

So they did. Annie wasn't sure exactly how following a sheep trail would help, but Niall had already turned off the road and her mare decided she didn't want to be left behind. It didn't take long before they reached a small glade where the animals grazed near a tumbling burn. Niall stopped beside it and dismounted. "We can rest the horses here for a few minutes."

As Annie started to dismount, her leg buckled. Niall was beside her in an instant, his hands around her waist, steadying her. "Easy there."

Annie put her hands on his arms, feeling the rock-hard definition of his biceps. The touch was comforting. She hadn't realized she was so shaky. Suddenly, the enormity of what had happened in the past twenty-four hours—the real danger she had been in—swept over her like one of those rogue waves on Loch Linnhe. She clutched Niall tighter and looked up at him. "If ye had nae come—"

"'Tis over, lass. Try nae to think about it."

"I thought….they said…that ye were dead."

Niall smiled. "'Tis a good thing they thought that or they might have finished me off with a bullet."

"Doona jest!" Annie gripped him harder. "I could nae bear the thought that they had…killed…ye."

Niall's eyes darkened as he looked at her. Holding her gaze, he encircled her waist and drew her closer until her breasts pressed against his chest, and then he bent his head.

Annie stopped breathing. The mere graze of the first kiss was a gentle caress, barely there, the second teasing, his warm lips playing with her. Then Niall nibbled lightly at one corner of her mouth before slowly sucking her bottom lip between his.

Annie felt dizzy and about to swoon, even though she had managed not to while abducted. His tongue probed hers as he deepened the kiss. Instinctively, her arms went around his neck as she opened her mouth to allow him entrance. Niall groaned, his tongue delving deeper to taste all of her.

The experience was heady, like sweet mead. Instinctively, her tongue sought his, circling and looping, playing tag. Her nipples tightened and her breasts grew heavy. Annie rubbed against him, seeking the friction that would bring pleasure.

Niall broke away, his breathing short. "I want to taste all of ye, Annie, but 'tis nae the place. We are nae safe yet."

Annie drew a shaky breath. "Ye are right. We must ride."

Niall nodded and boosted her into the saddle, then handed her the reins. He vaulted onto his own horse and turned to her, his eyes darkening again and his gaze intense. "But tonight...*tonight* we can finish what we started."

****

They forded Loch Lomond a short time later, leaving Campbell lands, and rode south along the coastline toward Glasgow. While they rode, Annie recounted what the MacDougall leader had told her. She still shuddered at what might have happened once the riders returned with the news that she was not Briana Campbell, but with each passing mile a little bit of tension eased. By the time Niall decided to stop at the village of Drymen, she felt almost like her former self.

Almost.

"Do ye think it safe to get a room for the night? Perhaps we should camp—"

"Nae camp," Niall answered as he helped her down. "I doona intend to take your virtue on hard ground. A nice, soft bed sounds much better, nae?"

Before she could reply, he had taken her arm and walked into the inn. This time he didn't even ask if two rooms were available and, instead, ordered one with a large bed along with instructions for a hot bath, two meals, and a bottle of wine.

Annie followed him tentatively up the stairs, her teeth worrying her lower lip. He had obviously not forgotten the kiss they'd shared. Of course, she hadn't forgotten either. Just recalling how his mouth had felt made her insides melt and her core grow warm and damp. With the juggling of the horse's gait, her breasts had not stopped tingling all afternoon. She wanted to experience the pleasure of rubbing herself against Niall's bare flesh. Her body quivered in anticipation, knowing what it wanted.

And that was the problem. She was no virgin. There was no virtue for Niall to take.

What would he do when he found out? Shun her? Most men would. Even worse, what if he thought her lack of a maidenhead meant she had been loose with her favors? She hadn't. There had only been that one time…but what difference did that make to a man? A single woman who was not chaste was considered a wanton in society. Nothing more than a trollop. Annie couldn't bear to have Niall think of her like that. She loved him, even if he didn't love her. Better that he not find out about her past.

Just how she was going to keep him uninformed about that, she wasn't sure.

****

Niall looked at the clock on the mantel over the fireplace in the public room. Had thirty minutes been enough for Annie to enjoy her bath? He'd been through this routine before with her, but this time he wasn't waiting for her to fall asleep. This time he wanted her waiting for him. She'd asked for privacy for her bath, so he could only anticipate she wanted to ready herself. Just the thought made his cock stir. Truth be told, he'd have enjoyed *helping* her with her bath, but that could happen once she'd gotten used to shared intimacy. Besides, after tonight, there would be no way she'd refuse to marry him.

He gave her another fifteen minutes, although it seemed more like fifteen hours, before he walked back upstairs. The door opened to near darkness, the only light being the dying embers in the brazier and a single candle by the bed. Annie was already in it. Niall grinned and moved closer, then stopped, the smile disappearing from his face.

She appeared to be asleep. Not exactly what he'd expected, but then maybe she'd been more tired than he thought. But there were other ways to revive her energy. Niall removed his shirt and sat on the edge of the bed to pull off his boots and socks. He was reaching for the laces of his trews when she spoke.

"Please doona remove those."

Niall looked over his shoulder to find her looking wide-eyed at him. She had the covers tucked nearly to her chin, but her arms were on top of them and he could see she was wearing her shirt. He hadn't thought of

Annie as being shy, but then he was not in the habit of bedding virgins. He'd never deflowered any girl. He let his hands drop.

"Doona fash. I can remove them later."

Annie shook her head as she sat up, still holding the sheets in front of her. "'Tis nae a good idea."

Niall frowned. Where was the woman he'd kissed earlier—the one who'd kissed him back with passion? Annie had practically crawled into the corner where the bed sat against the wall. She must have been more traumatized than he'd thought. She'd not only been abducted, but threatened with rape. He should have considered that.

"Ye need nae fear me, lass. I will nae hurt ye."

Her eyes blinked at him like an owl's. "I ken that."

That was good. Perhaps she just needed to relax a bit. Niall glanced at the wine she'd left untouched when they'd eaten their meal earlier. "Would ye like a drink? 'Twould calm your nerves."

"I am nae nervous."

Not nervous? She looked about as skittish as a foal and he had the distinct impression she would have liked to bolt from the bed, but he blocked her way. What in the world was wrong with her? He wished he knew something—anything—about easing a maiden's worries. He'd already offered marriage, but maybe he could soothe her with words of reassurance.

"I will nae get ye with child, if that is what ye are fashing about. 'Tis ways to prevent that from happening." Her eyes grew more owlish and he hurriedly added, "I will try nae to hurt ye either." Annie made a sound that sounded almost like a squeak. Even in the dim light, Niall could see her face had paled. Was she that scared of pain? "I promise ye, I will go slow. I will even stop if ye say so." Hell. Where were those words coming from? Going slow would be difficult enough, but stopping? Niall grimaced. It would be nigh to impossible, but he would do it if he had to. "I give ye my word as an honorable man that I will respect your wishes."

Annie stared at him, her eyes dark against her white face. "Re...respect?"

"Aye." Niall moved closer to give her a kiss, but her hand came between them. "Please doona do that."

Niall pulled back, confused. Was Annie playing a game with him? He didn't think she was the type to play coy and hard-to-get. He'd never seen her flirt. She didn't even accept compliments graciously. And now she was acting like she didn't want him touching her at all, even though she'd been quite willing to be in his embrace this morning by the burn...

Suddenly, the truth struck him. Annie had reacted to him earlier because she'd been in shock. She had needed someone—anyone—to comfort and assure her she was safe. That was all. The kisses meant nothing. They were simply the physical response of a female body to a male one as relief—or gratitude—replaced the threat of danger. It was one of the reasons warriors of old pillaged villages after winning bloody battles. Human instinct was, after all, *human.*

"Forgive me. I mistook your interest this morning." Niall reached down to get his boots and grab his shirt, shrugging into it as he walked to the door. "I will see ye in the morning."

"Wait!"

Niall hesitated, his hand on the doorknob. He should

go without turning back. He didn't need to hear any excuse she was about to give. He started to open the door.

"Wait!" Annie called again. "Where are ye going?"

Niall took a deep breath, closed the door, and turned around. "I am going to get another room for tonight and leave ye in peace."

"Ye…ye doona have to do that."

"I think it would be best."

"But…" Annie inched toward the edge of the bed. "We have stayed in the same room before."

Did she not have any idea of how she affected him? Perhaps not, since he seemed to be the only one harboring fantasies. "I was wounded and feverish the last time, hardly able to…" Niall stopped abruptly. There was no need to finish the sentence.

"To what?"

Niall sighed. Apparently he was going to have to finish the sentence after all, although he didn't know how Annie could be so daft. "To do what a man wants to do when he finds himself in bed with a beautiful woman. Do I need to be more clear?"

Pink suffused her face as Annie shook her head. "Nae."

"Then ye ken why I must leave." He managed a brittle smile. "I would nae be able to keep from touching ye."

"I…would nae mind if ye touched me," Annie whispered.

Niall stared at her, sure he had misunderstood the barely audible words. "What did ye say?"

"I said…" Annie cleared her throat. "I said I…would nae mind if ye touched me."

291

"*What?*" The word came out before he could stop it. The woman was going to drive him completely barmy, if he wasn't already there.

Annie cleared her throat again. "I said—"

"I *ken* what ye said, lass. I want to ken *why*." Niall clenched his jaw when she said nothing. "I must warn ye that men do nae like women who tease them with games."

Annie seemed startled. "I am nae playing a game."

"'Tis what it looks like from where I stand."

"I did nae…mean to tease ye, Niall. Never that."

Damn it, he believed her. She looked too miserable to be playing at anything. "Then why are ye blowing both hot and cold?" A thought came to him. "Are ye afraid I will nae respect ye if I take your maidenhood?"

Annie started to cry.

Hell! He'd never seen Annie cry, not even when she was attacked by unruly mobs. Niall dropped his boots and went to sit on the edge of the bed, tentatively holding out his arms. She started to move toward him and then stopped. He dropped his arms. "What is it, lass? What is wrong?"

"I…" She wiped at her tears with the sleeve of her shirt. "I…want ye to respect me."

He felt more confused than ever. It wasn't like he just planned to tup her and then ride away in the morning. She had a perfectly decent marriage proposal, one that she'd see as advantageous once she realized how pleasurable a coupling could be. "'Tis a natural thing for a man and woman to be together. Ye will see. Why would I nae respect ye?"

Tears pooled in her eyes again, but she defiantly brushed them away. Niall watched as a range of emotions spread across her face, as though she was doing some inner battle with herself. Then finally she squared her shoulders and lifted her chin.

"I am nae a virgin."

Niall stared at her, speechless. Of all the things he'd half-expected her to say, this was not one of them.

"There. Now ye ken."

Niall found his voice. "But how—"

"How many? Just one."

"I was nae going to ask how many," Niall said, wishing he could wipe the sadness from her face along with the tears. "I was going to ask how it happened. Nae that 'tis my business."

Annie clasped her hands in her lap and looked down. "I let a man I thought to marry ruin me. 'Twas my fault."

"'Tis *nae* your fault!" Anger like a red-hot poker seared through Niall. "The bastard trifled with ye. If he still lives, I will kill him for ye."

"He is nae worth it." Annie managed a trembling smile. "Anyway, he ran off."

"The man deserves to die if he made promises he did nae intend to keep."

"I am thankful I did nae increase because of that mistake. 'Twas a bitter lesson," Annie said, "but I have learned to live with the fact that I am spoiled goods—"

"Ye are nae spoiled goods."

Annie studied him. "Ye truly do nae think so? Be honest."

"I will be as honest as I can be." Niall held out his arms. "Come here, lass."

****

Annie felt her eyes widen as she looked into Niall's face and found nothing of contempt or condescension or criticism there. Instead, his eyes darkened to near charcoal, burning into her with an intense gaze.

She moved closer. Niall's arms came around her and his mouth descended on hers. It only took the first touch of his lips for her to have total recall of how pleasurable the morning experience had been. One of his hands crept up to cradle her head, angling it to better fit his intention and she parted her mouth willingly to accept him. He tasted slightly of whisky, the smoky flavor adding to the peat smell from the brazier and the fresh scent of the soap he had used earlier. But none of that mattered since the tantalizing things he was doing with his expert mouth made her thoughts blur. There was only sensation as he teased, his lips brushing along hers one minute, increasing the pressure the next, then nibbling at a corner and sucking her lower lip before deepening the kiss once again.

His tongue explored her mouth fully, while his hand slid down to cup a breast, his thumb grazing the nipple as lightly as a butterfly lighting on a leaf. The barely-there stroke came again and Annie felt herself arching into his hand for more. Niall chuckled and worked his way down her throat, his warm mouth making wet, sucking sounds as his clever fingers rolled her now taut nipple between them. Annie groaned and pressed closer.

And then she was on her back, with Niall looming over her. He shrugged out of his open shirt and, seconds later, her shirt was gone too, leaving her completely exposed to him. Instinctively, her arms moved to cover herself, but Niall caught her wrists.

"Ye will nae cover yourself to me." He placed her hands down by her sides. "Ye are a beautiful woman, Annie Ferguson, and I intend to enjoy every square inch of ye."

He took a moment to boldly savor her nakedness. Annie felt heat arise in her face and flow through her body, the fiery hotness following his roaming eyes as he slowly let his gaze travel from her breasts down her belly to her core and back to her face. She probably looked like a pickled beet.

Niall reached for her breasts again, cupping both of them this time, pushing them together, then bending over her to put his face between the plump mounds. Annie made a whimpering sound as his thumb began flicking fast and hard across a hardened peak. Then she moaned in earnest as his mouth covered the other one and he began to suckle, lightly at first, his tongue laving the areola, pressing the nipple flat and then catching it lightly between his teeth as it popped back to erectness. Niall tugged gently and Annie pulled his head down, demanding more. He obliged, suckling harder and drawing deep. Annie felt herself shudder as sharp tingles raced downward to the pulsing center of her core.

Growling, Niall sat back momentarily to remove his breeches. The cool air hit the wetness of her breast where his mouth had been and Annie shivered, not from cold so much as missing his body heat. And then she shivered again as he stood to shed the last of his clothes and she saw his proud manhood jutting out at her. She swallowed hard. She'd only seen one other man's penis before and it hadn't been so...*big*. Tentatively, she reached out to touch it. Niall grasped her hand.

"If ye do that right now, I will nae last to finish what I have planned."

Annie looked up at him, a bit bewildered. "I ken what comes next."

Niall grinned. "Do ye?"

"Aye. Ye will spill your seed in me." She looked again at his thick, hard length. "I think ye are ready."

Niall's grin widened. "I am more than ready, but I have nae pleasured ye enough, lass."

Annie stared at him. He didn't think she'd enjoyed what he'd just done? Good heavens, she could practically feel herself dripping. "But ye have pleasured me. 'Tis your turn."

"Nae yet."

"What…" she started to say and then gasped as Niall spread her thighs apart and nestled between them. Before she had time to grasp what he intended to do, he'd placed her legs over his shoulders and she felt his warm tongue lapping at the juice that flowed from her like overspilt milk, taking his time before licking slowly and leisurely along her folds. Annie gasped again and then nearly levitated as his mouth covered her thrumming nub and he sucked on it hard. Something clenched deep inside her belly and her thigh muscles corded around his head, locking him in place as her body shattered.

"Oh, my…" The words were lost as Niall slid up her body and she felt the large tip of his shaft nudge her entrance. She barely had time to register that it felt smooth as satin over hard steel before he began to push and she felt herself being stretched wide. She stilled, adjusting to the strange sensation of slowly being filled.

Niall paused. "I am nae hurting ye, am I?"

"Nae!" And it was true. The first time had hurt like Hades, but Niall's cock inside her only felt like heaven. Annie wiggled beneath him. "Nae! Doona stop."

"I have nae intention of stopping, lass."

Niall finished his thrust and withdrew as slowly as

he had entered, until he was nearly separate from her. Annie made a mewling sound in her throat and wrapped her legs around his hips to keep him in place. "Doona…nae yet…"

Niall laughed. "I am nae going anywhere, lass."

Annie nearly cried in relief as he filled her again. She hadn't known her body could actually ache for such a thing. But it did. Every nerve ending felt like it was on fire as Niall kept his thrusts slow and even, teasing her by nearly leaving and then coming together again. She began to writhe beneath him, wanting…*more*. But Niall continued to tease, alternating now between his slow, easy rhythm and moving harder and faster, which just made her want…*more*. Much more. Annie's hands grabbed Niall's shoulders, her nails raking across his back as her body began to undulate in earnest. Heat seared through her, the flames spreading through her veins like molten lava. Sound faded and her sight dimmed, her only concentration on the joining of their bodies. She had no idea where hers ended and Niall's began. There was only…sensation beyond belief. And then, just as she began to float on air, a final hard thrust came, butting against her womb and she erupted like a long dormant volcano.

It took several minutes before Annie could actually claim her arms and legs again. She felt boneless—even the effort of moving seemed too much. Niall had rolled off her but kept an arm looped over her stomach. She finally managed to turn her head to find him propped on his other elbow, watching her intensely.

"I…that was…wonderful," Annie said, thinking how inane and inept those words were, but she had nothing else to describe their coupling.

"Aye, 'twas," Niall answered and pushed wet strands of her hair away from her face. "And 'tis what we can enjoy every night once we are married."

Married. Reality returned like a cold dose of ice water from a burn. He was still insisting they get married. No doubt he thought that what had just taken place would persuade her to say yes. Maybe he had even *planned* to seduce her into it. Lord knew the man was good at what he did. Annie closed her eyes. For most women, this would be enough. A man who made wonderful love to her *and* wanted to protect her.

But she didn't want protection. Or maybe she *did*—she couldn't deny that being rescued a time or two had saved her from harm—but she didn't want a man to marry her out of a sense of duty or responsibility. And she knew now that Highlanders had a strong sense of honor. She'd not only seen it in Niall, but also from his brothers and Ian MacLeod and even Owen MacLean. They would all fight in a flash to protect a woman. It was in their blood. It was what they did. That didn't mean they loved any of those women—other than Ian and Jillian, obviously.

Niall had never said he loved her. The word had not even come up when he proposed marriage. He hadn't even actually asked her if she would become his wife. He'd simply presented the idea as a good arrangement so he would have the legal right to protect her according to English law. Honor. Duty. Responsibility. Not love.

Love was the only reason she would even consider giving up her freedom for marriage. But her pride could not let her tell Niall that. If she did, he'd simply say the words to make her feel better. He wouldn't *mean* them. Love was not something someone could ask for. It had to be given freely without pressure. She knew because she loved Niall with all her heart. But she could not marry him knowing he might never feel the same way. Better to let him think a career was more important to her. She took a deep breath and pulled the sheet up.

"I have nae changed my mind."

Niall frowned. "*What*?"

"I have nae changed my mind."

"Ye doona have to repeat it." Niall sat up and stared down at her. "After what we just did…ye cannae tell me ye did nae enjoy it."

Annie sat up too, careful to keep the sheet in place. "I did enjoy it. 'Twas heaven."

"Then why—"

"Because coupling is nae…" Annie stopped, horrified she'd almost said *love*. "…I mean, bed sport is fun, but 'tis a common reaction between men and women, nae?" It was a lie on her part, but she didn't give Niall a chance to answer, just quickly added a second one. "I want to stay an independent woman. I will find another job."

"Doona be ridiculous. I can help—"

"I ken ye can help," Annie answered. "But the answer is the same. I will nae marry ye."

Niall stared at her for a moment longer, then rolled off the bed and grabbed his clothes. Pulling on his trews, he headed for the door and opened it before he turned around. "Just so ye ken, what happened between us is nae a *common* reaction."

And then he was gone.

Chapter Twenty-Five

Annie woke before dawn and threw the covers back, ignoring the cold floor on her bare feet and the chill in the air because the fire in the brazier had gone completely out. She made hasty work of her ablutions in the near icy water left in the basin and donned her clothes just as the first streaks of pale lavender were lighting the dark sky.

Was Niall still here or had he left in the night?

It had taken only a moment to pull the nightshirt over her head last evening, but by the time she'd gotten to the door, Niall had disappeared. She'd contemplated getting dressed and going down to the public room where he was probably having ale, but reconsidered when she heard the raucous laughter drifting up the stairs. Most of those men would already be in their cups and, if Niall wasn't there, she would become the target of lewd remarks and lecherous looks and maybe even worse. She certainly didn't need Niall to rescue her once again. Rationalizing that perhaps he needed some time to think about and understand what she'd said, she'd retreated back to bed, waiting for him to return.

Only he hadn't.

She opened the door and poked her head out. All was quiet and the other doors in the hall were all closed. Was Niall behind one of them? She couldn't very well start knocking, though. Her stomach rumbled, reminding her that she hadn't eaten much of the dinner last night because she was too nervous about Niall's reaction to finding out she wasn't an innocent, modest maiden.

That thought made her smile. She was much too opinionated and outspoken to be thought modest. Her worldly views and strange ideas about women's independence weren't at all conventional either. But, more to the point, Niall hadn't been upset that she'd given away her virtue. If only she thought he actually loved her…

Annie pushed away that fantasy. It had become all too obvious when Niall hadn't returned to the room that he didn't. Well. She was wasting time wool-gathering. If Niall hadn't already left, she might be able to catch him if she waited in the public room. They needed to talk.

To her surprise—and relief—Niall was seated at one of the tables having breakfast. Or rather, breakfast was being served to him by an attractive, smiling maid whose generous cleavage was showing above the peasant blouse she wore. Annie narrowed her eyes. Had Niall spent the night with the girl? Had there been any empty rooms available? The idea of another woman curled up against him, naked, enjoying having him do the things he'd done to *her* made Annie's female parts heat while the blood in her veins turned cold.

Niall looked up and caught her gaze. His expression was impassive and she couldn't tell if he was still upset with her or not. Neither could she tell from his bland expression if he'd sated the barmaid's needs last night either. Drat it.

"I believe we'll need another plate," Niall said to the serving girl as Annie approached his table.

The girl gave Annie a look that was none too

friendly and flounced off. Annie stared after her, chewing her lip as she sat down, then she turned to Niall. "Did ye…"

He raised a brow slightly as her question trailed off. "Did I what?"

Annie felt her face warm. She'd almost asked him if he'd spent the night with the serving girl. "I meant, why did ye nae return to our room?"

His brow rose higher. "Why would I?"

She didn't much like the tone of that question. She wasn't sure what he meant either. "We need to talk."

"Talk?" Niall shrugged. "Ye made yourself quite clear last evening. There is nae more to be said."

But there was! She wanted to explain that she wasn't rejecting him, she was simply rejecting the idea of marriage. But then, she'd also have to delve into her reasons and that would probably bring about another argument or, worse, a declaration not sincerely meant. Perhaps it was best to postpone that discussion.

"I did nae mean to put ye out, Niall."

He shrugged again. "I managed."

Anne frowned. Just whom did he manage with? The serving girl? Or maybe some other woman who worked here? Annie remembered there had been several in the public room last night. She couldn't *ask*, for heaven's sake. Her mouth seemed to be functioning on its own though.

"Did the inn have an extra room, then?"

A corner of his mouth lifted. "I was comfortable enough."

That wasn't answering her question, blast it. But then she realized he wasn't going to. From the quirky smile, he was probably enjoying baiting her. Her temper began to rise and she lifted her chin. "Forget I asked. It is nae my business."

Niall gave her a level look. "We can agree on that, at least."

Argh! The man was infuriating. Annie opened her mouth to retort and then snapped it shut as the maid approached with a bowl of porridge and a plate of coddled eggs and ham. "Thank ye," Annie managed to say between nearly gritted teeth.

"Ye had best eat all of it," Niall said after the girl left. "Since the roads are good from here to Glasgow, I rented a carriage for ye."

Annie looked at him, startled. Was he abandoning her after all? "Are ye going to ride with me?"

Niall shook his head. "I will ride behind to make sure we are nae followed. If we doona stop except to rest the horses, we can make the city by nightfall."

"But it took us almost two days on the trip up."

"The leg wound made for slower going," Niall replied. "I am sure your mother will be anxious to see ye."

Which really meant Niall was anxious to be rid of her. He wasn't even riding in the carriage. It was also obvious he did not want to spend another night at an inn with her. Annie fixed her eyes on her food so he wouldn't see her disappointment. She wouldn't have minded a repeat performance of what they had done, if for no other reason than to prove to Niall she wasn't rejecting *him*. Annie gave herself an inward shake. Liar. It wasn't about rejecting Niall. It was about how good the whole experience had felt. She really, really, *really* would have liked that one more time.

But Niall evidently didn't agree.

****

Ten hours had never lasted so long. By the time they sighted Glasgow, the gloaming had descended, mirroring Niall's darkened mood.

Annie Ferguson was the most stubborn woman he'd ever encountered. Next to her, his sister Margaret seemed as docile and agreeable as a spring lamb, a description his brothers would no doubt feel made him a candidate for London's Bedlam. But it was true. Ninety-nine percent of young women *wanted* husbands, if for no other reason than to have someone provide a house and funds. He'd avoided the parson's noose often enough. And now—*now*—when he'd made an honorable offer of marriage because he wanted to protect Annie, she was the one woman who didn't want to get married.

Obstinate creature! But even she couldn't deny what had happened between them in bed last night had been nothing short of fantastic. Niall might not understand how a female's mind worked, but he damn well knew when a woman had been pleasured. And Annie had responded with unfettered passion just as he had always suspected she would. He admired her strength and independence. He knew there would never be a dull moment in her presence. But, most of all, the thought of having her in his bed nightly had been consuming him for weeks. He finally understood why his brother Alasdair had been so besotted with Bridget. For the first time in Niall's life, the thought of settling down, remaining faithful, and having a family appealed to him.

Family. Niall's mind jolted from his doldrums. Lord Almighty. He may already have gotten Annie with child. He hadn't taken his usual precautions because he'd assumed that she would agree to marriage once they'd physically coupled. Most single ladies expected a marriage proposal if they'd been caught in a compromising situation and they demanded it if liberties were taken beyond a kiss or two. Physical coupling certainly met both standards. But then, Annie Ferguson was the other one percent.

Contrary woman.

But, back to the point that had caused him alarm, what if Annie were already carrying his child? She would have no other choice then but to marry him. And, as much as the idea of a bairn was intriguing, he did not want to force Annie into a marriage. She would hate him forever.

The carriage pulled up in front of her mother's boardinghouse and Niall dismounted to open the door and offer his hand. Annie looked at it as though she weren't quite sure if he was hiding a dagger in his sleeve. He supposed he shouldn't blame her for acting suspicious about a touch of gallantry, since he'd been acting a bit boorish most of the day. They'd hardly spoken the two times they'd stopped for rest breaks, and he'd bought her a box lunch to eat as they travelled, so he wouldn't have to make conversation.

Annie put her hand in his and stepped down. She'd taken off her gloves and the slight touch of her bare hand only made him remember how other bare parts of her had felt—her soft breasts smooth as satin, her flat belly silky, and the warm juncture between her thighs slick.

His cock stirred and he adjusted his riding coat. He cursed inwardly. Maybe he should have taken the tavern wench's offer last night to share her bed with him, so his memory of shared intimacy with Annie would have been diluted. The last thing he needed was to entertain thoughts of having her naked body entwined with his once more. That was not going to happen.

****

When Annie went downstairs the second morning of her return, she was surprised to have Niall join her in the breakfast room a short time later. Since their return home, he had made himself scarce, generally breaking his fast before she came down.

Niall had stayed away from the boardinghouse for most of the daylight hours since they'd gotten back. Owen had assured her that Niall was busy with Aidan and what had taken place at Henderson Shipping while he had been gone, but Annie knew Niall was avoiding her. He only came to the dining table in the evening after everyone else was seated and any conversation she tried to make with him had been met with polite, neutral responses. Even her mother had noted the formality in his behavior, although she was probably relieved that nothing untoward seemed to have transpired during their time away. The memory of what did happen was as clear as the water of a mountain burn in Annie's mind.

She missed having Niall in her bed, drat it all.

"What are ye doing here? Ye are usually gone by now."

He arched a brow. "I ken ye doona prefer my company—"

"I dinna say that."

The brow went higher. "Ye did nae have to. Ye were quite clear—"

"Ye never gave me a chance to explain," Annie interrupted, her temper rising.

"'Tis nothing to be explained."

"Aye, there is! I did nae mean to insult ye when I

said I would nae marry ye. I…*liked* what we did." She felt her face heat and hurried on. "'Tis just that I doona want to be dependent on a man."

"Ye have made that point quite clear." Niall shrugged. "I understand."

Annie frowned. "Then why have ye been avoiding me for three days?"

"I thought it would be best." Niall gave her a direct look. "I…*liked* what we did too."

Heat coursed through her. She looked around to make sure they were truly alone, then turned back to Niall. "I would nae mind if ye came to my bed again."

Niall's eyes darkened, but he shook his head. "I will nae use ye like that."

"Ye are nae *using* me if I am willing."

"I will nae treat ye as a doxy."

"I am nae that."

"Exactly," Niall said. "So we are agreed."

It was a statement, not a question. Annie huffed a breath. Stubborn man.

"But to answer ye," Niall said, changing the subject before she could argue, "ye have an appointment with the magistrate this morning. Have ye forgotten?"

How could she forget? "I remember. Owen has offered to accompany me."

Niall's mouth tightened. "I will escort ye there."

Annie nearly rolled her eyes. She would never understand the rivalry between the two of them. Owen might have flirted a bit—although she suspected that was more to get a rise out of Niall than it was because of real interest in her—but why did that matter if Niall was not planning to accept the invitation she had so blatantly extended?

As if on cue, Owen came through the door to the breakfast room. He gave Niall an appraising look before he gave a half-bow to Annie. "The carriage is waiting whenever ye are ready."

"Ye need nae bother with this," Niall said. "I will attend Annie."

Owen's eyes narrowed. "Ye have nae been doing that lately, have ye?"

Niall narrowed his eyes too. "I swore to protect the lass."

"So have I…in your absence."

"Ye can both escort me." Annie placed her napkin down and stood before the two of them engaged in fisticuffs. She swept out the door to the foyer, both of them following her, each muttering something in Gaelic she didn't understand.

They both leaped in front of her, shouldering each other to get to the carriage door first. Annie sighed. Truly, she would never understand the competitive streak in either of them. At least, they weren't wearing their tartans with the accompanying swords and assortments of knives, so they should all arrive at the magistrate's looking relatively normal. She hoped.

****

MacQuarrie's office was fairly large, but it seemed small since so many people occupied it. Aidan was seated in the far corner and nodded. Niall looked around. Apart from the magistrate, his assistant Charles Curtis was there along with Tevis Shaw, the excise man, and two men Niall had never seen before.

"Please be seated." The magistrate gestured to chairs that had just been brought into the crowded room by his clerk. "And, thank you, Miss Ferguson, for attending."

Niall caught a fleeting glimpse of confusion on Annie's face, although she maintained her composure. "Thank ye for…having me," she responded as though she'd just been invited to high tea instead of an inquisition. Niall almost smiled. *Never show fear.* He admired her for that.

MacQuarrie shuffled some papers on his desk and then smoothed one out before he cleared his throat. "I have only a few questions for you, Miss Ferguson."

Only a few questions? This time, Niall was confused. They'd all thought Annie was going to be in for a grueling session of accusations. It was why he and Aidan were here, to provide support. Hell, it was probably the reason MacLean was here too. No one wanted Annie to face this battle alone.

Annie looked serene, but Niall could see how tightly her hands were clasped in her lap. He moved his chair slightly forward.

"Please go ahead and ask," Annie said, sounding once more like she was nobility granting a favor.

Her voice shook slightly, but Niall didn't think anyone else would notice. He felt proud of her. Stubborn she might be, but she also had the self-determination never to back down.

"Let me remind you," MacQuarrie said to her, "that your answers are witnessed by all the men in this room."

Annie's chin came up. "I will nae lie, if that is what ye are meaning."

Niall inched his chair a bit closer. The magistrate looked at him and Niall met his gaze with a blunt stare. The man looked away.

"I am not implying that you would lie, Miss

Ferguson, only that what you say will become part of the record for this proceeding."

Annie nodded. "I understand."

"Very well. When did you first become aware that Archibald Haines was smuggling opium to the States?"

"I did nae ken about that until ye and Mr. Tavis showed up at the office," Annie replied.

"Explain precisely what your duties were."

"I was to manage the office and keep records of inventory. Shipments received and shipments going out. Mr. Kingsley double-checked all my figures. Ye can ask him to verify that."

"We have already taken a statement from Mr. Kingsley," the magistrate replied and then looked at his notes again. "At any time, did you see or were you aware of a second set of books being kept?"

Annie frowned. "A second set? Nae. Never. There was only one set of ledgers."

The magistrate studied her. Annie held his gaze but Niall could see her fingers were nearly white from being held so tight. He moved his chair again and MacQuarrie turned to him and a corner of his mouth lifted.

"Your intention to defend the lady is obvious, Mr. MacDonald, but is not necessary."

"Nae?"

"No." MacQuarrie looked at Tavis, who nodded and then turned back to Niall. "Miss Ferguson is free to go."

Annie stared at him and Niall frowned. "Please repeat that to be sure we heard correctly."

"I said Miss Ferguson is free to go." The magistrate shuffled the papers again and withdrew another one. "After the second set of books was discovered, Mr. Haines confessed to the smuggling operation and said the only reason he'd hired a woman was because he did not think she would ever suspect a thing. Apparently, he was right."

Annie opened her mouth and then closed it. Niall bit back a smile. He could almost see her hair turning brighter as her temper simmered. But at least, she was holding her tongue in front of the magistrate.

The man looked down at the paper he was holding. "After a bit more investigating, we were able to track where Mr. Haines' profits had gone. It seems the gold was invested by a Gordon Monroe, who had been keeping the books for Henderson Shipping as well."

"Henderson Shipping?" Niall asked and glanced at Aidan before looking back at the magistrate. "If the line was being used to smuggle opium, none of us had knowledge of it. I will swear to that. In fact, that bookkeeper was gone by the time I got to Glasgow."

MacQuarrie nodded. "It seems that Munroe was keeping a second set of books as well as a percentage of the profit from other dealings through Henderson Shipping too." He turned to one of the men Niall didn't recognize. "This is Mr. Graham, the original bookkeeper."

"I can nae tell ye how sorry I am that this happened," Mr. Graham said. "I've been ill with consumption and asked my nephew to fill in for me. I had nae idea he was so dishonest until I returned last week and started checking the books." He dabbed at his eyes with a wadded linen handkerchief. "I did nae want to believe it. I even held my peace until yesterday."

Aidan spoke from his corner. "From what Mr. Graham says, it looks like Henderson Shipping has lost several thousand pounds."

"So where is Munroe?" Niall asked.

"He ran off—actually, disappeared would be more accurate—several months ago."

Niall frowned. "Are ye searching for him?"

"We are," MacQuarrie answered, "although he may have changed his name again."

"Again?"

"Aye," Mr. Graham spoke up. "My nephew's name is Gordon Graham, nae Monroe. That was his mother's name."

Owen, who had been sitting quietly on Annie's other side, suddenly looked alert. "Gordon Graham? Did he work for a London investor about a year ago?"

"Aye, he did," Mr. Graham replied. "Did ye ken him?"

Owen nodded. "I clerked for Nathan Rothschild and Gordon worked for another investor just down the street. He disappeared from London when his vowels were being called in by men he'd lost to in the gambling hells."

"I had nae idea," Mr. Graham said, his voice cracking. "I would nae have let him jeopardize the shipping line if I had kenned. I hope ye believe me."

Aidan exchanged a look with Niall. "That will be up to Robert Henderson and his father to decide, but ye seem an honest man."

The man's eyes grew suspiciously bright. "Thank ye."

Niall nodded. "If we are through here, I would like to escort Miss Ferguson home."

"Of course," the magistrate said and gestured to the other man Niall didn't know. "There is just one more thing."

"I am Oliver Nolan, Archibald Haines' business partner. *Former* partner," the man corrected. "And I, too, had no idea in what he was involved. However, just before this whole sordid mess came to light, Archibald asked me if I wanted to buy his half of the warehouse business. He indicated he had a proposition for another venture and needed capital. I accepted the offer since there had been several disagreements between us over the past months." He looked at Niall. "You submitted an offer to purchase the property two days ago?"

"I did." In his peripheral vision, Niall could see Annie's mouth had dropped and she was staring at him. He kept his attention focused on Nolan.

"Well, the price you offered is a good one," Nolan said. "If you will come to my office this afternoon, we can take care of the paperwork."

"I will be there by thirty past three o'clock," Niall answered, and Nolan nodded.

As they rose to leave, Niall glanced at Annie. She had closed her mouth, but there were a dozen questions in her eyes. He just hoped she'd wait to ask them until they were alone and he was ready to answer.

Chapter Twenty-Six

As soon as they were outside the magistrate's office, Niall made the surprising move to allow Owen to escort Annie home, saying he needed to have a word with Aidan before going to Mr. Nolan's office. Annie suspected Niall was simply not wanting to answer the barrage of questions swirling in her mind.

So it wasn't until evening, after they'd eaten and retired to her mother's small, private parlor, that Annie was finally able to ask what had been on her mind since he'd revealed the startling news.

"Why did ye buy the warehouse?"

Evidently, she wasn't the only person whose curiosity had been piqued. All conversation ceased and everyone in the room focused their eyes on Niall.

"It seemed the practical thing to do."

"Practical?" What kind of an answer was that? Annie folded her arms across her chest. "Ye need to be more clear."

Niall raised a brow. "Practical is a simple word, nae? Purchasing the warehouse made sense to me."

Annie frowned. "It made *sense*? Ye are the one nae making sense."

"Perhaps I can explain?" Aidan asked and then continued, "Niall and I have both gone over the ledgers at Henderson Shipping. One of the major costs incurred is storing goods waiting to be moved to either the States or the Continent. I will be extending our kelp trade by opening an office on Skye and I know Owen is thinking of doing the same on Eigg and Rhum. We all need a warehouse that is well insulated to keep the kelp bales—as well as woolens—dry. Haines' building does that and owning it will keep our expenses down."

Annie looked back to Niall. "So ye are going to manage the warehouse, then?"

"I doona ken if I will have the time." A corner of his mouth quirked up. "I thought ye might be interested in doing that."

"Me?" She was so surprised her voice squeaked. She tried again. "Ye want me to manage the warehouse?"

"Aye. Ye do have the experience, after all."

"But…" Annie eyed him speculatively. Was he having fun with her? He was smirking a bit. "For weeks, ye have been trying to convince me the job was nae a woman's job. *Now*, ye want me to do it? 'Tis unkind to jest—"

"'Tis nae jest," Niall replied. "Ye have told me often enough that the job was important to ye. I should have listened better. Ye should be able to do as ye wish. Ye should have your freedom and independence. Ye were right and I was wrong."

Annie's hands dropped to her sides and she almost fell off the chair. Her mouth opened, then closed, then opened again. She felt somewhat like a gaping fish flopping around. For Niall to admit he was *wrong*, especially in front of Owen MacLean, was an amazing feat in itself, but to support her decision to work? Why was he doing such a thing?

It was a question she asked her mother an hour later, after the men had left to have a celebratory drink at

Walkers and the two of them were cleaning up the kitchen.

Her mother gave her a wry look. "I did nae think I had raised such a daft daughter."

"Daft? I am nae daft. 'Tis just that after weeks and weeks of arguing with me about working because I want my freedom and independence, why does he suddenly have a change of heart?"

"Perhaps ye should ask him that." Her mother dried the last dish and put it in the cupboard and closed the door. "But if ye are asking my opinion, I would say that the man loves ye."

****

Loves ye. Annie repeated the phrase to herself as she prepared for bed. Was it possible? Did Niall love her? He certainly had never said as much. Not even when he was buried deep inside her. If he'd had such feelings, wouldn't he have said something *then*? Och, she was being silly. Even though Niall had taken his time to pleasure her thoroughly—how could she forget the adept touch of his hands caressing her breasts and the expertise of his fingers bringing her nipples to hard, little peaks? Nor could she forget the deep, passionate kisses they'd shared or how his mouth had felt lapping her juices and then skillfully sucking her sensitive nub until she practically rose from the mattress? But bed sport did not equal *love*.

But what if Niall *did* love her? She had no doubt he'd been acting out of some Highlander Code of Honor when he'd intervened with the men leaving the Virginia Street office building or when he'd showed up at the Trades Hall the night she'd been pelted with the rotten cabbage. She'd assumed that escorting her everywhere—even the Sunday when the club had demonstrated outside the church—was another part of that code. Or maybe it was some kind of male competition with Owen. But could Niall also have done all those things because he cared for her? And the real rescue, getting her away from the angry mob of weavers and then riding with a wound he didn't mention…she'd thought that he felt he was responsible for her safety. *He is a Highlander*, Ian had said. But even if all that were true, that Niall had been acting out of a sense of duty, including tracking her abductors, it still didn't make sense that he would put her in charge of managing the warehouse.

Ye should be able to do as ye wish.

Ye were right and I was wrong.

Did Niall say that because he finally agreed with her? Annie hadn't seen any softening in him toward that idea at all. If anything, he had distanced himself and hardly spoken on the last day of their ride. He had even refused to take her to his bed again. So maybe offering her the job was a gift of sorts? That he understood how she felt?

Ye should have your freedom and independence.

Annie felt a chill run down her spine. What if offering her the manager position was a *final* gift? What if it was his way of saying goodbye? She'd refused to marry him, after all. Twice. He'd said he didn't think he'd have time to manage the warehouse himself. Maybe he wasn't even planning to stay in Glasgow. Maybe…

She heard footsteps in the hall, the sounds of Owen and Niall talking as they went past her room to climb the stairs to the next floor. Annie paused in brushing her hair and looked at herself in the mirror. She was nearly three-

and-twenty. Did she truly want to be a spinster?

Work was important. She liked the feeling of earning her own money and not having to be dependent on a man. But did it have to be an "either-or" situation? Niall had offered her the manager's job. He would let her keep it.

But did his offer of marriage still stand?

Annie grabbed her robe and wrapped it around her, then opened the door to peer into the hall. It was empty. She padded out on bare feet and went up the stairs. She hesitated a moment and then knocked softly on Niall's door.

He opened it, his gaze taking in what she was wearing and travelling back to her face. "Ye should nae be here." He looked down at her bare feet and her night rail under the lightweight cotton wrapper. "And nae dressed like that."

"I need to talk to ye," Annie said and walked past him before he could close the door. "First, I need to thank ye for the job."

Niall frowned as he latched the door. "If ye think ye need to thank me with your body, I do nae require it."

For a moment Annie wondered if she'd made a mistake in coming up. Maybe Niall really didn't want her. Maybe once had been enough… Annie lifted her chin. Niall was not Broderick. Anyway, she was already here.

"Ye are welcome to my body, but 'tis nae the reason I am here."

His eyes raked over her again. "Say what ye have to say, then, and be gone before ye are compromised by someone seeing ye. I will nae force ye into a marriage."

Annie swallowed hard. "What if I changed my

mind?"

Niall gave her a wary look. "On what?"

"On marriage."

"*What*?"

The incredulous expression on Niall's face almost made Annie falter, but she might as well blurt out what she was feeling. If Niall rejected her, so be it.

"I realize…I mean, I think…" Blast it. The words were hard to say. "Do ye care for me?"

He looked at her as though she'd taken complete leave of her senses. Maybe she had. "I mean…well, ye would nae have done so many things to protect me if ye did nae care. I ken ye Highlanders have a code ye follow and ye feel ye have a duty and responsibility—"

"I care for ye."

Annie stopped. "Ye *truly* do?"

Niall looked heavenward as if praying for patience. "Do ye think I would have spent so much time—nae to mention trouble—following ye around like a moonstruck calf if I did nae care?"

His choice of words made Annie smile. "I would hardly say ye acted like a moonstruck calf."

"Ye ken what I mean," Niall answered. "'Tis true I started out only thinking to protect ye—mainly from yourself—but my feelings changed. Ye managed to vex me and make me want to stay at your side at the same time. Ye are stubborn and opinionated and—"

"Are those your idea of compliments?" Annie asked.

"Aye. At least, in a way. Ye never have liked flattery," Niall said, "so I might as well speak truth. Ye are willful and obstinate and tenacious, to boot. I never expected to fall in love with ye."

Annie's heart stilled. "Ye...*love* me?"

Niall threw up his hands. "Ye doona think I would have asked ye to marry me if I did nae?"

"But ye did nae *say* it."

Niall looked bewildered. "Did I have to *say* it?"

"Aye, ye daft man. 'Tis a word a woman wants to hear. Even one who does nae care for flowery compliments."

"I thought I *showed* it."

Annie quieted and then nodded. "Ye did. I was just too stupid nae to see it."

"Stupid is nae a word I would ever use to describe ye," Niall replied. "Headstrong, mulish—"

"Enough," Annie said. "My answer is yes."

"Yes?"

"Aye. I love ye and I will marry ye." Annie tilted her head. "If the offer still stands."

Niall smiled. "It stands. I love ye, Annie Ferguson."

She smiled too. "Then *show* me."

And he did, drawing her body close and covering her mouth with his.

A word about the author...

Cynthia Breeding lives on the Gulf Coast of Texas with a very non-spoiled poodle-mix and enjoys walking and horseback-riding on the beach, as well as sailing.

www.cynthiabreeding.com